LITTLE PRAIRIE
FLOWERS

Robert Anthony Brown, Sr.

WESTBOW
PRESS®
A DIVISION OF THOMAS NELSON
& ZONDERVAN

WestBow Press books may be ordered through booksellers or by contacting:

WestBow Press
A Division of Thomas Nelson & Zondervan
1663 Liberty Drive
Bloomington, IN 47403
www.westbowpress.com
844-714-3454

Scripture taken from the King James Version of the Bible.

ISBN: 978-1-6642-1313-5 (sc)
ISBN: 978-1-6642-1315-9 (hc)
ISBN: 978-1-6642-1314-2 (e)

Library of Congress Control Number: 2020922891

Print information available on the last page.

WestBow Press rev. date: 12/08/2020

CONTENTS

BEFORE IT ALL BEGAN

❀⤸

March 11, 1863

"Not much happening to tell about today," spoke the Reverend Arder, the hoary headed preacher and telegraph operator. "The Rebel ship, Nashville, was sunk in Georgia, so I hear." He looked into the eyes of his wife, Prisca, remembering the day the war had begun. "Not much happening now, but it will get worse, and a whole lot more men will die."

"Shame," she spoke softly, rocking in her chair in the small telegraph office. "I am relieved that we live so far away from the killing."

"Not far enough. This worrisome telegraph tells me more than I want to know."

She looked up from her knitting and asked, "who is the message for?"

"Can you figure?"

"Mr. Williston?"

"Yes," he muttered. "From his kin in Arkansas."

Prisca went back to her knitting and gently rocked in her chair. "Odd, isn't it? You never hear him speak of any kin in Arkansas. You think he's interested in the conflict?"

"Sure. I'm interested too," he answered. "It's tearing our country apart every day."

"It ain't our country."

"It soon will be, dear. Nebraska is close to statehood. We might find ourselves caught up in it yet."

The front door opened. In walked a tall, well-built man with speckled hair and thick eyebrows. His boots drummed as he hurried across the floor to the desk where Reverend Arder sat.

"Speak of the devil," Arder exclaimed.

William Williston's dark eyebrows drew downward.

"We were just talking about you. You got another telegram."

William took the paper eagerly and read it quickly. Then he stuffed it in his vest pocket. "Thank you, Reverend. Hello Mrs. Arder. I have one to send too." He gave the paper he had been clutching in his left hand to the aged preacher.

Arder read it and looked up. "You're heading back down there?"

"Yes. It's business."

"Back to Arkansas?" asked Prisca.

"Yes ma'am."

Reverend Arder raised his eyebrows. "I reckon you will be bringing back more of those flowers your children love so much."

William grinned. "I reckon so … or maybe just the seeds. I bring back flower seeds for them every time I go somewhere." He chuckled. "Sometimes I have to bring back the plants just to get the seeds out of them."

"It's something how they can get 'em to grow so pretty out here. I've seen 'em blooming in the scorching summer sun and in the chilly fall and spring."

William nodded and turned back to watch Mrs. Arder. "It's sort of like the knitting you're doing there, Ma'am. The flowers will be a reminder of me while I'm gone and … and in case something happens and I get detained for a long spell."

She stopped rocking and knitting. "I do wish you would stay away from the South. There's a big fight going on."

"I know."

"And you might get caught up in it."

William smiled at her. "Then I would sure appreciate you praying for me." He turned back to the minister. Reaching in his vest he lifted an envelope and handed it to Arder. "This is what I talked to you about Sunday. Will you keep it in a safe place and if something bad were to happen to me on this trip, make sure it gets into the hands of my dear wife?"

"Sure I will. I told you I would."

Prisca leaned forward from her chair, concern in her voice. "Is it a will, Mr. Williston?"

"Something like that. The preacher here knows about it. In case I don't make it back – or if anything ever does happen to me, I want Sadie to know where I hid my valuables."

"Oh my," she uttered. "It sounds like you're expecting something bad to happen on this trip."

"These are dangerous days down South. The Yankees are keeping all the fighting down there. Anyway," he looks back to the elderly man, "I don't want to tell my family where it's hid or they might be in danger."

Reverend Arder squinted. "In danger from who?"

"You never can tell. There's a lot of mean folks out there."

"You don't need to tell a preacher that."

"And I haven't always been a good soul. I had a life before I married Sadie. Somebody might be holding a grudge against me and take it out on my family. So, put it in a safe place and give it to Sadie only if I don't make it back."

"Why don't you put your treasures in the bank?"

"I don't trust them."

"But you know the government is close to creating a national bank with a lot of securities."

"It's not secure enough for me. I know how easy it is to rob a bank."

"You do?" remarked the minister's wife, looking up from her knitting with disbelief.

He chuckled. "What I mean is that banks are too easy to get into. I would prefer to stay with our original plan."

The preacher nodded. "I know the perfect place to hide it," he said, folding the envelope and sliding it inside his light coat. "I'll put it there tonight. But I'm not a young man."

"Seventy-three," Prisca interjected.

"Yeah. I'm seventy-three and I might get sick and go home to the good Lord before you do, William."

"Then you might tell someone else about the envelope – someone you trust. Not your wife either."

Prisca cackled. "I'm not as old as that old coot."

"No, ma'am, I'm sure you're not. But I don't want you to be in danger either – in case someone comes looking for my valuables."

Prisca suddenly looked anxious. "You frighten me, Mr. Williston."

Reverend Arder went on. "I'll tell the young minister, my assistant, Smythe, the one who joined me last year. He really is quite young – and inexperienced – but you will have two of us who know the whereabouts of the letter."

"Thank you, Reverend. I plan to leave in the morning. Don't say anything about this to my family. I want them to be safe."

Arder nodded in agreement.

"Mr. Williston, sir," began Prisca. "I feel as though there is something about this trip you're not telling us."

"Prisca, dear, that is his business." He held out his open palm to his customer. "We'll take care of everything. Now that will be two dollars."

William Williston tendered two large, golden coins that jangled noisily during the exchange. He bid the couple good-bye and vacated the little square office. Arder was admiring the pretty gold coins. These sure are some shining gold pieces," he said. "I suspect William might have brought these back with him from California when he was out there panning some years back."

"Reckon so," his wife agreed. "Folks say he struck it rich out there."

"Well, gold ain't everything. It's just street pavement in Heaven." He bent low and lifted a small metal box from under the counter when a sharp pain abruptly stabbed him in the chest.

"I really do worry about him," stated Prisca just before she heard the rattling of the metal box when her husband set it down hard on the counter top.

Reverend Arder didn't answer. She looked up and saw that he was laying across the counter with his arms tucked beneath his body. "Jacob! What's the matter?"

He raised up clutching his chest. "I'm Okay now. Its passing."

"No you aren't. You look so pale. It's your heart again, isn't it?"

"I'm sure it is."

"Then come on. We are going to see the doctor."

"No. I told you I feel better now."

"But you don't look any better. I guess this whole thing with Mr. Williston has upset you."

Reverend Arder scoffed. "That has nothing to do with this. You know I have heart troubles."

"Well, this sure didn't make it any better." She helped him slip on his longer winter coat. "Let's go and no argument from you."

The elderly couple left the shop and turned over the sign on the door that read, *BE BACK SOON.* Holding his arm, the woman escorted her husband across the mucky main street of Glensbluff, Nebraska towards the doctor's house. She wore that same worried expression on her face that she wore for Mr. Williston a few moments before. Reverend Arder grabbed his coat at the buttons, pressed his fist against his heart and panted with quick, shallow breaths.

WHEN IT ALL BEGAN

March 12, 1863

William Williston galloped on his pale horse across the Nebraska plains with a great deal on his mind. The War Between the States had been underway just over two years. His heart felt heavy as he left behind his wife, Sadie, and their six children and headed straight south, into the South, the Confederacy – where graves outnumbered the living and a dollar couldn't buy a pouch of hard tack. Northern soil was yet unscathed, but southern earth was scarred and bloodied. He could hardly believe it was already 1863 and the war was turning dreadful.

There was business to be done in Arkansas that could affect the outcome of the war. That was where he was born, though he had no close family still living in the south. The old homeplace was his now, since his parents and sisters had died, and a nephew and his family now lived on the property. But it was important enough business to make the trip, an enterprise that some thought could shorten the conflict and save thousands of lives from Virginia all the way to New Orleans. He had to go. Since he was too old to fight, confirmed by his speckled hair and aching joints, he knew that using his mind and intuitive strategies in this outlandish scheme were the best contributions he could make to his nation.

Not a man to worry about much, this day William felt the weight of a barn on his shoulders. He wasn't so much worried about himself, but about his wife and children left behind. He knew he could be in grave danger in Arkansas. Before he set out on this trip, he gave some seeds to his little ones and told them to plant them in the pots in the barn during the cold days so they could come up and grow strong before being set out on the new family cemetery – the place he would be buried someday. It sat on a little knoll overlooking their happy home.

What he worried about the most was the note he gave the minister. He hoped it would get into the hands of Sadie if something did happen to him and he didn't return. He wished he could have told her what it said, but he knew he had made a lot of enemies through the years and he didn't want her to be put in a terrible predicament of having to make hard choices. She and the children were going to be well off if he didn't make it back. He made sure of that. So, he would have to trust that Reverend Arder would take care of it for him – if it ever came to that.

He could hear the steady hoof beats of his mare, Cherish, as she kicked up the dry earth. A prairie bird, startled by the noise, darted into the sky with humming wings and disappeared. He pulled back on the reins and looked down at the spot where the bird had been roused. A large ginger and yellow butterfly flitted across the vegetation beneath him. But something else caught his attention. He drew Cherish to a complete halt and dismounted. Stooping down, he gently touched the lovely Butterfly Weed blooming rather early in the spring.

The pretty flowers were rooted in the dry and rocky open glade, clumped on top of their short, hairy stems, and displayed their umbels of radiant yellow-orange flowers amidst their spear shaped leaves. It seemed as though the butterfly he had just observed was one of the flowers that had miraculously come to life and fluttered away.

This was Sadie's flower. He even gave her that nickname while they were courting. "*My Little Butterfly Weed.*" It looked the color of gold, the same color of the ore he had mined in California years ago and the same color of the rock that fell into his hands and that he hauled back in a wagon. William knew the Butterfly Weed bloomed into the late summer and he would be passing this way again soon enough to pick some fresh ones for his wife. But he wanted one to take with him to Arkansas. It's nectar that attracted so many spirited butterflies would remind him of his patient wife while he was away.

So, he snatched a small handful of them, dampened a kerchief from his canteen, wrapped it around the stems, and stuffed them inside his saddle bag. While in Arkansas he would inhale their pleasing fragrance and think of home. William re-mounted Cherish and proceeded south with the sun bearing over his shoulder. He was sure that he could make Kansas in good time, take care of the crucial mission in Arkansas, and be back in Nebraska as swiftly as a flitting bird.

AFTER IT ALL BEGAN

❀ ⌇

September 1865

The carrot-colored moon was not quite full but seemed to sit directly atop the jagged rocks on the horizon and cast a radiant hue across the scene. A different horse cantered across the plains at full speed guided by the rigid form of a man riding bareback. In the generous light, he looked sleek, and reedy. He quickly glanced back at the men chasing him. Five of them – or six. He couldn't tell. But he could hear their thunderous hoof beats and the cracks of their guns. Bullets whizzed by his hair so close he could overhear them.

Up ahead he saw the jagged rocks and the earth rising into a swollen bluff. That may be his only chance, he thought, to take cover and hope he can fend them off. He knew who these men were – not each man – but the one who was behind it, the one who wanted him dead bad enough to hire them, the one who was once his friend. "Come on boy," he spoke to his silky, black Mustang, the one he stole from the Calvary in Arizona. "Get me to those rocks."

The rider directed the horse with his knees and leaned over its head to dodge the flying lead. As he neared the rocks, the horse slackened his gate, reared, and nickered. The rider slid off and ran for cover. The men in pursuit dismounted at a short distance, slapped away their mounts, and crouched to the ground. There was little sanctuary on the open plateau, except for the promise of darkness. The men began emptying their guns towards the rocks.

The lone defender realized his hopeless situation. Even his horse had bolted off. So close to the Williston farm, he thought, a mere handful of miles from safety. But close wasn't good enough. Now he would die on the open plains and buzzards would graze on his flesh in the morning. He wasn't afraid of dying, but his spirit felt crushed inside by the thoughts that one friend had betrayed him and another friend he himself had let down.

So, the brave man rapidly scaled obtrusive boulders, fitting his boots into crevices like stairs. He determined to fight from the highest crest and take down as many as he could. A couple of men in the darkness seemed to drop. But as he stood there boldly firing his last bullets, he felt a sharp pain. One burned deep inside his chest. He froze as he felt the sting, the warmth of blood, and then realized he was teetering. He looked down. The fall seemed inevitable. Darkness swallowed him like a blanket. Even the florid of light rebounding from the moon through the clouds could not penetrate the blackness.

ONE

Late March 1866

Beautiful, feral prairie flowers would soon be blooming sporadically across these barren Nebraska plains, so early in their summer, imagined Sadie Williston. The unadorned woman, almost forty now, had seen many varieties of flowers in her years of living on the Nebraska grasslands. There would be many more blooming soon, flourishing in the sun and creating the most spectacular view comparable to Heaven itself. Her husband, William, loved to behold them more than gold – well, almost. Perhaps the heavy snow left behind in February and March would help nurture the premature flora to survive.

Sadie, the mother of nine children, three of them already lying beneath the rich soil in small graves on top a knoll near her sod house, had planted some of those flowers each year from seeds her husband brought back from New Orleans. *He had spent far too much time in New Orleans at the start of the war,* she thought. She quickly erased the thought from her mind – so tired of wondering what her William had been up to way down south. Three years ago he left for Arkansas and never came back.

She wearied of speculating about him. It brought her no answers and no William. Back to the flowers, she corralled her mind. William had often gone on business for weeks, but she never knew what he did – for he never spoke of it when he returned. She never knew why he felt compelled to go off so much – three or four times within a year. But the last trip never ended. She caught herself again. Her mind was drifting.

She was a widow now – at least she might as well be. She had no husband at home at night. Some town folks said he had run off to California again where he found his gold. She doubted that. He had no desire to go back to California since all the gold was gone. A few Gossips claimed he was living it up in New Orleans and had found someone else to share his life. With his love for gambling, that was possible; but she didn't believe that one either. He was dead, she decided. He had to be. The war between states had ended with Lee's surrender a year ago, and she was convinced that the conflict had something to do with his disappearance. All she could do was wonder.

She admired each of the young florets, started in pots in the barn, as she strolled towards the knoll to the graves of her young children, Laura, and Alfonso, and the baby born too early who rested in Laura's tiny arms. The flowers would soon dress the grave mounds like new garments, scurry down the slope, bend with verve past the sod barn, and inch nearer the well house. They would reign in their full glory until overthrown by Fall.

Smooth Asters would soon pop up everywhere, tiny florae with violet blue and white rays and yellow centers like little saucers. They would scatter in loose, panicle-like clusters. Colossal bumblebees would hover, anxiously humming about them, and would pause to sip some succulent nectar. They would be followed by Butterfly Weed – her nickname. It grew in clumps a few inches high and featured umbels of bright yellow-orange balls atop reclining, hairy stems with narrow, spear-shaped leaves. They resembled small bushes.

The hoary blue Vervain, another favorite, would grow several feet high. It's scary, square stems looked reddish. Their toothed, lance shaped leaves advanced in pairs up the stem. On some days they might look purplish-bluish and would flourish in spectacular, elongated panicles. A cottontail rabbit or two often came out into the open to nibble on the foliage, tempted by the attractive blooms late in summer. The cardinals and field sparrows, and sometimes the slate-colored juncos, would declare them enticing too. They were not shy about eating the seeds or much of anything in the drought of summer.

And lastly, her children's favorite wildflower, the Petunias, would soon spread out like food on a banquet table at a prairie wedding. They were so charming with boundless character that reminded her of the old ladies at church who loved to dance with younger men. They sprung up in low growing clumps producing light purple, tubular flowers that arose in delightful clusters at the leaf bend. She imagined them all on the springtime prairie and tears pooled in her eyes as she thought of her missing husband and their children resting beneath the earth. After moments of reflection, she lifted the hem of her long dark shift and headed towards the well.

Sadie remembered walking this same path last year at the end of the summer, to water the plants on the graves... when out of the corner of her eye, she saw something. She glanced over to the shaded area by the sod barn among the clumps of grass and supposed she had merely seen one of the indolent dogs sleeping. She intended to shoo off the lazy animal.

"Get up from there," she called out, detouring towards the barn. But as she grew closer, her demeanor changed. Her eyes widened. Her voice quivered. "O my goodness!"

It wasn't a dog at all. It was a man clad in dirty clothes lying face down. She could see the skin on the back of his neck and it was dark with dried blood. She cautiously lowered her hand and touched him with her fingertips. He didn't react. Was he dead? She called out for her children. While waiting for them, she struggled to roll him over on the clumps of grass and dry dirt. He was breathing, his chest slightly rising and falling. Then she gasped. Blood stained his vest. Through the torn shirt she saw a gaping hole in his breast. The smell of putrid flesh gagged her. Then she observed his dark face.

He looked young, a bit younger than her, but older than her children. She suspected he was an Indian... or part Indian... with those high cheekbones. Whoever he was, he was hurt badly. She had to help him quickly. He must have staggered in during the night and collapsed by the sod barn where the shade concealed him. *A lot of good her watch dogs were*, she thought. She recalled the story of the Good Samaritan and understood that God had given her this opportunity to try to save his life. She called out again – for anyone in the house. She had to move him inside or he would die.

That was how Ned Ames came to live on the Williston property last year. Evelina, Anton, and Amos came out – and Preacher Pearsall too, who was staying with them for a while. They carried the wounded man into the house to one of the beds in the back bedroom and there nursed him to health. It was quickly determined that Ned had been shot in the chest. He had nearly bled out before it miraculously stopped.

At first, they feared they would never get his fever down. They couldn't call the law in case that was who had shot him, and they couldn't send for a doctor, less the shooter might discover it. So, she sat by him, placed cool, wet rags on his forehead, and washed down his muscular frame until the dried blood was gone. He muttered something unintelligible. Yet, in a few days he came to, sat up, and began to eat some chicken broth. Preacher Pearsall prayed for the man, even though he repeatedly informed them that he had no compassion for Indians.

But who was this strange man they discovered? And where did he come from? His mannerisms and speech indicated he was an eastern gentleman, but he had worn a low holster like an outlaw. His skin was blended like potatoes and gravy, light and dark. Was he an Indian or Mexican? And why did someone shoot him? Sadie had to worry about her family, especially the little ones; for if he were running from the law or an enemy who wanted him dead, someone could come riding in letting bullets fly. The preacher guessed that Ned was running from the law. He said he didn't trust the man, as he was a good judge of people. Though he bore no grace in his heart towards Indians, he had to agree that it was only by some miracle that the man survived. God kept him alive for a reason.

The stranger didn't seem to want anyone to know why he was

in Nebraska or what had happened to him. He claimed to be part Apache with some white in him. But his eyes filled with anger when he spoke of growing up in the southwestern territories where he took a lot of ridicule and abuse until he could take it no more. One day some soldiers started knocking him around and tried to put a cow brand on him – a hot one – and he decided he wasn't going to be punched around anymore. Maybe he didn't mean to, but he killed one of them with his bare hands and knocked the other one senseless.

No one then believed Ned's version of the events; so, he ran for his life. But all that was years before the war. He gave indication that the killing had nothing to do with what happened to him this time. He told his story earnestly and with a dour, stone face, admitting that he had been wounded in ways that were not physical. Then he thanked them endlessly for saving his life. Due to growing up in an Indian mission, he spoke English with perfect dialect and inflection, like a school master himself. Yet, who shot him… and why they tried to kill him, he would not divulge. His silence seemed to indicate that he knew who and why. He was certainly a fugitive from something.

Sadie trusted the outsider for some reason – intuition – and believed him to be no threat. *She could see it in his ruddy eyes*, she thought. They looked like miniature pools of lamp oil, murky, but glimmering. She simply prayed that whoever shot him wouldn't show up slinging guns on her farm. Sadie was known all over the territory for taking in people who had nowhere to go, like the preacher and the widow, Miss Lenora. But Ned Ames was the first one she took in who was running from something. No one asked any more questions and graciously accepted him on the little farm.

When the wounded gentleman healed up over the fall and winter, the hole in back of his shoulder where the bullet came out, healed too, but left an ugly scar. He soon started helping around the farm doing odd jobs and hunting for food along with her sons, Anton and Amos. But he seemed as skittish as a cat and kept his eyes sharp all the time. She just couldn't believe that this English scholar could be a killer. Ned was a mystery.

Being part Indian – or maybe because he was hiding from

somebody – he chose to live outside. He stayed at night among the cluster of bushes and trees along the Republican River branch. They saw him every now and then, and he took a liking to her children, even putting up with her oldest daughter, seventeen-year-old Evelina. Evelina was just at that age where she was in a foul mood most of the time and couldn't get along with anyone. She hated living on the plains and wanted to live somewhere that was exciting and had multitudes of handsome young men to dance with, like New Orleans. But, to her younger children Ned seemed kind and fun to be around, especially the two youngest girls, Lillibet and Lutie, and her littlest son, Ammon. They took a real shine to him and played games together with him around the house when he came in from his den. Still, Ned was clandestine. What secret was he hiding? Who was he constantly watching for over his shoulder? At times he disappeared for days and even weeks before returning, just like a tom cat. No one knew when he would show up.

Then Ammon got sick. It was the same cholera that took out Lenora's husband, and stole away so many other folks around the territory. Ned came in more often and sat by the boy's side, worry etched all over his face. Then Ammon fell into a deep sleep, his death sleep, as folks would say, and Ned could not come around anymore. He couldn't bear to watch him die. As Ned wandered off into the far outdoors once again, Sadie placed a damp rag on Ammon's forehead and sat by his side and prayed. She prayed selfishly that God would spare her poor child, but quickly added that God's will be done. Finally, she instructed Anton to get things ready early by going up on the little knoll where the wild flowers blossomed so beautifully all summer and dig his little brother a small grave.

TWO

꧁ ❦ ꧂

Sadie paused by the well house in front of her bleak sod home and stared longingly into the distance. Where could her William be? She contemplated his disappearance nearly every waking moment, even after all the time that had passed. Hadn't she been patient enough all these months to hear something from him – or, at least, about him? A faithful husband would never be gone so long without sending word to his wife and his family, she supposed. Not one letter. Not one telegram. Was it even possible he might still be alive?

Beyond the broken-down corral and the shallow pond, she gazed, her mind lost in time what seemed a life ago. She vividly recalled the last day she saw him. He had eaten battered eggs and biscuits that morning and sipped a couple tins of hot, black coffee – like he did every morning. She had baked biscuits and packed beans and dried rabbit to take with him on the arduous journey to Arkansas. William wore his regular traveling clothes, but made certain he packed his Sunday shirt and tie. She stretched up on her toes to kiss him goodbye while he wrapped her with one arm and drew her firmly to his muscular chest. He opened the door and closed it slowly on his way to the sod barn to pack his saddle bags and ready his horse. The closing door and the gentle latching of the handle was the final memory she had of him, the last time she heard his cheery voice, the last tangent of his whereabouts she could claim to know. He rode off then, right in the middle of the war between the states, and simply vanished from sight.

The night before he left he assured her that he would hurry home as soon as his business in Arkansas was finished. Soon? What did that mean? It meant never at all. He said he had one more thing to do on the farm to get ready for his trip, and after he finished that he would come in for supper. It was nearly dark then. What was it he had to do? She didn't think it important, but, in just a little while, before darkness swallowed him, he came back inside for his final supper.

During the long years he had been away, their daughter Laura had died and was buried on top of the cemetery bluff beside Alfonso – where the purple and white clovers were anxious to bloom, along with the smooth asters and petunias, and an assortment of more wild flowers the children had transplanted. The war had ended. The farm had suffered drought and snowstorms, had fallen into disrepair, and many of the animals had perished. But William did not come back. No one in Arkansas had seen him or had knowledge of him. Not the banker. Not the law. None of his acquaintances. Not even his nephew who lived on the old family place. How could she go on not knowing?

"I just can't believe what a beautiful day it is," spoke the aged widow, Lenora, inside the cozy house. Lenora had moved in with Sadie and her family immediately after her husband, Henry, died. They had no children living and all her family back in Maryland had died or moved off. Sadie didn't mind her moving in.

"Yes, it is," Sadie answered her. She lifted her eyes from the washtub and stack of dirty dishes to look out the half frosted window pane. "At least the sun is shining."

"I just can't believe what a beautiful day it is, "Lenora said again.

"Yes." This time Sadie wiped the glass gently with the edge of her apron. Outside it still looked bleak, like winter, and flat without color, except for the white of lingering snow patches in the shade of the barn and, of course, on the russet earth.

She turned to look back at the old, grey haired woman rocking in her chair, and pitied her. Her mind was like a child's now, in many ways. The rocker stopped suddenly, and the woman leaned forward as if she were going to get up. But she didn't. She only spoke. "I just can't believe what a beautiful day it is." Then she rocked hurriedly.

Sadie said nothing. She turned back to the window and allowed her eyes to follow the two bundled up figures of her sons walking up the cemetery bluff with a shovel and a pick in their hands. They were past the well house, turning near the pond – like marching in a processional – to dig another grave for when Ammon would depart this life. Ammon lay in the next room beneath the heavy blankets and the watchful eyes of his sisters, his breathing measured and one foot already imbedded in the Promised Land.

"I just can't believe what a beautiful day it is."

Sadie sighed heavily and collapsed her shoulders, grabbing a soapy dish with one hand and a rag with the other. She scrubbed forcibly, even though the plate was clean. A teardrop welled in each eye and rolled down her cheeks. Lenora stopped rocking and placed both arms on the rests. "I just can't believe what a beautiful day it is."

"Perhaps because it is not a beautiful day," she snapped at the old woman. "It's cold like it's still winter, and the boys are outside digging a grave for little Ammon in the cold, hard ground." She dropped the dish and the rag and spun around. "Perhaps that should convince you that it certainly is not a beautiful day. This is my fourth child to bury since we settled on this prairie. First Alfonso, then Laura and the baby, and now little Ammon… and I'm getting ready to go back by his bedside and sit with him again, to watch him breathe his final breath on this earth. The worst of all is that my William has vanished from the earth and nobody can tell me where he is." She breathed with much effort and choked back the tears. "And dishes don't wash themselves." She turned back and tried to compose herself. "Where is that girl?"

Sadie glanced out the window, then swiftly turned back towards the sitting room in one uninterrupted move. "Evelina!" she yelled. She grabbed a towel that was draped over a chair, dried her hands, and dabbed the tears on both cheeks. "I reckon she's outside with the boys. I reckon that's where they all got to, except Lutie and Lillibet sitting in yonder with Ammon." Sadie didn't really need Evelina to dry the dishes. She just wanted to feel her presence or hear her voice while the boys pummeled the soil. "In just a little bit they'll be coming in that door and telling me the little grave is dug. I tell you, Lenora, I don't see how they got the shovel in the ground as cold as it be. I don't know how they could get the shovel in the ground any ways."

Lenora continued rocking, this time slowly and easily. Sadie draped the towel across the back of the chair and glued her eyes on the sad, hoary haired woman lolling there in her tasteless grey dress and a clump of her drab hair up in a bun. She looked at Sadie, bewildered.

"I'm sorry Lenora," she spoke. "I didn't mean to snap at you. It's just that… it's not every day you bury your child. I didn't mean to bite at you."

Lenora smiled and kept rocking unmindfully.

"I reckon it doesn't really matter," Sadie spoke mostly to herself. "You won't remember this conversation anyways." She touched the ancient woman's shoulder and petted her piled up hair. "You poor thing. You have nobody at all. How can I complain?"

A short time later the door opened only a few inches. It was Anton, her eldest son – only thirteen and already wise to the cruelty and unfairness of the Nebraska plains. "The grave is digged, Ma," he announced solemnly without bothering to come inside. She could feel the cold draft from the outside… and from his words.

Sadie and Lenora glared at Anton's bundled up face through the space in the door. "It didn't take you long," Sadie commented not really knowing what to say.

"It wasn't easy," he explained like he had been plowing the field. "We cut it up with the pick axe and the dirt sort of just fell apart. The ground isn't frozen, just rock-hard and in big clods. You know the seeds the girls planted in the barn are up and wanting to bloom a little already, like summer time. Don't know how they can live when it turns cold like this. Must be God."

"Thank-you, Anton. Your little brother sure did look up to you."

Anton lowered his eyes inside his snug cap and made no reply.

Sadie was back to her full composure now. Her grieving had been mostly spent over the past couple of weeks. There weren't many tears left inside her. Just anger. She thought about the flowers meant to go on the graves. She told the girls it was too early to sow them, but they wanted to start them in the barn early so they could make the graves look pretty. She called back to Anton. "Tell your sister to come inside. I need her help."

"Which one?"

The question seemed to surprise her. "Evelina."

"She's not out there. Lillibet and Lutie ain't out there neither."

"They're with Ammon. Where is Evelina?"

"Don't know. I ain't sighted her in a while." Anton closed the door hurriedly.

"Where could that girl be?" Sadie asked aloud, not expecting a reply from Lenora. She looked out the window to see Anton hauling the tools to the barn. The sun, oddly enough, was glowing like summer, and melting the final remnants of snow. "Evelina's soon going to be seventeen and she's become quite a handful not having a father around." She glanced at the old woman. "That girl is my greatest trial. What will become of her?"

Lenora smiled as though her head were filled with pleasant thoughts of prairie flowers in full bloom down by the stream – Wild Petunias, Black Eyed Susans, and lovely Lupines. She nodded her head continually as if she were keeping time with a tune at a barn dance. She seldom spoke, except to sing a hymn or to repeat herself. Was she singing or talking to herself or to her husband's ghost... or maybe even to God?

Sadie smiled sympathetically. "Looks like I'll have to finish up the dishes myself, Miss Lenora Belle, honey. That girl must be outside somewhere. I know she's not in there with Ammon and the other girls." She paused and looked out the half-frosted window again and wagged her head slowly. "Poor, poor little Ammon. He was always a frail child. Only five years old. He never did have a chance to live his life properly. My heart is breaking something awful, Miss Lenora. First my little children...and then William disappearing..." She swallowed and choked back a tear. "I reckon all I can say is the Lord must know what's best. He has to know something that I can't see cause I can sure make no sense of it."

Lenora stopped rocking once more and leaned forward, scooting to the edge of her seat. She looked like she wanted to say something again; but whatever was on her mind couldn't seem to make it to her lips. Then the same words quickly slipped out. "I just can't believe what a beautiful day it is."

"Me either," answered Sadie, placing her arm across the woman's shoulder, and leaning over to kiss her on the cheek. "It is a beautiful day. It may be a bit too cold and the wind is howling like a coyote, but at least the prairie flowers are soon gonna be blooming all across our family's three tiny graves. That is my only hope, Miss Lenora, dear, my hope that somehow something beautiful might come of all this."

THREE

✿⚮

Evelina was nowhere to be found. Where could she possibly be? It wasn't like she could find many places to hide on the open plains. A depression here, a boulder there, a mound of dirt heaped high by the wind, covered with a trace of snow. But she wouldn't be out there, not even in her favorite place, the copse of trees on the edge of the property – not in this cold, thought Sadie. She knew her daughter hated the plains living and talked often of running away to New Orleans to look for her father.

"Your father isn't in New Orleans, young lady," she would scold her.

"Town folks say he is."

"You can't believe everything you hear in town."

But the more she thought of Evelina running away, the more her motherly suspicions rose. She gasped and placed her hand on her heart. Would she really up and run off? Sadie remembered that there was a new fellow in town her daughter had taken a liking to. She met him coming out of church one Sunday and spent an overstretched while talking with him beneath the widespread church tree while the family patiently waited in the wagon. *Would Evelina run off like she always threatened to do?* Her mother pondered.

Evelina was her rebellious child if there ever was one. Her eldest daughter and eldest child, almost grown into a woman now, had become as wild as a plains buffalo ever since her poor daddy disappeared. She could not understand her daddy just running off and discarding his family in Nebraska, not to see his wife and children again. But she knew, as did the town's folks, that he had a commanding weakness for money and risking it flagrantly to get more. Evelina had heard the gossip often that William Williston got caught up in some business scheme or amassed a huge gambling debt or fell for some young saloon girl. Evelina would never believe those tales, but she pretended she did when she wanted to argue. Her daddy could never really do wrong in her eyes.

She called out her daughter's name while the frosty wind slapped her in the face. She thought about William as she hurried towards the sod barn. She remembered very clearly the day she met him in Arkansas, back in late '49. He had just arrived from California where he made it rich in the gold rush. All he talked about then was his gold and getting more of it. By then the gold mines were swarmed with prospectors and life in California was dangerous. William vowed he'd not go back there; instead, investing his gold and making more money in the east. They fell in love with each other. William was a remarkably handsome man, strong as a bull and as gentle as the fallen dew, traits that helped her look past his one, glaring flaw…the love of money.

They moved from his family home place in Arkansas before the War Between the States began, knowing that war was inevitable and that no one they knew in the South was interested in settling the succession matters peacefully. The Willistons didn't own any slaves and didn't want to. William made it clear to the townspeople back home in Arkansas that he didn't believe in making another human being his slave and wasn't about to fight for the right to do it. *All people are made in the image of God*, he would say. There were other issues behind succession, but this was the one everyone talked about. With his gold and money, they moved up north and bought the farm she lived on now.

When the Homestead Act came about, she and William watched an influx of new families move to the area and quickly the little, nearby town of Glensbluff began to grow. Nebraska was their home now, even without William. Because of her strong Christian faith and desire to help the less fortunate, people still came from far and near to find refuge on the Williston farm. Sadie turned no one away who sought help. Her family, blood kin or not, grew like the town.

"Evelina!" she cried out once more, crossing the yard. She saw Anton and Amos outside the barn with weary, forlorn expressions on their faces. She looked around at the three little graves. Amos' twin brother, Alfonso, was the first grave. Then Lillibet's twin sister, Laura and the little still born baby, was next. The third grave, freshly dug, would soon become Ammon's.

"Anton!" she called. "I'm huntin' for Evelina. I can't find her."

Anton and Amos both stopped and turned at the same time.

"You sure you haven't seen your older sister?"

"I told you, Mama, I ain't seen her."

But Amos volunteered. "I saw her."

"Where?"

Amos recoiled as his brother shot him a nasty glare.

Sadie offered her own punishing glower. "Ok boys. If you know where she is, you had better tell me for the sake of the seats of your pants." She knew the boys were too big to whip; and she didn't have the strength to do it anyway. "Ok Amos, you know something of her whereabouts?"

He glanced at his older brother quickly, then back towards his mother's stern face with his sheepish eyes. "I think I saw her going towards the barn."

"You think." Sadie gave her boys a look of doubt and turned away tromping on towards the sod barn. The barn was built against a small butte, just like their home, and was reinforced with timbers. Most of the settlers had no wood, except what they brought with them in their wagons – or even the wagon wood itself. But William managed to buy wood with his gold and had it shipped in by train. He picked it up in wagons and hauled it north from Omaha to their new land.

Their home had what looked like a face on it, formed with windows and doors – unlike many of their distant neighbors. It seemed that the windows were eyes and the door was an open mouth. It seemed to be smiling all the time. A happy face. The barn, however, was simple and unattractive. It was reinforced on the inside with beams and rafters, but the outside looked like the side of a hill. Sadie jerked the door open, scuffing the hard soil. As soon as she put her nose inside, she smelled it. Smoke! She knew instantly what it was – tobacco. Right away she knew that her unruly daughter was hiding.

"Evelina Louisa Williston," Sadie barked like a cavalry officer. "I smell smoke. You better hope I'm wrong, but that is tobacco I smell."

Only silence. Nothing moved but a chicken cocking her head side to side as she strutted across the floor.

"Come on out where I can see you – now."

The windowless barn was too dark for her to see her daughter or even a small puff of smoke, but Sadie strained her eyes to find her. It made no difference either way. She knew smoke when she smelled it. She had been raised up back east around tobacco. She grabbed the fat straw broom leaning by the door with both hands and started across the dirt floor.

"There's no use hiding," she said. "I know you're in here and I warned you about this before. I ought to wear out your backside with this broom I got here in my hands. Come on out and stop acting like a spoiled child. Just imagine – a girl smoking tobacco! I want to talk to you."

Coughing sounds! Sadie heard it coming from the stalls in the back. "All right. I hear you barking like a sick mule. That's what tobacco does to a young girl."

From the darkness appeared a young woman with long auburn hair, wearing a pale dress that dragged the ground, her hands clasped humbly against her waist.

"You gonna deny it?" asked her mother.

"What's the use of denying it? You can smell the smoke."

"Where did you get that stuff from?"

No answer. The chicken pranced across the floor between them.

"Tell me who gave those things to you."

Evelina sighed. "It was only one."

Sadie placed one hand on her hip and leaned back. "I don't care how many there were. I want to know who gave it to you."

"Mama!" the young woman protested. "I'm almost grown now. You can't tell me what to do no more."

Raising the broom with one hand and holding it out like a scepter, Sadie quaked it at her daughter. "Oh yes I can, girl. You are right about one thing. You are almost grown. Almost! I'm still your mother and you still live under my roof."

"Believe me," Evelina snapped back. "It's not because I want to live here. I'd give nearly anything to move back east. Why can't we live back east like sane people do instead of out here on these wasted plains? I hate it here."

Sadie knew she had never beaten her daughter with a broom stick and never would. But oh, how she wanted to. "That's enough. Your father brought us to this land because he…"

"Yeah, I know. With all his gold. But where is he now? Running around New Orleans gambling it all away." She watched her mother's eyes grow like saucers, just as she hoped they would. "Well, everybody in town is saying."

Sadie knew that her daughter was speaking only from her hurt. "You know you don't believe that, child?"

"People in town are still talking. They all are. Why don't we just pack up and move to New Orleans and you'll see it for yourself."

Sadie was speechless. She released a deep breath. "I need to put a stop to you going into town. They're putting silly ideas into that brain of yours. Your father wouldn't just run off. You know that. Something happened to him."

The young girl coughed again. "Yeah. Then where is he? Oh, what does it matter?" She slapped the dirt off the hem of her dress, frightening the lone chicken. "He's still not here and we won't ever find out where he went. So, what good is it to have a daddy we can't find?"

Sadie twirled the broom upside down and leaned on it. "Evelina, stop talking foolishness. Your daddy loved you and he wouldn't be gone unless something disastrous befell him. And stop changing the subject. Smoking is what I'm talking about. It's bad for a woman and it makes you smell like a camp fire."

"Smoking ain't so bad. Men do it all the time and it ain't hurt them." The chicken turned and approached the hem of the girl's dress. Evelina kicked at the bird.

"But you aren't a man. And I wish you would stop saying ain't. That's another bad thing for a girl to do. They sure don't talk that way back east. Now I asked you who gave it to you."

"I won't tell."

"It was that new fellow in town, wasn't it?"

"No ma'am."

"What's his name? James?"

"Jamie – and he doesn't even like tobacco."

Sadie rolled her eyes. "Is that what he told you? I'm gonna tell him he's done spending time around you and to move on. Who is he anyway? He's not from these parts." Sadie didn't give her time to answer. "He works for that crooked outfit in town – that lawyer, doesn't he?"

Evelina stomped her foot on the black dirt. The light from the door in front of her lit up her angry scowl. "He ain't like them. Besides, it wasn't him. That's not fair to accuse him all the time just because who he works for."

"That's a good enough reason for me. But I accuse him also because he's always trying to ruin my eldest daughter's character. Yes. He needs to stay away from you."

"It wasn't him, Mama," the girl cried. "You never believe anything I say. Jamie didn't do nothing wrong. Why, I haven't even seen him since church let out last Sunday."

Sadie grinned. "Yeah. Hanging around outside the church. Why didn't he come inside for service? Is that when he gave it to you?"

"I promise you on my daddy's grave he didn't."

"Your daddy doesn't have a grave, Evelina – not one we know about. He can't be running around in New Orleans and in a grave at the same time."

"Oh, what does it matter!"

"If that fellow didn't give it to you, then who did? I can't stand here and hold on to this broom all day."

"I promised I wouldn't tell you."

Sadie jabbed the wooden handle of the broom in the soil like a spear. "That's all the more reason to tell me. Someone who would ask a girl to make a promise like that to begin with has to be a wicked man. Who was it?"

Silence followed again.

"Well," her mother pressured her. "Do you want me to go get Preacher Pearsall now and bring him in here to talk about tobacco?"

"I thought you didn't know."

"Know what?"

"Who gave me this tobacco," Evelina replied.

Her mother looked momentarily muddled and then speared the soil again. "If I knew, I wouldn't be standing here asking you." The chicken jumped, flapped her wings, and disappeared behind the stall. "If you don't tell me who gave that tobacco to you, I'm going to take you to the minister and we're going to get to the bottom of it."

"He told me never to tell you, Mama."

"Who?"

"The minister." Evelina just stared at her.

Sadie suddenly understood. "The minister?"

Her daughter stepped closer into the light and her face turned white as she nodded.

"No. Not the minister," cried Sadie. "Tell me he didn't give it to you." Evelina lowered her gaze, but Sadie raised her voice. "Not the man of God." She looked directly into her daughter's eyes. "If you are lying to me…" she shook the broom bristles at her again.

"No, mama. I thought you knew it was him all along."

The woman sighed. "Why would he do such a thing. I guess I shouldn't be surprised with all that he's been through, but…. when even the minister…"

"Don't blame him, mama." Evelina regained her nerve again. "I'm a woman now. Leave me be to make my own choices."

"I reckon I can't blame the minister after what happened to him. He's fallen from his calling. But I can certainly blame you. You're too smart to have taken it." Sadie could only shake her head as she released the broom handle allowing it to fall against the wall. Exasperated, yet humbled, she spoke as if all her breath had escaped. "Come on, child. Anton just finished digging Ammon's grave on the hill."

"But he's not dead yet."

"No."

"And I'm not a child."

"No. I suppose you're not; But your little brother will soon be gone. I thought you would still be sitting in there with him instead of hiding out here in this barn. Come on. Let's go sit with him together." Sadie put her arm around her daughter's waist and escorted her to the open door. "Now isn't the time for me to be worrying about smoking, I reckon … or about the poor, backslidden preacher." The two women walked together towards the smiling house. "I can't stay away from Ammon any longer, even with all the work there is to get done. I have to be sitting there with him and holding his hand when he leaves this life. Besides, we need to give your sisters a rest. They've been in there with him all morning."

"I'll sit with him, Mama. You've been up half the night already. And you have to get everything prepared for the burial – when he does die."

"We'll both sit with him," answered her mother. "Ammon won't be here among us but a few more hours or days. I can do the chores any time when everything is over. Right now I must be sitting with him trying to somehow say goodbye to my poor, little child." Her voice broke. "Another one of my little children is leaving this world."

FOUR

❧

Anton handled death about as well as any thirteen-year-old fatherless boy growing up on the harsh Nebraska prairie. Anton was the oldest boy. He would turn fourteen in less than two months. That made him feel more like the man of the house since his father had disappeared.

Anton was a strong boy. He had to be with only one brother left, Amos. That is… after young Ammon dies. Amos helped with the farm work – and he was barely eleven. Amos and his twin, Alphonso, arrived on a cold and snowy night two days before Christmas and filled the festive season with pleasant cries. Alfonso did not live long after he got the stomach trouble and couldn't eat without bringing his milk back up.

Anton recalled hearing how their mother lost another little baby that was born much too early; and they never even gave her a name. She looked like a miniature porcelain doll. She died soon after Laura, Lillibet's twin, and was put in the same box with Laura, resting on top of her stomach with her little hands across the baby's body, as though Laura was the little thing's mother. *How strange*, he thought. *The nameless baby was born on Ammon's birthday, August 14th. And Laura was only five when she died, the same age as Ammon now.*

Life wasn't fair, thought Anton. *Babies shouldn't have to die, and mothers shouldn't have to put them in the ground before them.* He struggled to understand God's will when so much bad was happening all around him. Life just made no sense. He handled it the best way he knew how – *just don't think about it* – he decided. He couldn't figure out life anyway, *so why bust yourself trying*? He just had to accept death as the way it was and trust God to have a reason behind everything. Even harder than dealing with death was the disappearance of his father three years ago. That was even harder than digging graves. He was forced to become the man of the house at such a young age and try to be a father to his younger siblings.

The one he pitied the most was Lutie, born last, their mother's widowed child – as the neighbors called her. After their father left for Arkansas in early 1863 his mother realized she was expecting another child. She had planned to tell him the good news when he returned from his business trip, but she never got to tell the news. So, the Williston's bore nine children and soon only five would remain. These uncertain days pressed on his thirteen-year-old mind and he felt responsible for the welfare of the brood.

Anton was physically strong, but he had a tender heart. He believed his daddy must be dead or he would have come home by now. When he had dug Ammon's grave, he felt the tears well in his eyes and nearly mold on his cheeks. His brother watched him but he didn't think Amos noticed the tears. Anton was too proud, trying so hard to be the master of the house and shoulder the responsibility of their missing father that he grieved only privately. He felt like a failure. He couldn't offer his family any answers or give them any comfort about his missing father. No matter how hard he tried, he could not discover the spot the hidden money lay.

He had plunged the shovel into the broken clods. The straggling strips of snow were soft from the sun dangling in the sky above them; but the ground beneath was still hard like his heart. Only by hammering the sharp pick axe into the ground was he able to get anywhere. Now that his mother knew the task was completed, and the pile of hard-bitten clods formed a heap beside the grave, he told his younger brother goodbye and started up the worn path behind the barn. It was his way of saying he wanted to be alone.

"Where are you going?" asked Amos as if he could not guess.

"To be by myself." Anton gave a dismissing glare.

"I want to go with you."

The older brother opened the sod barn door and slipped halfway inside for a brief moment and came out still wearing his father's heavy wool coat and Russian hat that covered his ears and neck, but now with a hole digger in his grasp. "If you came with me I wouldn't be by myself."

"You gonna dig some more?" Amos asked, rubbing his hands together to keep warm.

His brother held up the hole digger as though his brother had not seen it.

"But the ground is too hard for a hole digger."

Anton merely gave a nod and lowered his eyes as he turned away. Amos wished his brother good luck. Everybody on the farm knew Anton was going to dig for hidden money. That was all he ever did, into the spring and summer and through the fall. Constantly. Day and evening. He hoped to discover the spot where his father had hidden his treasure before leaving for Arkansas. Since his pa didn't trust banks, he kept his money hidden somewhere on the farm. He changed the spot often. Once he saw him bury it in a hole in the yard. Why didn't he tell someone before he left – just in case something happened to him, and he didn't come back? Like it did happen. Yes, Anton knew his father had to be dead or he would have come back. It made him furious to think about it.

Today the ground was sticky, like thick, damp, clay and Anton knew he wasn't going to penetrate the soil without a pick, despite the sun radiating through the clouds. He realized that he wasn't even going to dig. He was just going to go through the motions. He was still grieving. He was mad at his father, mad at him for burying his money without telling somebody where he hid it and mad at him for not coming back home. Today his digging was just for healing.

Somewhere on this property, he believed, his father's money was playing a cruel game of hide and seek. It was laughing at him. For all he knew he could have been walking on top of it. But any treasure on the farm was hidden far beneath the reaches of his youthful hands. Just as he couldn't find his father, he couldn't find his father's secreted money. Though he had already dug graves for his brothers and sisters, he could never dig a grave for his father. There was no body to put in it. If only he could know where he was, if he was living or dead, and what happened to him. The hardest part was knowing nothing at all.

He pounded the diggers into the earth. They barely disturbed the soil. No, he didn't believe in miracles – not any more. He didn't even know if prayer worked. Everyone he prayed for to live only died and the father he prayed would return one day was never seen or heard from by anybody in Nebraska or Arkansas or anywhere else. Yet he pounded the ground again. There had to be a soft spot somewhere. With all the open holes from the last two years, the field looked like a family of prairie dogs had invaded. Maybe one day he would find the treasure his father had buried secretly. But not today.

The diggers slipped through the top layer easily; then struck the solid earth. Another thrust. Rock. Another thrust. Clumps of soil like pebbles. Another thrust and this time the blade slipped and scraped across the tundra. Already Anton was sweating, big beads rolling off his brow into his eyes. He didn't care. This time he wasn't looking for anything. He was just mad – plain old mad. Last fall he had spent an entire day down by the river, forming piles of dirt on top of the soil like little gopher mounds for a half acre or more. Holes were everywhere. That day he was looking for something, for buried treasure; but he didn't find anything then. He didn't find anything this frigid day either.

He stopped and leaned on the handle panting like a driven horse. He jerked the Russian hat from his head and looked up at the creamy sky. "Ok. Where is it?" he shouted up at the scattered clouds, just like always. "You know where it is. So, show me."

He dropped the hat and leaned heavily on the stick, craning his neck to see the stream and the wintery bushes all along its path, then back the other direction to the open fields and the sod barn way up ahead. "Why don't you tell me where it is? That sure would save me a lot of trouble. Don't you understand me? We need that money. It belongs to us. Tell me where it is."

He stabbed the blades at the ground uselessly while sweating drops as big as bumble bees. Finally, puffing, and red faced he pitched the diggers high in the air like they were splinters and kicked the Russian hat as he turned aside. He labored to suck the cool air into his lungs. Placing his hands on his hips he heaved up and down as he panted. While surveying the vacant land, his mind spun. *Where could it be? It has to be somewhere around here.* This was the last place anyone saw his father – here, down by the water – the morning he rode off to Arkansas. How he had prayed so hard that he would find the buried money. But it would not be today... again.

The thirteen-year-old started back to the sod barn, clomping like a horse. He intentionally left the diggers... and even the hat laying there, knowing that he would only have to come back and fetch them once it came up they were missing. So, he would come back. Leaving them there on the ground seemed to satisfy his anger at the moment as though he were punishing them for their failure to find the location.

Anton handled death, and the ensuing grief, as well as any other fatherless thirteen-year-old boy on the harsh Nebraska prairie. He was tired, tired of everything. Tired of being the man of the family. Tired of searching. Tired of not knowing. Tired of being poor. And tired of digging small graves.

FIVE

❦

Three Months Earlier
January 1866 Smithsbluff, Kansas

B en Granger sat lofty on his large brown stallion as he and his men
rode into the small town of Smithsbluff, Kansas, a few hundred
miles south of the Williston farm. The townspeople, milling
about on the raised boardwalks and grimy streets went about their
late morning business. But this morning they hesitated and stared at
the six men riding into town as if they knew they were up to no good.

The sun above Smithsbluff adorned the sparsely clouded skies
like a fat pumpkin on a picnic cloth; but the wind puffed a cool
breath. Small patches of a recent snow still lingered on the corners
of the buildings where the sun paid no attention to them. Moisture
from the winter presence clung to the road allowing the horses' hoofs
of the six riders to stir up mud like dough on a rolling pin. The sun
and the snow were competing.

Ben Granger was noticeably the leader. He rode in front just
a head's length ahead of his former enemy and now partner, Siler
Penrose. During the war they fought on opposite sides and would
have killed each other if the opportunity had afforded it. Granger
still wore his blue cap and Penrose his grey one. They looked like a
pair of miss matched socks. However, now that the war was over they
had united under the common cause – or common trait they both

possessed – greed. They wanted money, or more accurately, they wanted gold. Their gold.

The big man's face had the appearance of an old wall that had stood outside too long in the desert, a wall that had weathered wind and sand until chiseled into a smooth monument. His skin was bronzed, glowing as though it had been rubbed down with oil. Creases ran above his bushy eyebrows and across his leather cheekbones. Crow's feet had left their imprints at the corners of each eye. A thick mustache covered his upper lip. His expression above the double chin was grim, but alert; his eyes searching, but drawn.

To the contrast, Siler Penrose, who reached the hitching post in front of the saloon seconds after his boss, was bug-eyed, thin faced, and dull looking. The hair beneath his grey hat stuck out like a dingy mop and the whiskers on his face sprouted like prairie weeds. Something about his expression said that he was the kind of man who would just as well shoot you first and talk later.

Granger and his men dismounted. He motioned them to scatter as though he had already given them assignments before they rode in; and they took off in different directions with strides that showed they knew who they were looking for. Penrose followed Granger into the saloon. It seemed almost empty at that time of the day, except for a couple of cowboys eating flap jacks at one table and a lone man standing at the bar.

The bartender raised his head. "We're not open yet, gentleman."

Granger spoke. "We're not here for pleasure."

"I am," barked Penrose. "Fix me up."

Rather than argue with strangers, the bald bartender frowned and set a couple of glasses on the counter.

"Not for me," Granger waved his hand.

The bartender poured tinted liquid into only one glass and Penrose quickly grabbed it and gulped. He took notice of the dirty caps on their heads. "I see you two fellows served on opposite sides in the war."

"We're on the same side now," answered Granger, looking much larger and heavier than he did on his ride. Penrose stood about six inches shorter. Both seemed sober and forbidding.

The bartender wiped the counter nervously. He sensed something was up as he had seen the other four men spread out through his town. "What brings you fellows to Smithsbluff?"

"Looking for a man. Abner Abercrombie. You know him?"

"Yes. Can't forget a name like that. He's been in here," the bartender stated. "Doesn't talk much."

"Doesn't talk at all," said Granger poetically. "Dare say you never heard him utter a sound. He's our friend from the war. He fought with Mr. Penrose here for the grey and got shot. He's lucky to be living."

"By one of yours," interjected Penrose to Granger, grinning. He noticed the look of surprise on the bartender's face. "Well, the war is over."

Granger grabbed the glass from Penrose before he could fill up again and set it down hard. "Do you know where we might find him now?"

"Yes, sir. You'll find him over at the jail."

"Oh yeah?"

"Your friend had a little too much to drink last night and started a fight with a fellow. Sheriff threw him in jail."

"Doesn't sound like our friend to start no fights," said Penrose. "What was it over?"

"You might guess."

"We are in no guessing mood, Mister," snapped Granger.

A sober look came across the attendant's face. "It was about the war," he replied. "Some other fellow was bragging on the Yanks and your friend just hauled off and hit him with a bottle over his head."

"Is that's right?"

"That's exactly how it happened."

"Well, what was the man saying?" asked Penrose, tapping his glass, and licking his lips.

"He was drunk and was just bragging about how the Yanks whooped up on the Rebs."

Siler Penrose chuckled and stared at the empty bottom of his glass.

"So," Granger interrupted. "You said our friend is in the jail?"

"Yes, sir. Sheriff Smith is holding him there."

Penrose grinned again. "Is that who they named this town after?"

"No, sir. Believe it was his family though. There's a lot of them Smiths still here. We got a Doc named Smith and –"

The big man's eyes seemed to say, *stop talking.*

Outside, Granger and Penrose were met by one of their men, Jasper Handshoe. Handshoe was a rough looking character like Penrose and wore his black hair cut short at the ears. "I found out about him," he announced.

"Yeah we know," said Granger, walking by him. "Where's the jail?"

"It's down yonder; but he ain't there no more."

"Well, where is he?"

"Gone," explained Handshoe. "The marshal came through early this morning and took him."

"The marshal!" cried Penrose. "For hitting a man on the head?"

"On what charge?" Granger asked.

Handshoe adjusted his hat and looked behind him as another one of the men, Bezold, approached. Bezold was heavy in the gut and his cheeks wobbled as he stopped to catch his breath before filling them in. "No charge against him. The sheriff said that Abercrombie was heading up north on some kind of business and the marshal said he could ride along with him."

"Some kind of business? I reckon we know what kind, but did the sheriff say?"

"Sheriff didn't know. He said Abercrombie wrote everything down for the marshal and he never saw the paper. He was just too glad to get rid of him."

"As if we don't already know where he's headin'." Penrose fidgeted and slapped his hand on his gun. "You think that weasel told the sheriff about the gold? If he did he might cause us a heap of trouble."

The large man in charge stroked his chin and looked towards the other end of town. "Whether he told the marshal or not, he's heading to Nebraska for the same thing we are. What are you waiting on? They got a big start on us. Let's get going."

The other two men, Taylor, and Moncrief, barely old enough to be men, joined the assembly in front of the bar just in time to hear Penrose's bellowing laugh. He slapped his hand on his holster again and seemed anxious to shoot. "Just let me catch up with that rascal. I'll handle him."

"All you gotta do is shoot him in the hands and he won't be able to say nothing," said Bezold.

The five men roared with laughter until Granger silenced them. "No wonder you lost the war," he said. "You just jump right into something without thinking. Maybe we need Abercrombie."

"Then what are we gonna do?" asked Handshoe.

Granger mounted his horse first and the others followed. "You men forget that before the war I was a lawyer – and still am. I know a great deal about the workings of the law. Come to think of it, there's no real hurry to get there. Maybe we should take our time and head directly to the courthouse in Glensbluff."

"But Abercrombie will get to the Williston place first," warned Penrose.

"And tell them everything," added Handshoe.

"That's why I am the Colonel and why I'm in charge of this venture," explained Granger as he pulled on the reins to prompt his horse. "The county courthouse in Glensbluff is where I figure to set up my office. There I'll get to work figuring out a good plan to take that land away from the Willistons."

"How can you do that?" questioned Penrose.

Granger chuckled again. "Now, Siler, I told you that I am the authority on legal matters in this outfit."

"What does that mean?"

"It means I also happen to be the authority on the not so legal matters."

This time all six men laughed heartily, and their horses faced north. The tall, hefty Granger swore in his saddle. "We will do this right if we ever want to get our hands on that gold. Nothing and nobody are going to get in our way, boys. Let's ride."

SIX

❀⁓

Back in Nebraska

adie knew she had to talk to the preacher about how he had corrupted her daughter with smoking, but other matters were pressing – like little Ammon. Still she thought about Preacher Pearsall often as she sat by Ammon's bedside. After all, he would be preaching his funeral and giving comfort to the family.

She had taken him in like she did all strangers. Reverend Joseph Pearsall was his name, but he said he was no longer qualified to be called Reverend. There was nothing reverent about him. They just called him Preacher. He arrived in the late summer, soon after the war ended, without horse, wagon, or family, and carried only one sack across his back. He showed up on her little farm exhausted, dazed, and angry. He was one hostile man to be called a minister. But he had his reasons.

Preacher Pearsall, his wife Annabelle, and their little one, Seth, were travelling by covered wagon to work with the Indians up north. After the war ended he felt called to move to the Dakotas to minister to the poorest of the poor Indians. That was his heart's calling. *Was* his calling. Not anymore. They were attacked by Indians, probably Sioux, and they killed his wife and child. He miraculously survived – or they permitted him to live in order to torment him.

But he was not the same as he was before his endeavor westward – so Sadie and the rest believed – even though they had not known him before. He just seemed liked a man who was not the same as he used to be, all crushed up and scattered inside. And now? He hated the Indians – all Indians no matter which tribe they were. He had lost his calling and had buried his heart and nearly lost his mind. *Stumbling in one's faith was not the worst of sins*, Sadie thought. It was understandable considering what he had gone through. She tried hard to understand. She knew it would take nothing less than the hand of God Almighty to restore him.

Still, she knew she must talk to him. After all, he was known as a man of God to folks, and could not keep living that way. Teaching her daughter to smoke tobacco of all things. They had graciously given him time to grieve since he moved into the little room attached to the front side of their sod home. But he had only depreciated. He was filled to overflowing with odium towards all people now, not just the Indians.

But today was not the best day for confronting the living. It was a day devoted to the dying, Ammon, quickly slipping away. Evelina, who sat with him through the night, sent word that he was fading like a blossom in the snow. As hard as it was to see his thin, delicate body pale with the ardor of death, Sadie knew she had to be with him when the moment came. She had other children to attend to, but he was her child too for a little while longer. Evelina was sitting by his side on the bed swathing his forehead with a damp cloth and looked up when her mother walked into the room. Lenora sat in her rocking chair beside the bed table and basin of water and rocked slowly, humming a tune Sadie recognized as *Rock of Ages*. Somehow the old widow knew.

"His breathing has slowed down considerable," said Evelina. "I think it's going to be soon."

"He still hasn't spoken?" she asked.

Evelina shook her head. "Nor drank a drop of water."

"Oh, my poor little child," she responded, her voice cracking and tears welling in her eyes. "Why so young? Why could it not be me?"

"The other children need you, Mama. They couldn't make it without you and Daddy both."

She sat down on the opposite side of her little boy and stroked his hair with her open hand, allowing the strands of blonde hair to filter through her fingers. "He would turn six in August," she reflected. "I remember so well the day he was born. I was carrying him inside me when we moved up here and he was born in this house. His lips are so dry. Can you try again to give him some water?"

"He won't take it."

"He has to. Give me the cup."

She handed the cup to her mother who raised his limp neck with one hand and placed the rim of the cup against his lips with the other. When she tilted it ever so slightly, the water simply ran down his chin onto the grey sheet. "Come on, my little baby. Take a drink for your mama. You got to drink something."

But Ammon didn't drink. He didn't open his eyes. He didn't even take another noticeable breath. The morning passed while his mother cradled his little head in her arm and gently rocked him side to side. Before the sun was high, Ammon gave up breathing all together, little by little, until the final shallow breath escaped his mouth like smoke from an extinguished candle. Her little child had left Nebraska and this life to awaken in the arms of angels.

Lenora continued her drone, purring like a kitten, unaware that anything had changed. Lutie and Lillibet stood in the doorway and watched guardedly as though coming into the room might grant death's power over them. Their faces were grim and their eyes moist. Amos went outside to tell his brother that Ammon was gone. The room was filled with peaceful humming and soundless weeping until the sun was no longer high in the sky over western Nebraska.

Preacher Pearsall had been compelled to come. He stood over the death bed beside Lenora and could not speak a word, not even to pray. It seemed as though he were the one who had died. The next day he stood over the small grave, mere resolution holding him up, gripping his heavy black book in his hands. The thick shadow of a beard covered his face like a mask of bees clinging to a hive. He flipped through the pages nervously and ironed one down with his open palm against the breeze.

"Behold, children are a heritage from the Lord," he read without feeling. "The fruit of the womb is a reward. At that time, the disciples came to Jesus, saying, who then is greatest in the kingdom of heaven? Then Jesus called a little child to Him, set him in the midst of them, and said, Assuredly, I say to you, unless you are converted and become as little children, you will by no means enter the kingdom of heaven. Therefore, whoever humbles himself as this little child is the greatest in the kingdom of heaven. whoever receives one little child like this in My name receives Me."

He read some more scattered passages and spoke a few words about little Ammon's brief time on earth; then prayed eloquently a prayer read like a script. When he spoke the final *Amen*, he imprisoned the book against his breast and stepped backwards three strides. That was his signal that he was done. Amid the tears and soft wails about them, Anton and Amos spooned the rich soil over the top of his tiny box. First a clod, then a handful, and finally a shovel load. The clotted dirt seemed unfitting to fall on their little brother, cold and cruel as they packed it down into a smooth mound. Deathly silence followed. Only a distant rooster crowed.

Finally, Sadie released a bursting breath. "Soon some little prairie flowers will grow over Ammon's grave like they do on Laura's and Alfonso's."

"Yes," added Evelina. "Big colorful clovers."

Lutie stood over the grave and wiped away a tear. "Purple ones. I like purple best."

Evelina smiled sympathetically. "That's sweet, honey. I like purple too. The Blazing Stars were Ammon's favorite. His grave will look so pretty with some tall Lupines and Coneflowers and some small wild Petunias that will soon spread out and cover the dirt like God's tablecloth."

"Are they purple?"

"Yes. Many of them can be. Pa brought a lot of colors back with him. We'll make Ammon's grave look pretty. If we must keep living on this wasted land, we might as well try to make it look beautiful."

"Evelina."

"I know, Mama."

Lillibet's eyes brightened as she smiled at the vision of florae, but quickly darkened. Her little chin drooped, and her mouth puckered. "But why did Ammon have to get sick? Why did he have to die? I prayed so much for him to get better."

"You'll have to ask the preacher that, honey," answered Sadie. "I have the same questions and I haven't found the answers yet. But we know God never fails."

"Flowers will make it look pretty," Lutie said. "But Ammon still won't be living up here with us."

"Yes, he will," replied her mother. "He will always be in our hearts."

Three graves holding four of her offspring spaced so close together in a row, thought Sadie as she stared at the little mound of earth that William started himself when Laura died. She looked just beyond Ammon's plot. *Who would be next?* She wondered, moving her eyes to each mound of earth. How much more could she bear? Was William already dead too, and would he one day finally be buried here? So many emotions stirred in her heart.

As much as she would have loved to sit by the graves and talk to her babies, or sing a song to them, or just ponder on their sweet little faces, the grieving mother knew she had to get back to the house and get busy. There was always labor to do on a farm. Her other children needed her more now than before. So did the other souls in her care. There was little time for grieving on a prairie farm.

The following day Sadie decided to talk to the preacher about the tobacco he gave to Evelina. She didn't want to. He was still hurting from his own misfortune, but it was something she needed to do. The preacher's room was off to the side of her house, opposite the kitchen on the other side. There was a short boardwalk William had built, connecting it to the front porch, and the room could be entered only from the outside. It opened into a tiny room first, like an enclosed porch stoop, before one stepped down into a widening foyer leading into a narrow hall. The door off the hall opened into the preacher's room and then outside through a backdoor.

She didn't mean to eavesdrop. She had pushed open the front door rather loudly, not meaning to sneak at all, intending to announce her presence. She even tromped intentionally across the wooden floor, across the small foyer filled with old books and odds and ends that they recovered from his abandoned wagon after he had arrived. They were layered with dust. His large Bible was lying open on a small table.

Through the next door that led to his sleeping room, she heard his voice. He sounded like he was in great agony. Her first thought was Ammon's funeral. Had his death affected the preacher deeply, so short a time after burying his own child? He was talking to someone. To himself? She should have turned and left but she didn't. She stopped, as though obligated to stand in that spot to listen. It sounded like a prayer.

He spoke forcefully. "Where are you, Lord? I don't see you… or feel you… or even hear your voice speaking to me anymore. Are you really there? I long for you, Lord God of Heaven. I do so desire to hear your voice. As the hart panteth for the water brook, so my soul longeth after you, the Living God. But you are awkwardly silent to me."

She heard some shuffling on the floor inside his room and imagined that he must have gotten down on his knees on the floor boards. "You have taken my wife and my child from me by the very hands of the ones I came to serve. Oh God, I am a wretched man, so filled with hate in my heart so much of the day and night. My joy and my peace have fled from me. How shall I ever get it back again? When will your spirit come back to me and restore the joy of thy salvation?"

Sadie turned to leave, feeling so guilty for listening to his heartfelt prayer; but she recognized the scripture he was pouring from his heart. *It's a Psalm of David*, she thought. "Thus, my heart was grieved, and I was pricked in my reins. So foolish was I, and ignorant…" He paused a brief moment, then cried passionately. "Whom have I in heaven but thee? And there is none upon earth that I desire beside thee. My flesh and my heart faileth: but God is the strength of my heart, and my portion forever."

As she backed away furtively to the door she heard more scuffling as if he had stood up and were moving across the boards. For outside there arose a distracting clatter. It was shouting. She recognized the voice, Amos, his raucous cries of alarm. *What on earth could be going on?* She wondered. When she opened the door she saw him dancing with anticipation.

"What on earth are you bellowing about?"

"Indians, Mama," he replied. "Indians coming."

SEVEN

he prairie woman raised her eyes to take in the broad landscape but saw no one. "Where on earth are they?"

Amos pointed beyond the sod barn to the open grasslands. She shaded her eyes and observed nervously. The preacher followed her out the side door and stopped beside her, shading his eyes too, and straining to spot some movement. "Are you sure?" he asked. "I don't see any Indians."

"Yes, sir. I saw them with my own eyes...way out there...way beyond the barn. I ran as fast as I could to warn you."

Sadie and the preacher remained motionless and scanned the view all the way to the horizon, still protecting their eyes with cupped hands. "I still don't see any," the preacher repeated.

"Just a ways... over that away," Amos insisted, stretching his arm. He hurried past the side of the mud barn where the wagon was kept; then turned his eyes back to see if his mother and the preacher were following.

Sadie gazed at the preacher to read his eyes; but they seemed as lost as hers – except that they were wild with fear with his bushy eyebrows arched, his nostrils flared like mountain caves. His face seemed distorted. "I can't see a thing for this sun." He sounded panicked.

"Amos?" Sadie started to chide him.

"No, Mama. I see them." His eyes moved steadily across the scene. "There they are. They must have stopped. Now they're moving again."

"Your eyes are younger than mine – oh! I see them. Well no wonder we couldn't see them. I was looking for a big party of them. There's only two."

"I see them now," said the preacher. "They're moving awfully slow."

"And I see just one horse," Sadie added. "You sure them are Indians?"

"Looks like Indians to me."

"Well, they seem to be heading this way." She looked at the man of God who had lost his family to Indians and wondered what his response would be. Would he cower and hide in the barn or would he be vengeful, grab a gun, and run out shooting. She couldn't decide. He looked worried. She was worried herself, wondering who they were and why they were coming their way, but their modest presence created no alarm to her. "They look like they mean to come peacefully."

"Or perhaps they are coming to kill us?"

"Not likely, Preacher. "There are only two and they have what looks like a crippled horse."

Amos agreed, "It looks like the horse is pulling something."

"A wagon?" asked the preacher.

"No, sir. More like he's dragging something behind."

"Your eyes are sure better than mine."

Sadie placed her hand calmly on her son's shoulder. "Go and fetch a rifle just in case, son."

While she waited for Amos to sprint to the house, the minister stepped backwards a few paces until he was behind her. "What are you going to do?" he asked. "Kill them before they get a chance to get us?"

"Of course not." The woman heaved a lengthy sigh. "Don't be foolish. It's just that we are alone out here and have to be cautious."

He stood there with his legs apart, arms arched by his sides, like a determined gunslinger ready to draw. He patted both hips and realized he wasn't wearing a gun. Though he never carried one before, he licked his dry lips and felt like part of himself was missing.

All he could see through his wide, glazed eyes were the band of Sioux Indians that attacked his wagon. He could even hear them in his head – their shouts and war cries, whooping and wailing as they circled the wagon, dust clouding the air, violently attacking. It seemed like he was swept back in time.

"God, help us!" he could imagine hearing Maggie cry as a warrior grabbed her from behind with a wicked smile on his face and jerked the bonnet from her head. "The baby!"

He sprung towards her ready to tear the painted man off his wife – with his fingernails if he had to – but then he heard the baby's cry. Samuel. A warrior instantly leaped into the wagon. Before he could take a step, another one of the wild brutes lunged for him with a broad knife. It missed him, but he fell backwards against the wagon wheel, stunning him. He could hear Maggie's piercing screams reviving him like smelling salts. He called out to God with raspy breath. *God help me.* Under the wagon he crawled and then scampered like a rabid dog towards the trees. But Joseph Pearsall was not running away.

Two Indians were chasing him. He looked frantically for something to use as a weapon. There – where their fire had gone out – a log. He grabbed it and in one motion turned and swung, knocking the first man off his feet. The second Indian pounced on him before he could recover, taking the both of them to the ground, rolling on the brown sward of dirt, across the heap of warm ashes, body against body, his nostrils reeking with the scent of sweat and raw flesh. He found himself on top of the painted man; and the creature beneath him was clawing at him as he brought his fist down on the warrior's lean face.

The last sound from his memory, he could still hear the Indians whooping behind him, Maggie calling out to God, and Samuel crying from the wagon. Then, suddenly, all around him swirled and went dark. He woke up some time later with his face in the dust near a lonely scrub. The rest was gone from recollection. He rolled over painfully and raised up – his head busting from the pressure behind his eye sockets, pounding like a blacksmith's hammer. He was alone, everything as quiet and as peaceful as a rippling fountain in a church flower garden. The birds in the trees chirped merrily behind him. He could hear their gentle songs.

But the thought suddenly came to him. *Maggie. The baby. Did God hear Maggie's pleas or Samuel's cries?* He stood up, staggered like a sick cow, and made his way towards the overturned wagon. The Indians were gone, even the one he struck. He expected the worse and knew in his heart he wouldn't find her alive. Did they kill her or take her and Samuel away to kill later? As he searched for her around the stripped wagon he saw something on the grass not far away. Maggie, her blue flowered dress half ripped from her body. He knew instantly that he would never hear her tender voice again saying, "*I love you, Joseph.*" Then he remembered Samuel. *Did they take him?* But, no. Samuel lay motionless in the wagon, bloodied, no longer with breath in his lungs to cry.

These were the images that visited over and over in his mind that very moment in time as he watched the miniature caravan plod along. They played over every night in his nightmares like he had a front row seat to a tragic play that always ended with the same closing scene. He buried Maggie and Samuel together in a shallow grave in the woods by a Black Chokeberry bush, still colorful with its flame red autumn foliage contrasted with its dark black berries, just like his life. That would serve as their only marker. The horses were gone too. Joseph felt more alone than ever in his life. Then he fell to the ground, exhausted, and slept for a whole day beneath the wrecked wagon out of the flaming sun. It was then he walked away and wandered like a dazed deer before he was found on the banks of the Republican River by a homesteader.

God hadn't heard his cries either. *Where are you God?* He wondered. He asked the question to himself once again, barely moving his cracked lips, as he gazed upon the travelers.

"What did you say?" It was Sadie's voice that drew him out of his nightmare.

"Nothing."

She gave him an inquiring look, drawing her eyebrows stiff.

Then she turned her attention back to the two walking figures and the slow treading horse as they grew closer. "I wonder what they want?" she asked, rounding the side of the barn, and narrowing her eyes on the shifting dust cloud.

"To kill us," spoke the preacher with chilling assurance.

"Will you stop talking like that? I wouldn't figure so since they seem to be crawling like turtles. Amos must sure have some good eyes because I can't even tell what they are. Looks like only a couple walking… and the horse dragging something. Maybe their belongings." She stepped closer a few feet and covered her eyes again. "One of them looks small enough to be a child." She dropped her hands and looked questionably at the minister. "They don't seem to be in a hurry, do they? Well, I reckon we'll know directly what they want, if they ever get here."

"That's what I'm afraid of," his icy voice followed. "They didn't come all this way for a picnic."

"They look harmless to me."

"No Indian is harmless. You ought to let Amos or Anton shoot them as soon as they get close enough."

"Preacher!" Sadie exclaimed. "Stop that foolish talk. They're as welcome on my farm as you are. Now we're gonna greet them with the love of Christ."

EIGHT

S adie couldn't decide what she thought about the intruders slowly approaching her smiley face home. They were Indians, alright – a woman and a small child of about six. The horse plodding between them was sorrel with colorful swirls; but her beauty was marred by dust on her coat, and a backbone that sagged like a washed-out gully. The animal was dragging something made of broken tree branches that carved out the soil like a blade.

"Looks like they're hauling somebody on it," she spoke. "Someone sick or injured."

"Or a trick," asserted the preacher.

Sadie made a face at him and rolled her eyes. Just then, the Indian woman reached the corner of the barn not far from where Sadie and the preacher stood. Anton ran up to them with a long rifle, followed by the rest of the family, including Lenora who held onto Evelina with both hands. They had heard Amos's warning cries too.

"You can put the gun down, son" she calmly directed her son. "We won't need it now."

He did as she said, setting the butt of the weapon down while the eyes of the Indian woman followed it until it rested on the ground.

"How can you be sure we won't need it?" snapped the preacher.

Gentle her answer, "Look at them, Preacher. What do you think?"

"You can never tell."

"There's a tired woman, a little child, and a sick body on the rack."

"You can never take chances with these people. Are they Sioux?" Sadie wagged her head. "No." She approached the old, Indian woman, smiled, and bowed slightly. "I think they're Pawnee," she answered.

The Indian woman looked ancient from the exposure to the sun and the clinging dust. Her lips were swollen, parched, and split. She had a round face with full chestnut colored cheeks, slanted eyes, and a long noticeable nose. Her hair, parted cleanly down the middle, looked dingy, and the long braids that draped each shoulder had frayed. The braids lay across the front of her dress, a plain garb with thin vertical stripes and a decorative lace collar. Her dress was also soiled and stained with what appeared to be blood. The child, about the size of her little girls, had a smooth, slim face and a thin strip of hair from his forehead to the back of his neck.

"Run and draw some water for them," she called to her boys. "And for the horse. Feed that starving creature. It looks like it might collapse. Evelina, you and the girls fetch some food for the woman and child. They look famished too."

They did as she said, excited to have some more visitors on their farm, since they went for days without seeing a new face; and they scattered in different directions. Sadie walked around the child, touching his cheek gently as she did. Then she moved directly to the body on the stretcher. She saw that he was an old man, much older and deeper sun baked than the woman, with grey hair rolled back on the top of his head. As sultry hot as it felt in the sun, the man was wrapped to his neck and all around his face with blankets that looked as though they had once been colorful. Loose strands of grey hair blew across his wide nose.

"Come over here and help me," she called to Preacher Pearsall, who stood at a distance watching the scene.

"I don't believe so," he replied, not moving an inch.

"At least help me find a place to lay the old man."

But the preacher turned and marched straight back to his room like a defiant child.

"Then fetch Ned, if you can find him."

Preacher Pearsall acted as though he couldn't hear her. He crossed the boardwalk without a second glance and retreated behind the door into his innocuous quarters. Frustrated, Sadie groaned again.

While they tended to the new arrivals, Ned showed up. He had watched the trio saunter in from his hideaway near the stream that fed the Republican River and hurried towards the house with his fresh string of rabbits. He had been checking his traps in the copse of trees behind the home when he saw them in the distance. He knew that they were Pawnee on the run after being raided by the Sioux. It was a common sight. He stroked the strange horse and took note of the contraption it had drawn across the empty prairie. He dropped the rabbits on the well house for the younger girls to take inside and hurried over to the shade of the barn where Sadie tended to the injured man.

"I'm glad you're here, Ned. The woman refused to let us take him inside."

"Pawnee," he stated.

"Yes. I thought so. And the woman and the boy – they just stand there like they're under some kind of spell."

"I am sure they are. Fear."

Evelina had taken the widow Lenora back inside, worried more about the preacher than she did the new arrivals, and skipped up on the boardwalk towards his room. "It's ok," sounded her comforting voice. She had opened the door that led to the preacher's room and called inside. "They're not looking for you. They're Pawnee Indians."

"I know," he growled, sitting against the wall in the shadows. "Makes no difference to me what kind they are."

"They're harmless."

"No Indian is harmless."

"You can't really mean that."

"I do. Now leave me alone."

Back outside, Ned looked alarmed. He cocked his head to one side and tightened his jaws. He narrowed his dark eyes and drew down the thin brows. Then he turned around as suddenly as he had stopped. Ned was not tall, but he was built like a buffalo, thick in the chest; and dark skinned like a Mexican. His arms that extended from beneath his vest were masses of bulging muscles like hills on a prairie. A long scar rippled down his right arm.

Noting his concern, Sadie grabbed his arm. "What's wrong?"

"Maybe nothing at all," he answered in his perfect English. "The Sioux are on the prowl." He panned the horizon. "If they are raiding the friendly Pawnee, then maybe we are next."

"Let us pray not," Sadie followed with searching eyes and a quiver in her voice. "Can you find out what happened?"

"I will speak to the woman."

"Can you speak her language?"

"I will use signs."

Ned squatted down beside the squaw who was holding the small boy with one arm. He and the squaw began gesturing with signs and sounds. Sadie left them and went inside the house to commence skinning and cooking the rabbits for the new comers. The grub her girls gave them was adequate for now, but she knew they needed a good meal.

Later that day Ned sat at the kitchen table with Sadie, Evelina, and Lenora. Preacher Pearsall was sitting in a larger chair in the living area surrounded by the smaller children. At their request he was reading to them a story from the Bible. They listened intently to his deep, animated voice.

Ned spoke over him at the table. "Their village was raided by hostile Sioux and Cheyenne. The woman said that most of her people were killed. Only a few of the women and children escaped and the last she saw of them they had sought refuge in the rocks."

"How terrible!" gasped Evelina. "Why do we live out here in this horrible forsaken ends of the earth?"

Ned kept his eyes on Evelina for a long moment. "Yes...well...they are peaceful Pawnee." He made the sign with both hands of pointed ears on his head. "This is the sign for Pawnee, the wolf people. They are friendly to white men, which is the reason they were attacked. These three survivors have traveled days from the east."

"Is the old man badly hurt? asked Sadie. "I wasn't able to tell."

"No. He was injured only in his legs when he was pushed down. He was already old and sick and will probably die soon."

Evelina protested. "We can take care of him. If his injury is not that bad…"

"It is not his injury that will cause his death. His spirit is gone," Ned explained. "In other words, he has lost his will to live. The woman is daughter in law to the man and her husband was killed in the massacre. The child belongs to her sister or someone in her family. I am not sure. She saw her people massacred, even the littlest ones. The warriors bashed their heads with stones and slung them against large rocks…"

"Ok. We don't need to hear that part?" cringed Sadie.

Preacher Pearsall stopped reading, though he didn't turn his head, and seemed to be listening.

"What can we do for them?" Sadie asked.

"You can let them stay here – at least until they might find another Pawnee camp. I will speak to some of the Pawnee I know. That is how I know a little of their language. As for the man, all you can do is give him a good death."

"No," Evelina protested. "We can help him."

"The old man has a will to die. You will not change that."

Sadie forced a deep breath. "That's all we need is another funeral. What will become of the woman and the little boy if they can't join their people?"

"They will die too. They are strong now, but they cannot live without their tribe. The woman made signs that she struck down the Sioux warrior who attacked her father in law. She hit him on the head with a tool she used for farming. She is not afraid, but she will die nevertheless without her family."

"Then we will be her family," stated Sadie, "much as we have become your family, Ned."

The rugged man looked down at the table cloth. "I am able to survive and take care of myself." He raised his eyes again. "But the woman and child are broken in spirit. The child will heal since he is young – if he can adjust to a new life. His family and his village are no more, and he may prove demanding for you. But the woman will mourn herself to death."

"You are a herald of good news," said Evelina.

"I only speak the truth."

Evelina was not one to forget how Ned Ames came to live among them; and she had an audacious manner of speaking her mind. "Yeah, you can take care of yourself Ned Ames – right now you are able. But don't forget that we were the ones who picked you up off the ground when you were shot in the chest and dying and we nursed you back to health. You would be dead if not for Mama and me."

Ned half smiled. "Yes. You are so right. I shall have died without you. I shall never forget your kindness."

"Shall?" The preacher scoffed. "Where did you ever learn to talk like that?"

"The British schoolmaster in Arizona was a strict grammarian. Talking proper is not a negative trait, Mr. Pearsall."

Evelina went on. "And don't forget that we've hidden you from the law or bounty hunters or whoever…"

"That's enough," said her mother.

"But I still don't understand why someone would want to kill you, Ned. You never would say. Was it Indians or white men?"

Her mother elevated her voice. "I said that's enough."

"But, Mama, I want to know why men are hunting him like a wild animal. What did you do Ned?"

"I would bet on running from the law," interjected the preacher in-between reading the Bible story. "There has to be some good reason they wanted you dead."

Lillibet and Lutie found the conversation interesting. "Did you rob a bank?" asked Lutie. "Or shoot a man?" followed Lillibet.

"Pay no attention to my nosey children, Mr. Ames, or to the preacher." Sadie hushed Evelina with a gentle pat on her leg. "Whatever reason he was shot and why he is hiding is his own business. I'm a fairly good judge of character and Ned is a good man. But this talk has nothing to do with these poor Indians."

"Thank you, Mrs. Williston."

Evelina always had to get in the last word. "Don't know why you can't tell us, since you wouldn't be alive if it wasn't for us."

Her mother gave another, firmer pat on her leg. "Now back to the Indians…"

"You already have very little food for such a large family," Ned went on. "And you take in many people, like the old woman here."

Lenora's eyes met his and she beamed a pleasant smile.

"You will not be able to care for every stranger who comes to this place."

"Listen to him, Mrs. Williston," chimed in the preacher, who was attending intently all along. He paused from his reading. "Mr. Ames makes perfect sense. Send them on their way."

"Don't be foolish. We can't just send them away with a dying man."

He mumbled. "That's one way to get rid of them."

"Preacher!" exclaimed Evelina. "Sometimes you make me wonder about your faith."

Ned turned about at the table and faced the preacher. "Because they are Indians?" He asked. "Is that why you don't won't them here?"

"Yes," he answered without hesitation. "That is why."

"But I am Indian too. Do you want me to leave as well?"

The preacher stared at the open page on his Bible. The children about him tried to look him in the eyes, curiously waiting for his response; but he wouldn't look up. Finally, he muttered. "You are only half Indian."

"It is the Christian thing to do to help them," claimed Sadie, confidently. "Just as we take everyone in, Preacher, I wouldn't dream of not taking them in." She narrowed her eyes. "You need to listen to that book you're reading to the children."

The cleric lifted his head this time and looked Sadie in the eyes. "It's a matter of survival," he preached. "The winter was a hard one and the food supply is low. We don't know what kind of season we'll have yet. It might be dry or the harvest even fail. You cannot give your food away to strangers when you might not have enough to feed your own family."

Sadie remained firm. "God will supply our every need according to His riches in glory by Christ Jesus, wrote the Apostle Paul. That's in that book there, Preacher. Philippians..."

"I know where it is."

"We will not turn away any soul who needs our help. And let me remind you, Preacher Pearsall, you were a stranger and we took you in and fed you. That's found in Matthew twenty-five."

Ned looked Sadie in her eyes. "Back to the Pawnee. The truth is the woman and child may not accept much of your help. Pawnees are proud people."

"They came here, didn't they?" she replied, tired of the conversation, and stood up dusting off her long dress.

"They came here like I did," he explained. "Running away from something. You just happened to be here."

Evelina reminded him once more of his providential blessing. "Aren't you glad we happened to be here when you showed up?"

Sadie smiled, proud of her otherwise rebellious daughter. "Let's go and find out what we can do to help them."

Lillibet volunteered a suggestion. "Why don't we make them a tee pee?"

"That is very thoughtful," said the dark-skinned man. "But Pawnee people do not live in tee pees."

"Then what do they live in?" she responded with an inquisitive look.

"The same thing you do...almost. They make dirt houses in the earth, like the barn."

"Then what are we waiting for?" Sadie rallied the troops. "Let's get to work making them a place to stay."

Preacher Pearsall slammed his Bible closed. "Go ahead, then. Put all your lives in danger. Starve to death this next winter. Who's to say the Sioux and Cheyenne won't come after them here and kill all of us too."

"That's a chance we'll have to take," the head of the house decided firmly. "I will not turn away anyone in need from my home. We will face with Christian love and trust in God whatever he permits to come our way, whether good or evil."

NINE

Nebraska Territory Near the Kansas Border

The two men rode side by side on their loyal horses. The robust man with the wide brimmed hat and handlebar mustache sat astride his lofty brown Kentucky Quarterhorse. A swirl colored pony carried the much smaller man. He looked older than the big man and as lean as a skeleton in the desert, with a sunken chest and protruding backbone. He scratched his scraggly beard and fanned himself with his hat. The heavier man wiped his brow. They dipped low in a shallow ravine and splashed across a narrow creek.

"Might as well let the horses drink," said the big man, Babb Stern. As he turned his body, the slighter man, Abner Abercrombie, could see the marshal's badge glittering in the hot sun. "I know we haven't come that far," added the marshal, "But we don't know how the water will hold out. Might as well take advantage of this creek and get a few swallows ourselves."

Both men dismounted and allowed their animals to banquet on the slow-moving water. A little upstream they knelt, cupped their hands, and gulped along with the horses. Then they filled up their containers for the hot journey ahead.

"You know, Abercrombie, I'm taking you only as far as Glensbluff. I've made it clear that I have official business further north in the territories. You realize that don't you?"

The reedy man simply nodded and wiped his lips with the back of his hand.

"You know there's a lot of talk about Nebraska territory becoming a state. Next year, some are saying."

Abercrombie jerked down the scarf from his neck revealing a tiny cavity on his throat where the skin had scarred over time and left the round indention. Stern noticed it as Abner splashed water on his face. "I reckon you're a lucky man to be alive after taking a shot right in your throat. It's a wonder you didn't bleed to death."

Abner didn't give any indication that he had heard the marshal; but he heard him alright. After letting their animals rest a bit longer, they remounted and started across the prairie at a respectable pace.

"Keep an eye open for Indians," said the marshal. "Some of the Sioux are being awfully rambunctious. If you see something just holler."

Abner offered a blatant look.

"I didn't mean holler." The marshal sighed. "You know what I mean. Reckon it's real inconvenient not being able to speak your mind. There are some outlaws I might wish that on, but..." The marshal let his words trail off. There was silence between them for a long minute. "Anyway," he went on where he had left off. "The Sioux and Cheyenne have been raising a heap of trouble in these parts lately. If they show up, we'll have to try to run – though who knows where to – or try to shoot it out. You're still able to shoot a gun, aren't you?"

Abner pulled out his pistol and dangled it by one finger loosely for the marshal's benefit. "Ok, Abercrombie. You don't have to get smart."

As they rode, the sun seemed to glow like a stoked fire. Both men pulled the brims of their hats lower to protect their faces from the striking rays. *It was awfully hot already for early springtime*, thought Stern. *Out here in the open where the rocks held the heat like coals.* "You really think this Williston fellow was telling you the truth?"

Abner Abercrombie dipped his hat.

"Maybe he believed it, but his mind was touched by sickness.

There was a lot of sickness in the camp, wasn't there?" Babb was getting tired of the one-way conversation. "Gold up here? Gold hidden on a farm?" He spoke mostly to himself. Then, grasping the saddle horn with both hands, he looked at his trail partner. "Buried some place on his farm, huh? You reckon he didn't know what he was doing?"

Abner shrugged his shoulders.

"You know where it is?"

This time he shook his head side to side.

"How in Heaven's name to you expect to find it? Did he give you a map or something?"

Side to side his head waggled again.

"Did he give you any idea about where to start looking?"

Another no.

"Well, good luck. You'll sure need it. Are you worried about those shady characters showing up – the ones from the prison camp?"

His *yes* gesture was emphatic.

"Expecting trouble, then? I've not heard of these men. Uh… Granger… and the other one… uh… Penrose. No, never heard those names in my line of work. And I've seen no posters with those names touting their prices. Doesn't mean they aren't outlaws; but I usually know them by name or from some wanted posters. You say they're heading up here too?"

Another shrug.

"But you think they want to get their hands on the gold too? If there is any gold." Another long moment of silence followed. "Is this Williston fellow even still alive?"

To each question the mute man nodded yes until the last question. He simply shrugged again.

"You don't know if he's alive? Was he still sick or hurt?"

Another nod. Then a sigh.

"Yeah. I know you told me all this already." The big marshal thumped his chest. "I got the paper right here in my vest pocket where you wrote it down. But what are you going to do if he's sitting right there when you get to his farm? Or if he's not there – maybe he's dead. And what makes you think his family will believe you anyway – if they are even there? You can't even tell them where the gold is hidden. They might think you a dupe and shoot you on sight. You figured on any of these possibilities?" He didn't wait for a response from Abercrombie. He didn't even turn to look at him. "Oh well, I'll take you up there to Glensbluff; but that's all I can do. I can't help you hunt for no fairy-tale treasure and I certainly can't get caught in the middle of a fight between you and those men. I say steer clear of the place and forget about the gold."

Abner shook his head vigorously.

"Ok. Ok. You do what you have to do. But mind you, you may get yourself shot... again. This time you might not be so lucky." He paused to wipe his brow. "Ah, maybe these fellows have forgotten about it all anyway and won't even bother to show up."

Abercrombie offered a little less vigorous head roll this time. It seemed obvious to the marshal that the mute man was expecting a reunion.

"You got some kind of loyalty to this rebel soldier, Williston, don't you? Made some kind of promise to him before the war ended, you say?"

To these questions, Abner did not respond with any gesture. He took a sip from his canteen, wiped his forehead, and fanned himself with his hat once more.

Marshal Stern looked dead ahead. "The wild prairie flowers are sure blooming pretty this spring. Can't say I'm much into flowers, but they sure do make the place look nice and peaceful. My daughter down in Abilene makes a big to do about picking them and putting them in vases at the hotel where she works. Bluebells." He smiled pleasantly and looked at his traveling partner. "I just hope it's peaceful for you when you get up to Glensbluff and over to the Williston farm. If I were you I wouldn't worry too much about meeting up with this Granger and Penrose. I'd worry a lot more about running into some hostile Indians who would part your hair for free."

Abner offered a weak grin and slowly coursed his head side to side at the poor attempt at humor.

The marshal grumbled. "Abercrombie, I sure do wish you could talk. It's hard to figure out your mind. Why, it's like traveling across these plains all by myself." He turned and seemed to be studying the frail, little man for a moment. "Wait a second! I think I figured this out. You're not going up there to get your hands on that gold. You're heading up there for another reason."

This time Abner pressed his lips tightly together and opened his eyes wide as he jerked his head down and up noticeably slow.

"Well," doled the large man. "I think you're taking a big risk – I mean not being able to talk and all. You're going up there to warn them, aren't you? So, that's what Williston asked you to do. Well, for all you know they've accepted that Williston isn't coming back and that he's dead and buried down south somewhere. Can't that be true?"

He shrugged his narrow shoulders again as someone disinterested.

"You ain't got the foggiest what you might walk into. I don't think you know much of anything, Abercrombie. I think Williston might be up there on his farm already and be the very one to shoot you when you ride up enquiring about some gold."

Abner motioned with one hand, pointing to himself and to the marshal.

"You mean me too?" said the marshal, catching on to the gesture. "I'm just taking you as far as Glensbluff. I don't plan on taking you directly to the farm."

Abercrombie nodded.

"It's out of my way. I'm heading further north."

Abercrombie stared at him and tapped his finger against his throat.

"That wasn't part of the deal."

This time the frail man grinned.

"I get it. You want me to do your talking for you. Okay. I'll take you to the farm and do a little introduction. But that's all. You know you can get me shot and killed too." The marshal wagged his head in disgust. "I tell you Abercrombie, if you wasn't a rebel soldier and had that hole in your throat, I would have left you sitting in that jail cell back there in Smithsbluff."

Abner jerked both legs and his horse broke into a gallop, moving slightly ahead of the marshal's steed. The lawman realized that this was his way of saying, "Let's just get going."

He called out to the man racing ahead of him. "I have a good mind to ride off and leave you here in the middle of nowhere, Abercrombie." He blurted louder, "Maybe you can find some buried treasure right here. Maybe those rambunctious Indians will help you dig for it."

TEN

nton and his younger brother, Amos, trudged along in the dark brown soil, ripping up the earth with a broad plowshare and laying it back like a deadly gash on her smooth back. The older boy shook the reigns and shouted at the old brown mule who was pulling the plow. "Get a move on, Kate. Ho!" His brother removed stones like a New England surgeon, slashing at them with the hoe and casting them into a burlap sack tied on the bar of the plow.

Back at the house Evelina had taken some food and water to the Indian family. Inside their crude little sod residence that everyone helped build, she knelt beside the old man, lifted his head, and poured water onto his cracked and swollen lips. Though they were parched, he refused to drink. He stared at Evelina with weak, but determined eyes. His flesh felt as tough as rawhide and looked the color of the bark on the gnarled river tree branches. He had chosen nobly to die.

The Indian woman spoke in her native tongue, but Evelina had no idea what she was saying.

"How do we bury a Pawnee?" Sadie asked Ned as they watched Evelina exit the simple home.

"Since they are alone, and their people dead, they will not be able to abide by all their rituals. They usually have a group of medicine men or religious men who lead the ceremony. I guess we will have to do the best we can."

"Yes," said Sadie, "It seems like we're always planning to bury someone, even before he dies." Her mind was on Ammon and her husband.

Sadie studied the Indian woman who came outside and squatted by the little hut-like structure. Her black hair was pulled tight across her head to her ears and parted down the middle. Then it developed into two recently tightened braids that fell across her breasts. Her forehead seemed wide and her nose long and obvious until it stopped just above her full brown lips. Her eyes were narrowed near like the Chinese women's she had seen in town; yet they still seemed large and lively as if filled with thoughts. She appeared to be thinking seriously about something – *perhaps her future*, Sadie imagined, *or the plight of the child.* She weaved from side to side as she softly chanted a dirge. "What about her?"

"She refuses to speak about the man," Ned answered. "She is quietly singing her death song for him. Her silence may be part of her ritual so she cannot talk now. Her mind is strong, however. Perhaps she is mourning the loss of her people, but I am wrong about her giving up hope. Her spirit is not broken."

"What do you mean?"

"The woman is a determined soul. Her hope or, perhaps, her anger is driving her spirit. I can feel her vigor. But she cannot do this alone. We must see to the burial ourselves."

Sadie looked out across the plain. "Where do we bury him?"

"A funeral pyre is the best."

"No. We can't do that. We have a small cemetery. We'll bury him there."

"That is not the Pawnee way."

"But we can't have a Pawnee funeral – unless you know how to conduct one."

He shook his head. "I have some Pawnee friends, but there is not time to consult them. It will not matter to the woman or to the boy for they do not have a people any longer and they will not expect the ceremony of their kind. They are strangers and orphans now."

"Yes," Sadie agreed. "We have to do this ourselves and he will be buried in our cemetery."

Ned looked surprised.

"What's the matter with that?" Sadie asked.

"That is your family burial ground."

"I'm aware of that."

"The old Indian man is not your family."

"Everyone on this farm is my family, including you, Ned. The Bible teaches that everyone is my neighbor too."

He looked back at the little sod structure and saw the woman rocking back and forth, now resting on her knees. The little boy approached her, placing his arms around her neck, and rocked along with her. "They are Indians. They are not your family. Your children sleep there."

"What does that matter?" she asked without waiting for a reply. "We all sleep the same, Indian or white... the rich with the poor, the young with the old. The grave respects no person. Besides, Ned, you are Indian too – at least half Indian. We are all God's creation."

"You may tell that to your minister friend."

"Don't look down on him, Ned. He has had his own share of troubles."

"So have I."

"Haven't we all?" the matron agreed. "Preacher Pearsall is grieving like the woman there and, in a way, he isn't in his right mind from all the sorrow he's had to bear." With that Sadie turned around. "Come on. Let's get everything ready for a funeral."

"Is he already dead," asked Lillibet who was listening from nearby.

"No, Honeysuckle, but we are going to be ready when he leaves this life – just like we were prepared for your brother. Sometimes the Lord gives us a mind to know ahead of time when folks are leaving this world."

"Has my daddy already left this world?"

"Not that I know of." *But he has left my world*, she thought.

When she strode up on the boardwalk near the door to his room and told him her decision to have a funeral for the old man, Preacher Pearsall grew wide-eyed and red faced and sneered. His reaction was as predictable as the rising sun. "My Maggie and little Samuel didn't have a funeral." The pitch in his voice escalated. "Their bodies were just left for the wild animals to devour and the sun to bake. I could only dig a shallow hole for them and cover up their bodies with a little dirt and rocks; so why should this Indian get a decent funeral? Let his body rot."

"You don't really mean that," said Sadie, looking startled and wounded, even though his bitterness was not really a surprise to her. "You're speaking from your hurt."

"Yes, I am. But I'm speaking the truth."

Lillibet stood by her mother's side on the porch. She brushed back her long, golden hair and stepped a few inches closer to the man of God, timidly, as though she were afraid of him. "Do you really don't like these poor Indians?" she asked in her meek, childish voice.

The question from a seven-year-old sobered him. He stuttered. "I don't dislike them. I just hate what they did to me."

"But that old man didn't do nothing to you."

"Out of the mouth of babes…" Sadie spoke.

"The old Indian man lost his family too," her soft voice sounded like a lullaby. "We're going to bury him with Ammon, ain't we Mama."

He raised his eyes to Sadie. "What does she mean with Ammon?"

"Just what she said."

"Not in the same graveyard with your children? I won't allow it."

"You won't allow it? He's my son and it's my land," argued Sadie. "You have no say in this." She stopped and released a lingering breath. "I realize you are hurting, Preacher, but it's the Christian thing to do."

"Christian thing! He's not even a Christian man. How can you even think of burying that Indian next to your boy?"

Sadie rested both hands on her hips. "You forget that I've lost three children and a baby… and possibly… a husband too. You are not the only one whose heart is throbbing."

"But they weren't slaughtered by Indians."

"No, they weren't. But they suffered and died, nonetheless. And I don't even know how my William died, if he is dead." She whispered that part so Lillibet could not hear her. "But that doesn't mean I have to be cruel to others because of my own sorrow. Lillibet is right." She placed her soil toughened fingers on the girl's soft blonde hair. "That Indian man had nothing to do with what happened to your family. What do you think he went through himself watching his entire tribe get slaughtered mercilessly? Just look at that woman and that child over there. Look at them closely!"

He turned his head reluctantly towards the side of the little sod house where the Indian squaw rocked back and forth on her knees with the child clinging to her like a baby possum to its mother. He couldn't see her face but he could hear her softly wailing.

Sadie pointed her crooked finger at the pair. "Only the Lord knows what they saw. Whatever she saw it was enough to snatch her mind away."

"What I saw took my mind away too."

"No," answered Sadie. "There's nothing wrong with your mind. It's your heart that's been snatched away."

Lutie, who had been petting her doll's hair on the edge of the walkway, turned her head and looked up at the preacher looming high above her like a giant. Just like her sister, her golden hair scattered in the breeze. "God loves Indians," she said. "He loves everybody, don't He Mama?"

"Yes, he does, Lutie, Honey," replied her mother. "Preacher Pearsall loves everybody too." She saw his lips tremble. "The preacher is just so sad about his own family."

Preacher Pearsall hung his head and studied the boardwalk beneath his shoes.

Sadie tried to see his eyes. "I believe the preacher came all the way out here to Nebraska because he knows God loves everybody, even the Indians." She took Lutie by the hand and helped her up, Lillibet clinging to her skirt on the other side. "Come on. We have a few chores to do to get ready for the funeral. I have to bring out the family Bible and find something good to read over the poor Indian man when he dies."

"Maybe he won't die, Mama," said Lillibet.

"If it be God's will, he will stay right here with us, child. But the poor man is very ill."

"Like Ammon?'

"Yes. Like Ammon."

Night soon fell and the old Indian man died. The next morning Ned helped Anton dig the grave, just a couple of plots over from where Ammon lay. Clusters of purple spiderworts brought back from one of Williams trips and started in pots inside the sod barn were stretch upwards like vines on Ammon's grave and would soon spread and bloom all across the little cemetery. The man's body, completely wrapped in cloths, was gently lowered in the grave. The Indian woman sat at a short distance, on her knees, but no longer rocking. She gazed into the sweeping skies. The little boy sat quietly beside her and didn't seem to comprehend what was happening. He looked bewildered by the woman's silence and the sight of the old man wrapped up in linens.

Ned spoke first. "I painted the old man's face with red paint. I do not know how to make their sacred red ointment, so this was the best I could do. He did not have a tribal costume and we do not have a bison robe to wrap him in before burial, which is their custom." He saw that Sadie was staring at him as though wondering how he knew all this.

As Amos and Anton shoveled dirt into the gaping trench in the earth, Ned went on. "It is believed that after death the soul ascends to heaven to become a star, if the man has been brave. This man's soul has departed and, he looked up at the blue skies, "is now soaring in the heavens above. That is all I know to say about him."

Each one of Sadie's family took turns throwing handfuls of loose dirt on top and the boys finished the task with their spades. The soil completed a smooth mound atop the earth. Then Sadie opened her heavy black Bible and began to speak, "Job cried out in the sixteenth chapter, my face is foul with weeping, and on my eyelids, is the shadow of death; Not for any injustice in mine hands: also, my prayer is pure. O earth, cover not thou my blood, and let my cry have no place." She turned the pages. "I don't know what to say over this man because I never knew him. Only God can judge his soul. I pray that God be merciful to him. So, I comfort my own heart with the words of Psalm 18. I will love thee, O LORD, my strength. The LORD is my rock, and my fortress, and my deliverer; my God, my strength, in whom I will trust; my buckler, and the horn of my salvation, and my high tower. I will call upon the LORD, who is worthy to be praised: so shall I be saved from mine enemies. The sorrows of death compassed me, and the floods of ungodly men made me afraid. The sorrows of hell compassed me about: the snares of death prevented me. In my distress I called upon the LORD, and cried unto my God: he heard my voice out of his temple, and my cry came before him, even into his ears."

Evelina gawked at her mother. "Those are not very comforting words," she said.

"I am not feeling very comforted," replied her mother. She closed the book first, and then her eyes. When they opened she continued. "But you are right. Let's listen to something more hopeful: I am the resurrection and the life. He who believes in me, though he were dead, yet shall he live. And whosoever liveth and believeth in me shall never die. Amen."

"Can we put some flowers on his grave?" asked Lillibet.

"Purple ones," added Lutie. That's our favorite."

"Yes, we can," their mother replied. "Just not today. Let the earth settle a bit."

"Do you think he liked purple?"

"I think everyone likes purple, Lutie."

"Even Indians?"

"Especially Indians. They love nature and God made a lot of nature purple."

Their older sister stepped up between them and took the hand of each girl in her own. "I will help you plant some wildflowers on his grave when the dirt settles. Then they will grow and bloom for a long time and new ones will come back every year. Everybody knows we need to be able to see something pretty out here in the middle of nowhere"

After the brief funeral ended, Sadie spoke a silent prayer over the grave. Anton watched her closely and, after she opened her eyes, he questioned her. "What did you pray for?"

She smiled and placed a hand on his strong shoulder. "I asked God to take care of the poor Indian woman and the little child and to be good to them... and watch over us too as we leave this little graveyard and go back to our busy ways."

Anton nodded. "I prayed too."

"What did you pray for?"

"I asked God if he would just send us some word about my pa, so we can know whether to pray for him or cry for him."

"That's a right good and honest prayer, son."

"That's not all," added the lanky boy. "I asked him to show me where Pa buried his money."

ELEVEN

T he boardwalk reverberated with the sounds of pounding boot heels as the three men paraded into Ben Granger's new office on Main Street in Glensbluff, Nebraska. Siler Penrose led the way displaying his gray Rebel hat with honor. He was followed by the swaggering gunslinger, Handshoe, and the new fellow to the bunch, young Jamie Quentin. Granger sat at his desk puffing away on his imported cigar between yellowed teeth. He raised his thick eyebrows when the men appeared in the doorway and dropped the quill he was holding into the receptacle. He lolled back in his chair. "Well," he began business like, pressing down his hair with the palm of his hand. "Did you find it?"

Penrose stepped forward. "No."

"Did you find the woman?"

"Yeah. She still runs the telegraph. But she ain't got it."

"Ain't got it?" Granger echoed. "Well, where is it, then?"

"She claimed he placed the envelope inside his Bible, and there was the Bible just where he put it. But just the Bible – nothing inside it."

Granger dropped his feet to the floor and sat up straight. "What happened to it?"

"She don't know."

"Don't know! Did you show her you meant business?"

Before he could answer, Jamie Quentin spoke. "Widow Calder is sixty-seven years old."

"I don't care how old she is," the lawyer snapped. "I want that letter Williston gave her husband when he left here."

Handshoe leaned back against the door frame and opened a pouch of tobacco. "How do we even know there is a letter, boss?"

"You said she had the envelope."

"I mean, how you know that letter had directions to the gold?"

"It's my business to know things, Handshoe."

"She was telling the truth," said Quentin.

"What? Are you her attorney or something, Quentin?"

Siler Penrose never took up for anybody but himself, but this time he felt sure of Quentin's conclusion. "He's right, Ben. She went over and checked his coat – the one he was wearing that day. Nothing in the pockets. So, we went to the undertakers and asked him. He said he didn't remember no paper, but he always threw everything away before he buried a body."

Granger stood. "Maybe he saw what it was and kept it for himself."

"Or maybe," added Handshoe brazenly, "He didn't see it and buried it with the old preacher man."

"Then I see you've got some options, fellers. You can get the truth out of that undertaker and that Widow Calder or you can fetch a couple of shovels and head out to the cemetery tonight."

Penrose took another step forward and dropped a paper on the lawyer's desk. "Or you might check this out."

"You got the map?"

"Yeah. It's a complete map of the property. Every inch of it down to the rocks and holes in the ground."

Granger sat down and snatched the map, opened it, and put on his spectacles. He drew it close to his face. "It's not as big as I assumed."

The Rebel smiled, showing his missing teeth. "Not a whole lot of places he could of buried it."

The heavy man at the desk studied it like he was looking at a treasure map. "You don't need a whole lot of places. You just need one place, a place nobody thinks to look." He laid it down and looked back at the three men. In a calm, well pleased manner he added. "Who says it has to be buried. There are other ways to hide gold."

"But I thought he buried it before he left?"

"That's where you guys come in."

"So, you like this plan better than huntin' that letter?"

"I haven't given up on the letter, but until we find it you and your boys ride out to the Williston farm and scout around the property lines. Right here." He pointed to a boundary on the edge of the diagram. "Don't go on their land, just scout around the boundary line."

"For what?"

"For wagon tracks or worn paths..." the lawyer grinned. "Anything that might give evidence that someone's been going over and back out of that property."

"Why don't we just ride in and tell 'em we're going to help ourselves to taking a look around?"

"That will come soon. Right now we do it my way and I want it to look all legal." He laughed. Handshoe joined in.

Penrose didn't seem impressed. "That sounds a might bit soft to me."

"Yes," the boss grinned. "We start out soft and then hit them hard." They hooted some more.

Handshoe, dressed in his usual aphotic dark attire, noticed that the new man wasn't enjoying himself. "What's the matter? You got no sense of humor?"

"I don't get it," confessed the young man with his sun blanched hair.

"You don't have to get it, baby face," the boss man explained. "I was working on something here, boys, when you came in. When I get the legal documents drawn up and ready, I'll have you take it out to Matron Williston and place it right in her hands. But now, we keep our distance and don't give them any reason to complain to the sheriff."

The pop-eyed Penrose scratched his scraggly beard. "Still sound like we're being too easy on them. What do the papers say?"

"You mean what they will say when I'm finished with them. This document will lay out our proper, legal claim to the land and will give

Mrs. Williston and her family no choice but to meet my deadline to get off our property."

"I thought it was her property," said Quentin.

"It was," replied the lawyer, pleased with himself. "Apparently Williston left a few strings in his documents untied when he came out this way and filed later under the Homestead Act. I found those loopholes and made them a little bit bigger. Don't worry. It will hold up."

"What about that sheriff?" asked Handshoe.

The beefy jawed lawyer chuckled and positioned his cigar between his teeth again. "Since you brought him up, let me reiterate…he's not a problem to us. He's old and tired and doesn't even half know how to read. He'll find it much easier on himself and the whole town if he goes along with us. And he will. What choice will he have when I own his deputies."

Handshoe snickered, but Penrose seemed anxious. Talking always worried him. He wanted action. "So, how long 'till we take them papers out to her?"

"It won't be too long, Siler. First things first." He lifted the map and folded it. "If checking the borders of the property doesn't produce any results, we go with our other options. Right now, I want you fellows to check out the farm like I said. If we can come up with some clue as to where he might have hidden the gold, we may avoid going through all the trouble of having to serve the Williston's these documents."

"It's no trouble for me," boasted the gunslinger with a huge smirk on his face and patting his holster.

"That's why I won't be sending you by yourself, Handshoe. Your gun isn't the only thing you're good at shooting off. The last thing we need is the U.S. Marshal showing up because some fool started shooting the place up." The grin quickly disappeared from Handshoe's face. Granger went on, "The way it is now, no one knows anything going on and I want to keep it that way. If we get careless and attract the real law up here every greedy man in the territory will be looking for that gold; not to mention they might just connect us to the missing gold. I thought I might send you out there to serve them, Quentin."

"What?" complained Penrose. "That squeamy baby face?"

"Squeamy isn't even a word, Siler. Besides, Quentin's got something you don't have." Granger moved his eyes to Quentin. "After all, I hear that you are kind of sweet on the Williston girl. She is a might pretty and feisty too."

The new man froze. He wasn't expecting that. "I just saw her here in town a couple of times when she came in for supplies and church…"

"And you haven't taken your eyes off her since." The big man leaned forward and planted his elbows on his desk. "Yes, she has taken a real liking to you. I think you will be the perfect one to serve the papers the first time we go out there. If we have to go with that option." He turned his eyes to Handshoe. "You'll go with him in case somebody there wants to give him trouble – if you know what I mean."

Handshoe slapped his holster again, this time much harder. "I know what you mean, boss."

"But you don't do the talking." He turned back to the new man. "Any problem doing this, Quentin?"

Quentin thought really hard about his employment on Granger's team. "No sir."

"I mean with your liking this girl and all, you won't let that stand in the way of doing business, will you?"

He thought about the girl he'd met. But he still answered, "No, sir."

Granger rose from his chair for the second time. "I hope not. You see, I'm certain this is the stolen gold, the same wagon load of gold Williston snatched from Penrose in Arkansas at the start of the war. You heard about that?"

Quinten stroked the beginning of a beard on his chin. "Yes, I've heard that. That's why I've joined up with this outfit. I'd like to get my share too. But the story I heard was that it was stolen in Colorado."

Granger walked around the desk and eyed the young man close enough to breathe on him. "It was. But Siler had to split up in Arkansas when the soldier boys got on their trail."

Penrose growled. "Yeah, the double-crossing swindler – and I ain't seen a bar of that gold since we split up. That gold was for the South. We stole it to buy guns and food and… we would of won the war if Williston hadn't stolen that gold from us. We were in it together and he got greedy."

"Don't get yourself all roused up again," ordered Granger. "I want my hands on it too. After all, it belonged to the North before you got your paws on it. I heard about it in the prison camp, heard that somebody knew where it was. I reckon that's how you and I became friends, Siler. If Williston hadn't been shot and his mind hadn't gone bad, we'd have that gold by now. I did everything I could to make him well. I even sent him to a missionary doctor who said he could get him right again. But Williston disappeared and we have no gold. There's enough for all of us to make us filthy rich and I won't let anything stand in the way of getting my hands on it. You fellows understand?" All eyes fell on Quentin.

"I understand," answered the new man. "Like I said, that's why I joined up with your outfit, Mr. Granger. Why do you think I first set my eye on that girl?"

He stared into Quentin's eyes for a long second; then broke out into laughter. "That's good, Quentin. That's real good. I like the way you think. You being sweet on this Williston girl is a smart move on your part… if you're telling me the truth." Granger spun and hurried back to his desk. "Any questions?"

Quentin was the only one to speak. "Why do you think the gold got up here to Nebraska territory?"

"Smart man," said Granger, biting on his cigar again. "Most of the men who robbed the gold are dead now. That's why it is so difficult trying to figure out what happened to it. After all, a wagon full of gold can't be easy to hide."

Quentin's interest seemed to peak. "How come you think it's up here on Williston's farm?"

"Because of one man."

"Williston?"

"No. Abercrombie," barked Penrose.

"Abercrombie?"

Penrose explained. "Abercrombie was an old soldier in the camp."

"The prison camp?"

Granger explained. "Yes. The camp I ran during the conflict. While Williston was in the camp recovering from his wounds, he let it slip to this Abercrombie that he had treasure buried on his farm in Nebraska and if he lived through the war, he was going to head back up there and dig it up. Abercrombie was wounded pretty bad himself; so he wrote it down on a scrap of paper and that paper got into my hands." He arched his eyebrows. "I had spies in the camp."

"Where is Abercrombie?"

"We'll find him soon enough."

"Well," asked Quentin, "Where is Williston now?

"Williston's dead," claimed Handshoe.

"We don't know that for sure, but we think he might be," added Granger. "No one has seen him since the war ended. The last we saw him he was sick and dying. The last I spoke to that young doctor who was tending to him, he told me Williston might not make it. I hope he is still alive. He's the only soul who knows right where he buried it. As for Abercrombie…who knows where he is right now. He disappeared for a while and turned up again after the war. We just missed him down in Kansas a while back. Slippery as grease."

Penrose waved his hand brazenly. "Don't worry about him. He won't talk."

"But he can write," said the boss adamantly. "When he was spotted in Kansas, word was he was heading this way."

"So, you think he knows where the gold is buried?" asked Handshoe.

"It makes sense. We're watching for him." Granger continued, chewing on the stub out of one side of his mouth. "I reckon he wants his hands on it too. He might know it's here but not exactly where it's buried. But if he doesn't know, hopefully somebody does."

"You mean his wife and youngins," spoke Handshoe more like a statement than a question.

"Yes."

"Do you think there's a chance this Williston could still be alive?" asked Quentin.

"I wish I could say there was," Granger summed it all up. "It's been too long after the war for him not to have shown up already. Of course, ghosts from that war do have a way of showing up when you don't want them."

The men gave long quizzical looks to their boss.

"Like in my nightmares," said Granger. "But in this case, I hope the ghost of William Williston crosses right on over to this side and tells me where he buried my gold."

TWELVE

T he dust had hardly settled since the three Pawnee refugees showed up when Ned Ames saw another stir of dust on the horizon from his camp by the stream. He crossed the farmstead and beckoned for Sadie, who was sweeping the dirt with her thick straw broom, and alerted her of the strangers on horses. "This seems to be a busy place all of a sudden."

"Who do you suspect it is?"

"I don't know." He removed his hat and rubbed his neck. "They look like white men,"

Sadie agreed, licking her lips and warily holding her eyes on the movement. "Find a good place to hide before they get any closer. I know you're a wanted man." She transferred her eyes from the swirl of dust and planted them on her friend. He looked with apprehensive eyes. "Don't worry, Ned. I'll take care of them."

The wanted man disappeared behind the long, smiling face house, slipping through where the barn cast its shadow. Sadie dusted her dress and straightened her hair with her tarnished palms and locked her eyes on the approaching horses. Who could they be? Could they have seen Ned? Suddenly her heart fluttered as she thought about her missing husband. Did they have some news about William? Could one of them possibly be him? He could have changed so much since she last saw him. How she had prayed for that homecoming! How she had been disappointed so many times before. She prayed then that they would at least be friendly travelers.

As they neared, she became certain they were unfamiliar faces. What did they want?

Two horses came to a stop beside the well house where Sadie stood. One horse appeared to be a Kentucky Quarter and held a big man. The other was a proud pony carrying a little man. Amos, Lillibet, and Lutie came running from the rain pond where they had been fishing for frogs. They stood in a row beside her like soldiers in order of their rank and examined the two men curiously. The Indian woman and her boy exited their new sod house and took in the scene anxiously – strangers from afar on tired and sweating horses. Sadie could smell the wet equine hides.

The tall stranger on the brown quarter horse tipped his white hat to Sadie and again to her children and leaned back in the saddle. He rested his thick, dusty brown fingers on the saddle horn, breathed deeply, and searched the woman's worried eyes. "Ma'am," was all he said as a greeting. The second man offered no greeting except that he nodded and tipped his small, rounded black derby. Sadie noticed the thick checkered red and white scarf wrapped around his neck and thought it very unusual that he would wear it like a noose. Then she quickly observed the twinkling of sunlight reflected from the silver badge on the big man's chest. She thought of Ned. "How might I help you fellows?"

"Babb Stern is my name," answered the first man with his resounding voice. "I am a U.S. Marshal from down Omaha way. This here is Mr. Abner Abercrombie from Texas. Are you Mrs. William Williston?"

Her heart leaped. "I could be. It would depend on what you want with her."

The high marshal sucked in a lungful of dry hot air and quickly surveyed the surrounding property. His eyes moved from the children to his left, to the small sod shack with an Indian squaw beside it, to the grand house that looked like it wore a happy smiling face, and lastly to the barn on his right. He saw a young man, Anton, standing just in front of the barn with a shotgun braced in both hands. He released the breath in half the time it took to suck it in. "We aren't here to cause any trouble, ma'am. I am heading up north on some official business and I detoured this way for the sake of Mr. Abner Abercrombie here." He gestured to the man wearing the odd scarf.

"Mr. Abercrombie has ridden a long way to see you, assuming you are her. I met up with him kind of by accident in Kansas. He has something to tell you – if you are Mrs. Williston."

Sadie sighed relief. It didn't sound like the marshal was here for Ned. "I reckon I am her."

"Good. What he has to tell you will probably be mighty welcome in your ears."

She looked at the silent man on the marshal's right, hopefully. "Go on then."

But the marshal spoke instead. "It's about your husband…"

A look of shock must have struck her face like a slap. "Is he alive?"

Marshal Stern turned and looked long at Mr. Abercrombie. The lawman's face was tanned, durable, and shaped like it had been chiseled out of desert rock; but Mr. Abercrombie's face appeared narrow and pale in comparison – like a man who had been sick for a long time. "That he doesn't know for sure, I'm afraid. The last time Mr. Abercrombie saw him he was still alive, but that was two years ago. He knew your husband and served with him in the rebel army back in the war."

The force of his news nearly took Sadie's feet out from under her. Anton sprung forward from the barn. "My pa wasn't in no army," he cried out, angrily.

"Settle down, Anton," she ordered. "Put down that shot gun. This here is a U.S. Marshal." She turned back to look directly at Mr. Abercrombie "How do you know this?"

Stern answered again. "He served with him in the rebellion, ma'am. He spent time with your husband in a prison hospital near the end of the war."

"Are you sure it was him?" she asked the silent man again.

Abner offered a slow and unconvincing nod.

"How can you be sure it was my husband?"

"It seems that it was him for sure," The marshal answered.

Sadie seemed nettled that the big man did all the talking. "Give me the picture," he instructed Abercrombie, who reached inside his shirt pocket and withdrew a small piece of paper, handing it to the marshal. He took it and passed it down to Sadie. She stepped up beside the neck of the lofty horse and took the paper.

Anton rushed to her side. "What is it?"

She saw the faded drawing of purple flowers, "It looks like the drawing William gave me when we got married. Butterfly Weed. That was our favorite flower."

"Then you know to read the scribble on the back," said the marshal.

When she turned the drawing over in her fingers, tears began to well up in her eyes. Anton took it from her and read the scribble aloud, "I am sorry I did not come home. I love you, my Butterfly Weed."

Anton looked up at his mother with question in his eyes. With the tail of her apron she smeared the tears across her cheeks. "That was the name he had for me when we first got married."

"But… how…?" Anton demanded to know.

Sadie kept the drawing and looked back up at the pale man. "Yes, how, Mr. Abercrombie? My husband had no reason to join up with no army. He left here on business in Arkansas and never came back."

The marshal sat quietly, cleared his throat, and began to speak. "I don't know about all that…"

"If you don't mind, Marshal Stern," said Sadie, "I'd rather hear it from Mr. Abercrombie." She then darted her blazing eyes to the thin, frail man with the scarf around his neck, "Why don't you tell me this yourself instead of having the marshal do all your talking?"

Marshal Stern cleared his throat again and leaned forward in his saddle. "He isn't able to tell you himself. He can't speak."

The slight man tugged on his kerchief and pulled it down to his chest, revealing a nauseating, discolored hole about the size of a half dollar in the middle of his throat.

Marshal Stern explained. "It seems that he was shot during the battle of Big Black River Bridge near Vicksburg and he hasn't spoken a word since. Just a miracle I'm sure that he didn't bleed out right there. But it took out his voice box. Well, that's his story."

Sadie looked at Amos and her girls. "You children fetch some water for these horses. They look awfully tired and thirsty."

"Thanks ma'am," said the marshal. "We won't be any trouble."

"You two fellows get down from there and come on in the house for something to quench your thirst too. Reckon we got some talking to do."

The two men stopped at the well and chugged some water from the tin, wiped their mouths, and continued on inside. Evelina prepared some fresh coffee; then removed the apple pie from the saving cupboard and served each man a large piece on yellow china that her daddy had brought back from California. Marshal Stern and Mr. Abercrombie sat beside each other at the roughhewn wooden table while the mute man motioned that he wanted something to write on.

"Abner has to write down everything for me to say to you," announced the marshal. "Let me see if I have something to scrawl on." He reached inside his vest pocket. "He filled up my other paper. All I got is this poster here…" He unfolded it and exposed the familiar face of a man. In large black letters it read WANTED NED AMES." Then he turned it plain side up for Abner.

Sadie's eyes blossomed like sunflowers when she saw the face of Ned Ames. She suspected he might be running from the law, but didn't expect to see the sketch of his face on a wanted poster. What was it that he hadn't told her? She prayed Ned would stay out of sight. If her mother's eyes had blossomed like flowers at sight of the poster, then Evelina's inflated like giant air balloons. Seeing the large, bold letters alarmed her. Her feral eyes darted to her mother and she drew in a sharp breath; but before she could speak, the marshal complimented her coffee.

"Mighty good. Hits the spot." Abner agreed by nodding. He had slipped the kerchief back over his throat. The marshal went on, "Pie's a plenty good too, like the one I ate at the hotel in Kansas. I'd been down to Abilene to visit my daughter. " He gestured to Evelina who waited close by the table. Evelina brightened at the mention of Kansas. She was hungry for news, for excitement, for anything dissimilar to the flat plains of Nebraska. "What's it like in Kansas? she asked.

Sadie introduced her eldest daughter to him.

"It looks about the same as it does up here."

"Are there any big cities?"

"Yes. But not like the cities back east. More like big towns. A lot of outlaws and rowdy cowboys frequent them and they can get kind of rough, like Kansas City or Dodge City. Those towns can get pretty noisy."

"Are there dances and shows and… lots of eligible young men?"

"Yes, there are, young lady. There are twenty men to every woman, I suppose."

Sadie quietened her daughter. "The marshal didn't bring Mr. Abercrombie all this way to talk about young men in Kansas. They're here to tell us something about your daddy."

Evelina sat the pot down hard on the stove. "Reckon this is the closest I'll ever get to a big city." She frowned at her mother.

Sadie rolled her eyes. "That's the last thing you need – a girl with your temperament all alone in a big city full of unrestrained young men."

"Anything has to be better than living at the ends of the earth."

The marshal sipped his coffee and avoided getting caught up in the family squabble. He talked for the injured man beside him, reading his scrawl and adding what he knew from their previous engagements. "Abner says – and call him Abner if you please. He writes…met William, Union prison camp Mississippi while back…'"

"When would that have been?" asked Sadie.

Abner wrote it down on the back of Ned Ames's face. "Early sixty-four. Don't remember. Were prisoners."

"Are you certain my William was in the army? The Rebel army?"

Abner nodded. He wrote. The marshal read. "After captured Big Black 'round Vicksburg stayed in prison camp Mississippi eight nine months."

"What was he doing fighting for Mississippi?" Anton blurted from behind where he stood by the door.

"He went down to Arkansas entirely on business," Sadie added.

Abner jotted down some letters. "Didn't fight for Mississippi," the marshal read. "Me and William part of Tennessee army corp."

"Tennessee," they all exclaimed. "Why would he be fighting with Tennessee?"

The marshal read. "All I know I fought with him Vicksburg... fighting for Bowen and army Tennessee. He shot in shoulder... figure was going to die... told me about the..." Here the marshal's voice broke off suddenly.

Sadie leaned over and looked at the scribble. "He told you about what? What Marshal?"

"His buried treasure."

"His buried treasure!" exclaimed Evelina. "What buried treasure?"

Abner, as was his custom, took to writing some more. "Gold hidden some place." The marshal read. "Figure he die without anybody knowing; so, told me about it."

"Gold on this farm?" Sadie scoffed. "My husband struck gold back in California around forty-nine and fifty. That was a long time ago and I have never laid eyes on any nuggets. You sure he said gold is buried here?"

Abner explained in letters again. "Said had lot gold hidden away place no one could find. Told me treasure buried on farm Nebraska. Told me four five times."

The marshal laid the paper down. It was filling up quickly.

Anton, who stood eagerly listening by the cold stove, sprung forward as though anxious to fetch his shovel. "Where did he bury it? Tell me."

Abner wrote like a journalist on a new story while the family waited petulantly. "Didn't get to tell. Told me Preacher knows where."

"Preacher? What preacher?" asked Sadie. "We don't even have a preacher here in Glensbluff since Rev. Arder died and Rev. Smythe left."

"Oh, no!" cried Evelina. "Preacher Arder died the day daddy left for Arkansas. Don't you remember?"

Sadie blinked rapidly. "You mean…"

"Yes," Evelina went on. "Don't you see. That must be who daddy told before he left where he hid his money."

"I don't understand," said the marshal. Did he hide gold or money?"

The mother interrupted her daughter. "I haven't seen either one."

"Daddy didn't trust banks," Evelina acknowledged.

Her mother agreed. "Yes. He often hid his money whenever he left on a long business trip, but he always told me where he buried it. This time he must have told Preacher Arder where it was, for some reason. Maybe there really is some gold buried here."

"Or maybe," the marshal speculated, "he knew this trip was going to be dangerous so he changed his routine."

"What do you mean?"

"I'm not sure I mean anything particular. I'm only saying that your husband might have feared something might happen to him – like it did – and he took precaution to tell someone else where the money was buried."

Sadie's eyes widened. "I've never thought of William's trips as dangerous, Marshal. Except maybe now and then losing a bundle of money to gambling. He had that one weakness. But why would keeping the hiding place a secret from me make his trip less dangerous?"

"To protect you," answered the marshal. Abner nodded in agreement.

"Protect me from what?"

"That I don't know, Mrs. Williston. Maybe he anticipated somebody coming here and looking for it."

Evelina wiped her hands on her apron and met her mother's eyes. "That makes sense to me, Mama. That has to be it. He told Reverend Arder where he buried it, but he died before he could let us know. If Preacher Smythe or someone else knew also, they would have told us by now where the gold was buried."

"But we have no gold," explained Sadie, exasperated, as she stood up and walked to the window. "Maybe William hid some money like he usually did, but certainly not a heap of gold."

"Did he give you any idea what this business trip was about?" asked the big lawman.

"No. He never talked about the business."

"Well, I don't know anything about all this. I just agreed to bring Mr. Abercrombie to you and I've done my part. Perhaps there is nothing buried here at all."

"Yes, there is," argued Anton. All eyes fell to him. "We know daddy always buried his money some place before he left on a trip. Why do you think I've been diggin' up the whole farm the past two years? We know he keeps his money hidden and we know he always tells somebody in case something happens. I'd been thinking ever since he didn't come back home that maybe this time he just forgot to tell someone. But it makes sense now. He must have told that preacher and he – he took it to the grave with him."

"But Mr. Abercrombie says it is gold – a lot of gold."

"I know," Anton insisted. "Daddy made his money from gold; so maybe he just calls it gold. It's been turned in for money by now. Or maybe he kept some little nuggets."

The marshal turned back to Abner. "You sure he never told you exactly what this treasure was and where it was buried?"

Abner wrote and the marshal read again. "In terrible prison camp. Men sick… dying… wounds… infections. Diseases took over. Williston's arm bad… lost lot blood. Tried to tell me, but mind went in out. Missionary doctor… Kansas… said arm rotting. Plan to take arm off."

Evelina grasped her forehead with her fingers. "Oh, no!" she wailed.

The marshal turned the poster over and waited for Abner to write some more, then slid the poster closer to read the scribble. "When came out of operation got fever – bad fever. I took care him every day. Started out talking right; then mind went and stopped talking." Abner paused and then wrote again. "I feed him… little food we had… pick him up… lead him around…"

"Oh, don't read any more, please," cried Evelina.

The marshal looked down at the poster and looked back up as he read the next line. "Went into brain... never knew nothing again."

"Is he dead?" asked Evelina. She stared at Abner for an answer.

THIRTEEN

❦⁓

Of course, Abner Abercrombie could not speak. His eyes did, however. They conveyed something... frustration...ambiguity. It was as though he wanted to say something this time, to explain his answer in more words than the paper could contain; but he couldn't. At last he let out a hard sigh and dropped his head.

"He doesn't know," substituted the marshal. "He told me the Union soldiers came and got the healthy prisoners right after that. Well, none were truly healthy. But the healthiest ones they transferred to someplace else. They moved Abner and he never saw your father again."

The sullen widow, at least she felt like a widow, sat motionless, as though she might be attending her husband's funeral. But she wasn't grieving. She was riveted in serious thought. "Marshal, if you don't mind me asking, what's your business in all this? How did you really come about bringing Mr. Abercrombie up here?"

"Ma'am?" He swallowed his coffee, set down the cup, and put back in the chair. "As I said earlier, I met Mr. Abercrombie...Abner... in Kansas a few days ago. He told me about your husband and the hidden gold, and I agreed to let him ride along with me while I headed up to the Dakotas. We kind of took to each other talking about the war."

"Talking?" Evelina's sardonic reply startled him.

"Well, you know what I mean."

"You must believe there is gold up here."

"No, ma'am. But I believe Abner does and he's worried that you won't get it."

Sadie seemed to gather her thoughts while she turned back to the fragile figure. "Do you honestly think there is gold buried here? Not that I doubt your sincerity, but maybe you were confused a little bit yourself at the time."

Abner penned his answer on the corner of the paper and the marshal looked it over. He read, "All he said... gold hidden in cave... no one could find."

"A cave!" Sadie doubted.

Anton argued, "There're no caves around here, mister. Just a few gullies or big holes. Pa did hide his money in holes sometimes, but they were small holes and ones he dug and covered up. Nothing that looked like a cave."

The marshal looked from Anton to Abner and back to Anton. "Well, son, Abner does seem to know things about your father – like him joining up with the Rebs."

"I still don't believe it," said Evelina.

"But he is certain that your father mentioned hidden gold and I reckon he wanted to let you know all this because he made it a point to tell him in the camp." Abner nodded in agreement and pushed the paper closer to the marshal with new words on it. "Yes, yes," the marshal sighed. "Abner intended to get the location from William, but before he could his mind went bad and they got separated." He apologized directly to Sadie. "I'm sorry to cause you so much melancholy, ma'am, but Abner wanted me to lead him up this way to tell you. I've come farther than I planned to come as I agreed to take him as far as Glensbluff. But he insisted that I bring him here to do his talking... and I've kept my word."

"But what did he tell us? We don't know anything more, except William was shot and he claimed there is some gold buried up here on our land?" She still seemed bewildered. "We don't know if William is dead or alive or if there really is any gold. We still don't know why you came here." She was still protective of Ned.

The big man scooped the last bite of apple pie and washed it down with coffee. "I'm sorry again, ma'am. It's just that Mr. Abercrombie, when I saw him in the jail, felt so strong that he had to come up here and warn you."

"That's what this is all about?" she inquired. "You came to warn us? Warn us of what?"

Abner scribbled some more. "Heard him say he worried about his family."

"Worried about what?" asked Anton.

The marshal read again and paraphrased. "It seems Abner wasn't the only one to hear about the hidden gold. He says your husband was worried that some greedy characters might make their way up here and cause his family trouble. He asked Abner to warn you."

Sadie looked surprised. "Then why did you wait so long to get up here to warn us?"

The marshal looked to Abner, but didn't wait for an answer. "Mr. Abercrombie was a sick man himself. But while he was in Kansas he discovered that those men your husband was worried about were making their way up here to find that gold right now."

"You mean today?" Sadie cried. "Coming up here for gold? They'll be awful disappointed."

"I gather they are not decent sort of men," the marshal volunteered. "They may be dangerous."

"Let 'em come," barked Anton. "We know how to shoot."

Lutie's eyes widened and she hurried to her mother's side, wrapping her little hands around her mother's arm. The frail man's wound caught her eye and she stared at his throat. Sadie placed her arm on Lutie's back and cuddled her closer. "Stop that talk, Anton. Marshal, you said there was a doctor from Kansas?"

"Yes. Abner had tracked down the missionary doctor there after the war and was trying to find out what happened to William. That's where I ran into him."

"What about the doctor?" she asked.

"He found him living there in Smithsbluff." He read Abner's scrawl aloud. "Doctor took off many arms, legs… all faces look same. Couldn't remember."

Sadie smacked her lips. "How can a man simply disappear, and nobody remember him?" She pressed her fingers against her throbbing temples.

Amos was sitting quietly by the doorway keeping an eye on the widow, Lenora, who rocked contentedly to her own tune. "So, did he take my pa's arm off?"

The marshal wiped his lips on a thick, cloth napkin and waited for Abner to finish writing. "Doctor not remember William. Lots men talked off heads when sick." He looked at Abner and briefly met his eyes. "Doctor told most dying…talk foolish and didn't know what saying."

Abner wagged his head side to side. He scribbled some more. "Doctor wrong. I hear William talk in right mind. Gold hidden somewhere. He worried for you."

There was complete silence, except for a creaking rocker in the next room where sat Lenora, the old widow, singing a soft tune and keeping in time with the groaning rocker.

Sadie loosened her hug on Lutie and sat up straight. "Well, thank you for the warning, Mr. Abercrombie. William hasn't made it home, yet. We haven't seen him or heard from him. We realize that it's possible he will never come home again." She studied the wounded man's eyes carefully. "This gold thing makes no sense. My husband did discover gold, but he kept little of it. If anything is buried here, it is his life's savings or what's left of it."

"Something is buried here, Mama," defended Anton. "Gold or money, I don't know what. But something is buried on this land. Pa buried it like he always did, but we ain't found it yet."

"That may be, son, but it sure ain't no gold hidden in a cave."

Evelina poured her mother a fresh cup of coffee and joined them at the table. Sadie looked in the cup at the mud colored liquid, tasted it, and went on. "Thank you for bringing Mr. Abercrombie up here to warn us, Marshal? And thank you Mr. Abercrombie for letting me know about William and his… his sickness. I'm afraid you may have wasted your time riding all the way up here. But our lives must go on with or without William or the gold."

Marshal Stern stood and thanked Sadie again for her hospitality. I need to hit the trail," he said. "I need to make good time getting up north."

"What about him? Sadie planted her eyes on the silent man sitting beside him. "Are you going on with the marshal or heading back where you're from?"

The marshal replied. "I promised to bring him here. I didn't say anything about taking him with me. If he rides off on his own, he'll have nobody to do his talking for him."

"You mean you're just going to leave him?" asked Evelina. "This pathetic, barren place at the end of the world?"

Her mother stood too. "I'm sorry for my daughter's brashness, Marshal."

"Well, that was the agreement."

"And leave him here?" Evelina repeated.

"He's not my concern. What he wants to do is up to him now. I've done my part." He turned to fetch his hat and the star on his chest glittered from the sun coming through the window. "He agreed to this before we left Kansas." Abner scribbled on the paper again. "He says he's not afraid to ride back by himself."

The large lawman lifted his hat and held it against his chest. "I do thank you for the coffee and pie." Abner turned the paper over revealing a sketch of Ned's face and the large WANTED letters across the top, and wrote something in the margin; then slid it towards his friend. "There is one more thing Mr. Abercrombie wants to tell you. He wants you to know the names of the men who might be showing up here to look for the gold." The marshal recalled what Abner wrote during their journey. "Ben Granger was a colonel in the Yankee army. He commanded the prison camp where your husband and Abner were held. After the war, he and his bunch started raiding towns and stirring up trouble in the west. According to Abercrombie, Granger joined up with a prisoner in the camp, a Rebel major named Siler Penrose. Apparently, they both heard about the gold and believe it to be here on this farm. You might be in danger if they show up."

Abner hurriedly scribbled something else on the sheet. The

marshal snatched it up. "He says that Ben Granger was a lawyer before the war. Might be a tricky one." He folded the paper and put it back in his pocket. "Just keep an eye open for this Ben Granger and Siler Penrose and the rest of their cohorts. Just in case, let Sheriff Potts know if they come around."

Sadie touched Abner on his arm gently. "Do you want to stay with us? "We don't turn anybody away in need."

He nodded to say he would.

Sadie thought about Ned Ames's face on the paper and requested the marshal give it back to Abner. "So he can write on it."

"Sorry ma'am. I need this. That's who I'm looking for."

"You are?" Everyone's eyes grew as large as plates.

As he opened the door, Sadie called out, "Marshal, by the way, who is that man on your poster?"

"That is Ned Ames."

"What is he wanted for?"

"Murder."

"Murder?" whispered Evelina, alarmed.

"Yes. Watch out for him. Word is that he's up here in these territories somewhere close by. If you happen to see him, shoot him first and then ask questions. But don't worry. When I track down a wanted man, I always find him."

FOURTEEN

ome time had passed by on the Williston farm without a visitor. But this would soon change. Siler Penrose slumped in the saddle. His two cohorts were pushing their mounts on both sides of him as they journeyed onto the Williston property just ahead. Siler was a still a bit of a gaunt man, like many war veterans who had tasted sickness while confinement in insanitary death camps, and wore the marks of sunken cheek bones and hollow dark eyes a man could almost look through. His upper body seemed stretched and narrow like a hay bale banded, while his legs bowed awkwardly to fit the stirrups. Despite the scraggly beard, there was something in that hollowness to observe – something not good, something ghostly, and something soulless.

The animal he was riding seemed brawny compared to its master. She was a Kentucky born American Saddlebred that Siler often bragged about pilfering from a dead man after the war. He called her Kami after a French saloon girl he met in New Orleans. The creature was lofty and snorted and jerked her head in spherical motions as though she had been schooled in a traveling circus. Siler seemed to like his horse lurching about. She revealed a pride and independent temperament like his own over those inferior to him. The horse was part of his act.

That act was intended to intimidate people who stared up at the beast only to see a ghostly figure riding astride her broad shoulders. Siler still wore his grey hat with his *major* insignia pinned to the brow; and he chomped down on one of Granger's cigars between his crooked teeth. He had fought in numerous battles and even once stood side by side with General Beauregard for a photograph near Vicksburg.

During one battle, he took a bullet in the lower leg that came out on the other side and killed the horse beneath him. He crawled out from beneath the lifeless flesh and had slightly limped ever since. Before his capture, while in a cavalry charge, a fragment of exploding shell penetrated his lower back barely missing his kidney. It stayed in there for over a year before working its way to the top where he pulled it out one night, cursing and screaming. He survived the months of infection, but not without it taking a toll on his constitution.

Not many men were tougher than Siler Penrose, though they looked tougher. Not many were meaner either. He was meaner than his boss, Ben Granger, who was the meanest Yank he ever fought against during the war – and after. They would have killed each other under normal circumstances in war but they soon came to realize the common desire of both men's hearts during a heated argument one night in Tennessee, the state Siler hailed from. Money. Gold. The stolen gold. Penrose once had his hands on it until Williston betrayed him. He wanted it back. He tracked Williston down and forced him into the army. After their capture, they found themselves under Colonel Granger, the prison commanding officer. It was there that they learned about the missing gold from a note that Williston apparently gave to Abercrombie. Penrose and Granger presumed it to be up north on Williston's farm. The common love of money packaged the former enemies snugly together on the same side.

Neither of these soldiers cared about right and wrong. They cared only about themselves. They saw people as nothing but interruptions to be dealt with in order to get what they wanted. They set their eyes on Nebraska and the small Williston farm. They had to find the gold they heard so much gossip about in the notorious prison camp. Siler knew it was going to belong to him again. When Siler Penrose wanted something, nobody stopped him and his boys from getting their hands on it. Nobody.

Sadie welcomed Siler and his boys like everyone else when they stopped their horses short of the well house to stare at the Indian woman and her boy – until she heard him speak and saw through his dirty grin. This was one of the men Abner Abercrombie had warned her about. So, she stepped back sensibly as his horse raised up and stamped the ground a half-dozen times.

He provided his name, then introduced his two hands, moving his head to each side. "This here is Casper Handshoe and over here is Jamie Quentin."

Sadie glanced briefly at the two young men straddling their horses on either side of Siler. She discerned right away that these men were no good. "What do you want?"

He smirked and nodded his skull. "I represent a Mr. Ben Granger." Penrose stopped suddenly, obviously distracted by movement, and took in the little sod house where the squaw sat just outside. "Pardon me ma'am, but why do you have Indians living in front of your house. I reckon I' ain't never seen anything like that before."

Sadie ignored the question. "You were saying…"

He shrugged. "Yes, Ben Granger. He is a lawyer in Glensbluff and he sent me here to tell you to get off his land."

"His land?" That stunned her mightily. "How come I never saw this lawyer in town before?"

Siler Penrose still seemed distracted by the movement from the sod house. The squaw left the boy sitting by the entrance and paced slowly away from the home towards the men on horses, not removing her eyes from them for a moment. She stopped and folded her arms defiantly and stared at the men with piercing, dark eyes, appearing ghostly and foreboding like a portent. "Strange," he commented to his men.

The young fellow, Quentin, glanced at the Indian. "What's the matter? Haven't you ever seen an Indian?"

Penrose rubbed his stubble with his fingertips and shook his head. "Not like that one and not living on a farm. She looks like… like she knows something."

Handshoe scoffed, "If you want I can learn her a few more things, like it ain't polite to stare."

"Forget about her," said Quentin.

Just then Evelina and Anton walked past the well house and stopped just past the sod hut. Anton carried his rifle with both hands across his stomach. He studied the squaw with interest and then turned back to the men on horses. It seemed that the woman knew something wasn't right. Abner Abercrombie followed them meekly at a distance and stopped at the well, holding himself up by the wooden handle. He knew too.

"This is our land," stated Anton.

"I see you met Mr. Abercrombie," said Penrose with a wicked grin on seeing his former ally. "Howdy, Abner. Haven't laid eyes on you in a spell. Tried to in Kansas, but you disappeared." Looking back down at the matron, he went on. "He made it easy finding your place. He and that marshal were easy to track. Course we know right well where our land is."

Sadie sensed something was foul. She could feel the tension in the warm air. The Indian woman couldn't remove her eyes from them. "As my son told you, this is our land."

"I'm sorry ma'am," Siler spoke and then chuckled as he glanced at Casper Handshoe on his left. He gazed pompously down into the woman's anxious eyes. "It was your land."

Anton blurted out bravely, "This land belongs to my father. So why don't you get off it." He lifted his rifle higher against his chest.

Sadie started to speak until her attention was suddenly snatched away by something she had not expected to see. Her eldest daughter, standing near the well, appeared to be blinking her eyes rapidly and smiling at the young man called Jamie; and he was smiling back at her with a pleased expression in his eyes. She couldn't believe it at first glance, but there was no mistaking the infatuation. "Evelina," she called out, "Go back in the house."

"Why?"

"To tend to the girls."

"Amos is with them."

"Go back in the house and check on them."

Evelina knew why her mother was sending her away and frowned markedly toward her. She stepped back slowly as she turned towards Jamie, showing her pearly teeth to the handsome man as she smiled. She murmured through her grin, "That Jamie Quentin is sure a handsome fellow." Then she spoke a bit louder for her mother's ears, "And I never get to meet any boys my own age in this desolate country. When I finally do..."

Her mother talked over her. "Hurry now."

Evelina lifted her hem and huffed and stamped like Siler's horse all the way back to the house. There she turned back once more to glance at Jamie. She could see his blonde hair just under his hat lying across the brow of his bronzed face.

Sadie returned to the matter. "Tell me what this is about. I don't think I understand you."

"Mr. Granger is a lawyer and he claims his legal rights to this land."

"Like my son said here, my husband bought this land and paid it in full some years ago. We came here about the time the Homestead Act passed. We are the rightful owners..."

"We know all about your husband and his claim, ma'am. Might we speak to him?"

"He's not here right now."

Siler chortled and removed his cap to wipe his forehead. "Yes, we kind of figured that. 'Cause he's dead. And Mr. Granger has determined through all his lawyer work that this land was purchased illegally. He intends to take it."

Now Sadie was really getting upset. Her heart began to flutter. What did these men know about her William? Could there be some truth to what they said about the land? "We don't know that my husband is dead."

"Then, where is he?"

The woman refused to even blink. "What makes you so sure he is dead?"

"He fought under me in the war before we were captured. The last time I saw him he was shot and dying."

Sadie heaved a sigh and brushed the hair back from her eyes.

"Yes, but that doesn't mean he is dead. What kind of proof do you have that this is your land?"

"Yeah," snapped Anton. "Let me see it now or get off this land." He tensed his grip on the rifle.

"Or what will you do?" added Casper Handshoe from his mount, his hand slipping down to his holster. "There's three of us and you're just a boy."

"Quiet, Shoe," Siler barked. "I'd like to handle it that way, but Granger... We want no trouble today." He looked back at Sadie. "We just want our land. I don't have the proof with me today."

"You don't expect me to just hand it over to you without proof, even if this man is a lawyer."

"No. Mr. Granger will send you the documents at his convenient time, Mrs. Williston. He's still writin' it all up legal. We three fellows just road out here today to give you fair warning that this land was obtained illegally, and we aim to take it back. That's to give you fair time to pack up your things."

"You'll have a fight on your hands," warned Anton.

"He's right," added Sadie, looking back at her son with eyes that gave warning. "But not with guns. We want to see your evidence and then we'll fight you with the law."

"Mr. Granger is the law now," Casper mused himself.

Penrose grinned again and shook his head. "You can't win at this, ma'am. Granger is a good lawyer and he's got everything in order."

"Your definition of good might be a tad different from mine."

"Well, anyway, I reckon you might say it's good of Mr. Granger to give you notice."

"Thank him for me," she answered grimly. "But we aren't planning to go nowhere."

The skinny man took a deep breath and let it out all at once. His foreboding eyes darted to Abner Abercrombie, then back to the woman. "We done our job. Just don't say we didn't warn you ahead of time."

Penrose jerked the reigns of his angry horse and motioned to his two partners. "Good day. And good seeing you again, Abercrombie. Sorry you couldn't get a word in." Penrose bellowed with laughter. "If you knew what was good for you, Abercrombie, you and that Indian squaw will be gone the next time we show up here." The three men rode off together across the grassy plain.

"Mama?" was all Anton asked.

"I don't know, son. Don't fret about it." She turned to head back towards Evelina, who was now standing by the door with the younger children at her skirt.

"Don't fret about what? She asked.

Anton didn't give his mother a chance to answer. "But what about the papers? What if he really does have the right to put us off our land?"

"He doesn't."

"But what it he does?"

"Then we'll fight it – if it ever comes to that."

"I'm ready!" he shook the rifle in one extended arm.

"Not that way, son. Legally."

Anton bellowed. "Didn't you hear the man? He said that Granger is a lawyer. What chance do we have against somebody like that?"

"And what chance do we have fighting with guns against hired gunmen like them?"

Evelina stepped off the boardwalk. "He's right, Mama. Let's pack up and leave right now. This is finally our chance to get away from this awful place."

"This is your daddy's land. We're not letting anybody run us off."

Evelina didn't seem to hear her mother. Instead her eyes looked as though she had been captured in a spell. "Wasn't that Jamie so handsome sitting on his horse. If Daddy didn't do something right, then we should just pack up and head back east."

"Your daddy didn't do nothing illegal. We will be right here on this land when he comes home."

"Mama!" exclaimed Evelina. "He's dead. He ain't coming back and you know it."

Sadie hesitated before she spoke and decided not to argue with her daughter. Instead she released a breath and draped her arm across Anton's shoulder, walking him towards the house. He was as tall as she, and with that gun swinging in his left arm, he looked like a grown man. But he was still a boy, she reminded herself. "Don't listen to your sister, son. If your daddy was dead, we'd of heard about it by now." She knew as she spoke the words that she didn't even believe them herself.

Evelina hurried the children back inside the house where Preacher Pearsall waited. He stood with his arm looped through the widow Lenora's arm. Abner stepped up on the porch and joined them.

"But what if it turns out to be true and this land isn't really ours?" asked Anton. "What will we do then?"

"We'll pray, son. We'll keep praying that it is our land and that God will take care of this whole situation for us."

"And we'd better be praying that Pa comes home soon too," he replied. "Before it's too late."

FIFTEEN

❧

A few days passed and a soft rain fell steadily on the muddied streets of Glensbluff. The town consisted of wooden buildings joined to each other in two strips with the wide mucky street down the middle. A raised boardwalk ran in front of each store and office, covered by slanted roofs or canopies that kept the townspeople dry as they scurried from door to door. Horses and wagons trudged through the wet lanes leaving their tracks behind momentarily until the downpour obscured them. The overcast skies offered no relief in sight for the modest town.

Evelina stood under the dress shop canopy peering through the plated glass at the assortment of colorful materials. She still wore the cotton bonnet she put on when she left the house. Preacher Pearsall paused beside her facing the street and keeping his eyes on the storefronts on the opposite side. To his right he saw the sheriff's simple office, a decorative saloon called *The Lucky Dame*, the town's barbershop, and further down, the stables and livery. Turning his head the other way he saw the towering sign in front of the tallest building on the street, the Glensbluff Hotel. Beyond that, the wide road began to turn.

"I'm going to pick up the supplies," Anton called to his sister, glancing down the sidewalk to the general store. His brother, Amos, followed him while keeping his eyes on the saloon across the street. "Don't go too far," Anton warned. "We gotta get back before it's too dark."

He stopped after taking only a couple of steps. "You goin' into that dress store?"

"What for? I got no money for a dress." She looked back through the window. "I think I'll mosey on down to the restaurant and have something hot to drink."

"Hot!"

"It is a rainy day."

"Well, don't get lost."

She laughed. "In this town!"

Amos, who stood beside his brother obliged a mocking laugh. "He means on purpose."

Anton did not see any humor. "You know what Mama said. Don't even talk to no man."

Preacher Pearsall stepped back from the rain that was blowing under the canopy and pulled his collar around his neck. "Don't you two worry about Evelina. That's why your mama sent me."

Evelina rolled her eyes as the boys hurried on.

"I promised your mother I would make sure you were protected?" the preacher reminded her.

"Protected?"

"I mean safe."

"What could happen in this town?"

"Then, I should say, safe from yourself."

Just then the new man on Granger's crew strode up behind them. "Hello, Evelina," he spoke courteously.

"Hi Jamie," Evelina responded, smiling and blushing like a pink rose at the same time. Her eyes said it all – that he captured her full interest.

The blond-haired cowboy greeted the preacher and tipped his wet hat to the young woman. Preacher Pearsall merely nodded, unenthused. "I see you shaved," he muttered.

"It's good to see you again," Jamie went on, fixing his eyes on Evelina's lovely complexion and minding the preacher only slightly. "You look very pretty today."

"Thank you. But with all this rain?" She was fishing for more compliments. "And this old dress my mother made?"

"You look pretty every day. It's not the dress that makes you pretty. Your beauty is God given."

Evelina giggled like a school child. The preacher frowned.

"I'd be honored if you would walk with me... out of the rain, I mean."

"Why don't you buy me a cup of coffee at that restaurant down there?"

Jamie took her up on the offer. "A cup of coffee on a dreary, wet day like this would be nice...with you, that is."

"Just what I had in mind when we pulled into town." She reached for his arm. "We think alike."

Preacher Pearsall tightened his hat around his head and tapped the cowboy on the shoulder. "I'm afraid I have to go with you, mister."

"My name is Jamie Quentin."

"Mr. Quentin, her mother asked me to escort her while in this town."

"I'm not surprised. A young woman as beautiful as Evelina needs an escort. Of course, you are invited too."

Across the sodden street they hurried to avoid the mud slung by a passing wagon, proceeded past a few store fronts, and slipped inside the door marked *Mabel's*. Jamie and Evelina took seats at a small table in the back where there was no chair for the preacher. He slid into a chair at the next table and sat back away from the couple with his arms crossed like an owl watching his prey. There were only a few other customers inside.

"I was hoping you were coming to town today," the young man began. "It gets awful lonesome around here."

"I thought you were working," interjected the preacher.

"Yes, sir. But it still gets lonesome working around a bunch of dirty, unpleasant smelling men every day. I need a pleasurable interruption like this from time to time."

"Oh brother!" stated the escort.

Mabel approached the table and took their order. She returned quickly and brought two cups of coffee, setting them down before the young couple.

Preacher Pearsall was in no mood to sip any coffee. He sat and stared. "Why do you work for a man like Ben Granger, Mr. Quentin?"

"Preacher!" Evelina protested. "You are intruding."

"It's all right," Jamie answered politely. "And call me Jamie, please. I reckon there aren't many jobs for a young fellow in a town like this. A man has to take what he can get."

"Even if it means stealing the farm from Mrs. Williston?"

"Preacher, stop it." Evelina snapped.

But he didn't stop. "Do you realize this means you're also forcing Evelina and her family out of their home?"

"I hope it never comes to that, sir."

"That's Mr. Granger's plan, isn't it? He plans to set them out right in the middle of the prairie and take the farm for himself."

Evelina sat her cup down hard, rattling the saucer. "I didn't come here to talk about the farm. I came here to spend some time with Jamie. If you can't understand that then why don't you go outside and wait?"

Jamie touched her arm. "It's all right. It is raining. I understand what he's saying, and I don't blame him for being angry with me."

"Well, I blame him. Go outside, Preacher. That patch of dirt and shrubs we call home sure isn't worth arguing about. I hope he does take it. Why would anybody in his right mind want to live here? We'd all be better off moving away from this wilderness."

"You don't mean that," the preacher said.

"I mean it. Believe me."

"But it belongs to your father."

"What father?" The sound of her own voice seemed to frighten her when she realized what she had said. "And you hate this place too, Preacher."

Jamie touched her hand. "Don't speak to him so harshly. He's a minister."

"He's no minister – not any more. He gave it up when his wife and son got killed by the Indians." She stopped and covered her mouth. "I didn't mean it that way."

He stood up and pushed his chair back to the table. "I think I will go outside and wait."

"Don't be mad, Preacher. I didn't mean it."

"I'm not mad, dear Miss Williston," he answered. "I must admit it. You are right."

Evelina's attention was averted to the opening door before the preacher could move a step. The widow of Reverend Arder entered the little restaurant and their eyes met. She remembered the meek and pleasant wife of her pastor who went home with the Lord shortly after her father left for Arkansas. She observed Prisca carefully and could read anxiety in her eyes.

Excusing herself from the table, she met Mrs. Arder near the door. "Hello, Mrs. Arder. Are you well?"

"No, my dear, I am not."

"What's the matter?"

The timid woman spoke in a hushed voice. "They ransacked my place again."

"Who did?"

"Those new men in town. Those men who work for the lawyer."

"Ben Granger?"

"Yes. His men."

Evelina took her arm and drew her aside out of the doorway. "They ransacked your home?"

"No. Just the telegraph office." She caught her breath. "I was terrified. They shut the blinds and locked the door and then they said, 'where is it?'"

"Where is what?"

"They wanted a letter your father had given my late husband. I remembered your father giving it to him when he came in that day, but I thought no more about it until those men burst in and started demanding it. I thought they believed me, but they came back. How terrifying it was. You know that was the letter he gave my husband the day he left for Arkansas, just moments before my husband had the spell with his heart and died."

Evelina seemed concerned. "Yes. They didn't hurt you, did they?"

"No. But they said they would if I didn't tell them where it was."

"So, you didn't know where it was?"

"Of course not. I found the envelope in his old Bible after the funeral, but there was nothing in it."

"Do you know what the letter was about?"

"Oh, yes. I heard him. Your father had hidden some money somewhere and he trusted my husband to know where it was in case he didn't come back. You know, Evelina, we didn't have a good feeling about your father that day."

"What do you mean?"

"Well, it was just that…well it seemed like he wasn't telling us something."

"About what?"

Prisca glanced about as though she wanted to make sure no one heard her. "About his trip to Arkansas. It was like he was trying to keep something from us. Not that we need to know his business, but both of us just felt like this trip was different from all the others he had gone on. Oh, Evelina, I'm sorry I didn't say something to your mama, but when my husband's heart struck him, I… I just never thought anymore about it."

"That's Okay, Mrs. Arder. I'm just glad you're all right." Evelina turned back when she saw the widow looking at Jamie at the table. "Was that one of the men?"

Prisca studied the young man's face. "No. He works for Mr. Granger, I'm sure, but no. He wasn't one of them who ransacked my place. They were all older."

"We should go to the sheriff. I'll take you there now."

Mrs. Arder appeared alarmed. "No. We can't do that. One of them told me there would be a lot more trouble if I told the sheriff. They said they would strike a match to the church if I didn't cooperate with them. I'm not hurt. Just scared, I suppose. When I heard you were here in town, I thought I'd rush over and tell you about the letter, seeing it was your father."

"I'm glad you did. But now I'm worried about you."

Prisca let out a deep breath. "I'm all right."

"But what if they come back again?"

"It's strange," she began. "But I don't think they'll be back. I told them I didn't know where it was and expected them to get really rough with me. But they didn't touch me. After they went through the desk and all the shelves and made a mess of things, they warned me to keep quiet; and then they left. They even opened the blinds back up. Yes, it was truly strange. I got the impression that they just wanted to frighten me into being quiet. It was like they were satisfied that I truly didn't know."

Evelina looked back at Jamie and Preacher Pearsall once more. "Do you know what might have become of the letter?"

The widow thought hard a long second. "No, I don't honey. I didn't see him take it out of the envelope. But he must have because there was nothing inside it."

Preacher Pearsall stood up, but before he had time to push in his chair at the table, Amos came through the door to tell them they were finished loading the meager supplies.

The rain had slackened to a light drizzle, but the street was still murky and sodden with deep wagon tracks like miniature mountain ridges. Amos led them to the buckboard wagon where Anton sat with the reins in his hands. His clothes were filthy and soaking wet. "I thought you were going to keep an eye on her, Preacher."

He started to answer when his eyes suddenly diverted beyond the wagon to the boardwalk. There stood Siler Penrose and his sidekick, Handshoe. Handshoe was laughing. Preacher Pearsall broke his stare and he and Jamie helped Evelina to the wagon. "I didn't expect to encounter Mr. Quentin," answered the preacher, finally. "But I stayed with her like I promised I would. Who knows where she'd be if I hadn't."

Immediately upon seeing Penrose and Handshoe, Evelina turned back to Jamie. "Are those your friends?"

Before he could answer, Penrose called out from the boardwalk, "Hey Quentin. Your woman tell you where it is yet? Or did you have your mind on other things?" Both men hooted loudly.

Preacher Pearsall could see the situation had potential for getting out of hand. "You boys ready to head out?"

Amos jumped up to his seat. Penrose and Handshoe continued laughing and gesturing. For an instant, Preacher Pearsall felt like calling them out. He wished he had a gun on him in case something broke loose. He turned his indignation on Jamie. "If you're content hanging around men like his, then we certainly don't need to bring Evelina to town anymore."

"It's not Jamie's fault," the young woman protested. "He isn't anything like them."

"Yes, he is. He works right along with them."

Evelina looped her arm through Jamie's strong arm. "He is nothing like those men."

The preacher settled in his seat. "And you, Miss Evelina, if you're content to hang around men like him, maybe you should do some praying."

The wagon jolted Evelina as the horses began to move. Before she could reply to the preacher, Penrose cried out from the boardwalk, "I don't see why you're wasting your money on supplies seeing that you'll soon be off our land."

Jamie, standing in the drizzle up to his ankles in mud, called back. "Why don't you leave them alone?"

"I'm sorry," Penrose answered mockingly. "I forgot, Quentin, you gotta put on a good show in front of your girl. Just don't forget who you're working for and what we're after." He and Handshoe didn't laugh this time. "Come on," Penrose invited his partner, taking one of Granger's finest smokes out of his pocket and biting on it. "Let's go get a drink." The two men clomped their boots down the lengthy walkway until they disappeared inside the saloon.

The horses stopped when the wagon wheels mired. Jamie took the reins to help lead them out. "I'm sorry about those two," he said. "Mr. Granger doesn't approve of them acting this way and being disrespectful to a lady."

Preacher Pearsall scorned him, "You must be either a charlatan or a simple-minded man to believe that. You are just like them, Mr. Jamie Quentin." He turned to face Evelina in the wagon beside him. "Evelina, you poor, desperate child."

"Oh, Jamie," cried Evelina over the neighing of the horses. "Take me away from here. I don't like Nebraska at all. Please take me far away with you. Let's run off to New Orleans. Say you will, please."

SIXTEEN

꙳⌖

Evelina didn't run away – not then, at least. The preacher kept his word and made sure that she came home safely. But she wasn't happy. If she was cynical and bitter before the trip to town, her sardonic attitude became more noticeable when she returned.

"I hate this place," she repeated through the day to whomever would listen. She even told the widow, Lenora, that she was going to run away. "With that handsome Jamie Quentin... to New Orleans." Then she would talk about how much she loathed Nebraska territory. "Nothing is the same since my daddy run off." Then she cried and ran into the barn to hide her tears. At least she wasn't smoking, thought her mother.

A few days later a smile reappeared on Evelina's face. Two of Granger's men showed up at the Williston farm and one of them was Jamie. Casper Handshoe rode in beside him. Evelina rushed out to greet them and refused to steal her eyes away from the man she saw as her deliverance. Sadie peered out the window glass and recognized Mr. Quentin right away. She thought it odd that two of the hands would show up without either boss accompanying them. Sadie joined her daughter outside and asked the men bluntly what they wanted on her farm.

"Mama," her eldest daughter chided her. "That's no way to greet our guests."

"I don't treat guests that way," she replied. "Evelina, go fetch some water for the Indian woman and boy." Evelina didn't move far.

She kept her ears attuned. "Now I'll ask you fellows again, what are you doing here on my land?"

"We've been assigned to deliver these papers to you," answered Jamie politely while he held out a thick, folded clump of papers below his horse's neck.

"For Sadie Williston," added Handshoe, biting down on a twig between his yellowed teeth. "That you?"

"You know good and well it's me." She reached up and took the documents from Jamie.

Handshoe grinned, removing the splinter and examining it. "Those papers are instructions to get off the land that once belonged to your man, and the time Mr. Granger intends for you to do it. Better put – the deadline."

Jamie remembered he had been ordered to take careful note of her response – though they were instructed to take absolutely no action whatsoever. Granger wanted to make sure this all looked legitimate. He glanced over at his partner to measure his smug grin. He knew that Handshoe had a hard time following orders. Would he cause any trouble?

They observed the odd, round topped structure to their left, the same curious hut they had seen before. It seemed an out of place little dwelling made from sticks and grass and mud. *Still, much more unusual was seeing an Indian squaw and boy*, thought Jamie, *squatting down right beside the egg-shaped door like they were sitting in a Pawnee camp.* The woman and boy both appeared to be studying them too. Evelina finally drew the water from the well and sloshed the bucket as she struggled with the weight. This broke their gaze. She dragged the hem of her blue and white flowered skirt across the ground as she approached the woman and the boy. She stopped, set her bucket down, and poured the water into a clay pot.

"Aren't you a lovely sight to see this day," spoke Casper to the pretty Evelina.

Jamie smiled at her. His flaxen hair, sapphire eyes and brawny frame drew her gaze back right away. She smiled at him too, ignoring his partner, as though their smiles contained hidden messages.

Casper didn't like being ignored. "How would you like to spend some time with me in the barn," he said, splashing cold water on the pair's gaze.

"Settle down, Handshoe," order Jamie, replacing the smile on his face with a sour mien.

"Don't get so worked up. I mean after we're finished with our business."

"You have served your papers," spoke Sadie. "You may leave now."

"You best not put us off," Casper threatened. "You see, Mr. Granger wants us to see…"

Jamie interrupted. "…to see if you need any help with anything before we go."

Handshoe pressed his lips tightly like he had eaten a green persimmon. Then he blurted, "No. He wants us to let him know if you aim to pay any attention to the papers. They are legal."

"You don't know what legal is, Mr. Handshoe."

There was a stir behind Sadie, and she spun around to see the Indian woman standing now and wearing a troubled look. Back to Handshoe she turned. "You tell Mr. Granger I will read the papers; but I have no intentions of leaving my property."

The front door opened, and the preacher stepped through holding onto Lenora's arm. The younger girls followed with Abner Abercrombie. Amos and Anton approached from the barn. Visitors had a way of turning everyone out.

Handshoe sat up in the saddle. "Got the whole family out here now. That's good. Now you can all hear. This land belongs to Ben Granger and you have to be off it by the end of summer."

No one responded.

He grabbed the saddle horn and adjusted his frame. His eyes drifted towards the sod hut. "I can't hold this in no longer, but why you gotta Indian squaw living here on this farm?"

"We take in anyone who needs our help."

The man unexpectedly dismounted. "Well, that's awful nice of you, except that we don't like Indians. Not at all."

"Don't reckon it's any of your business," replied Sadie, "Seeing that this isn't your farm."

Jamie saw Handshoe's angry face and tried to reel him in. "We're not here to cause any trouble. We've already given her the papers. Now, get back on your horse."

"You ain't exactly my boss."

"Mr. Granger said to deliver the papers and that's all. Last I recall he is still your boss."

"Now it ain't gonna hurt to take a look, Quentin." The rough cowboy walked past Evelina, eyeing her from hem to hair, and reached the little sod house. The Indian woman showed no fear. She didn't flinch, even though he moved to within inches of her face, lifted his hand, and stroked her braided hair playfully.

"Leave her alone," demanded Evelina.

Sadie followed the man with grim determination to overtake him. Anton and Amos ran towards them and stopped only when they reached the heels of their mother outside the shelter. Jamie dismounted and went after his partner, calling out. "Get back on your horse, Handshoe."

"Why? What you going to do if I don't? These boys here ain't got no fast guns on 'em. Besides, I'm just having a little fun. What's in here?" He leaned down and peered into the structure. "Well, oh well, just... just nothin'." He patted the boy on his head.

"Get away from them," Anton barked.

Handshoe laughed. "What do you care?" He stepped back towards Jamie. "Now boys, we came out here to give you these papers that says this land rightfully belongs to Ben Granger. He's kind enough to give you a chance to collect your things and vacate this place. But keeping Indians on his land is not part of the gesture. They have to go."

"Come on, Handshoe," Jamie pleaded.

"Go bring me a lantern or something," he answered, ignoring the plea. "I've got a match." He pulled one out and struck it on his pants. It quickly burned out."

"I can't let you do that," said Jamie.

"What? You and me are on the same side here, you know."

"Not for this. We have our orders."

An angry snarl appeared on his face. "What's the matter with you? You afraid or something? You love Indians? Or are you just plain soft?"

Jamie's hand instantly slid down to his gun handle. "Stay away or I'll stop you. Granger gave me clear orders and I aim to follow them."

He noted Jamie's hand above his holster. "I wouldn't be so foolish if I was you." The gunman stepped forward a step or two, leveled himself with legs astride, and faced his partner. "You know I'm a lot faster with a gun."

Jamie swallowed hard and briefly met Evelina's eyes; but didn't back down. "You're going to have Granger and Penrose on our backs, you know?"

"So, are you going to draw on me or are you going to go and get the lantern?"

When he saw that Jamie attempted no move, the high-strung cowboy hooted and turned back around. As he started into the Indian house, the squaw stepped in front of him. With one back hand swing he struck her face and knocked her to the ground. The little boy ran to her side. Out of the corner of his eye Handshoe saw Anton and Amos come running. Whirling around, he faced them down with his gun drawn and pointing directly at them.

Evelina screamed. Sadie shouted at her sons to get back. Preacher Pearsall herded Lenora and the little children into the long, smiling home. Abner remained, looking as cool as a mountain stream. Sadie lifted the boy and sent him to the house with the other children.

"I don't want to hurt your boys, lady, so you had better keep them back."

"Why are you doing this?"

"I won't let no Indian stay on this property and that's final – if I have to shoot them down."

"Don't you realize," began Sadie, "That God made the Indians just like he made you and he loves them as much as he loves you."

"I don't reckon I believe in God."

"You will one day."

He froze as though his mind was trying to understand what she meant. "You heard me. Off this land now or I shoot."

"You can't kill her in cold blood," Jamie argued. "You're a mad man."

He grinned wide. "Maybe I am."

"Fast draw or not," Jamie spoke, standing his ground, "I can't let you do that."

"Then you will have to choose between me or her."

Abruptly a figure appeared from the shadow side of the long house. It was Ned Ames. His murky complexion and long black hair confused Handshoe. "I can't let you do that either," he spoke smoothly to the cowboy.

The sun blinded him. "Who are you?"

"Guess."

Handshoe seemed to suddenly recognize the dark face from a wanted poster as soon as he shielded his eyes. "Ned Ames." He grinned at the thought of finding the wanted man on the Williston farm. "It's been a long time since I saw the likes of you in Texas or, was it Arizona? And that voice, I'd recognize it anywhere. Granger figured you was hidin' up in the Dakota territories. Now, what a surprise."

Ned crossed the dry ground past Handshoe and reached the Indian woman still lying on the threshold. He gently helped her up. Handshoe stepped back a few paces just to watch him. Evelina ran to the woman's side and steadied her on her feet. As Evelina led her away from the sod house, the brave Indian squaw stopped and spit at Ned's feet. Before he could react, Evelina placed herself between the two and kept her walking ahead.

The dirty cowboy turned his eyes back to Ned Ames. "Guess I shouldn't be surprised seeing you here. After all, there's gold around for the takin."

"Ben Granger knows where I am. I suppose he does not trust you enough to tell you anything important considering you always were one to shoot your mouth off. Now, get off this land."

"What do you care about that Indian squaw?"

Ned faced the man with both hands arched above his hips. "She's a woman."

"An Indian woman. I hate Indians."

"I'm Indian too," challenged Ned, rubbing his dense curly chin hair.

"Then I don't regard you too high neither."

"You served your papers," warned Ned. "Now, you and your friend leave this land while you still can."

"Come on," said Jamie.

"So, you been watching us." The rough cowboy placed a chew in his mouth and tobacco juice soon dribbled down his chin. As he chewed and talked, it flowed from both corners of his mouth. He spit on the side of the sod house. "I don't reckon Mr. Granger's gonna like having Indians on his land; but especially when one named Ned Ames takes up for the rest of 'em."

"I said you and your friend get out of here," Ned repeated. "And make sure you tell Granger that he will have a fight on his hands if he wants to steal this property."

The cynical smile disappeared from Handshoe's fat lips. He spit again and slithered his arm across his mouth wiping away the brown liquid from the corners. He spit again and a boisterous laugh escaped his lips. "I take that to be an invitation." He readied his hands above the gun handles on his belt.

"Yes. An invitation to leave here. You don't want a fight with me."

Jamie narrowed the distance between him and Handshoe and pleaded with him. "Come on. Don't be an idiot. He looks like he's good."

"He's an Indian half breed. That's all."

Jamie lowered his voice, "He's that gunslinger, you know."

"I know all about him! There's a reward on his face." His grin broadened. "Why don't I find out how good he is?" The cowboy stepped back a pace, spread his boots apart, and lowered his hand a bit closer towards his loosened holster. Ned did the same, moving away from the sod house. All eyes were intensely glued to the two men. Jamie pleaded once more with his partner to have some sense, but the twisted cowboy's mind was made up.

Suddenly, Handshoe jerked his gun from the holster. There followed a loud explosion that rocketed across the empty plains. The pistol flew from Handshoe's grip as smoke escaped from Ned's gun barrel. The foolish gunman cried out in pain and fell to one knee as he cuddled his bloodied right hand with the other.

"You 'bout shot my finger off!" Handshoe cried out, wincing and dancing.

"Sorry," answered the gunslinger. "I reckon I'm a little rusty."

Jamie rushed to his partner's side and held him still. "I told you, didn't I?"

"Stay out of this!" He tucked his damaged hand under his armpit and squeezed his eyes so tight his face looked like a prune. Jamie walked him to his horse. "I'll kill you for this," he threatened Ned. "This ain't the end of it."

Sadie approached Handshoe. "Here. Let me look at that."

"Get away from me."

"You need to let me tend to that..."

Handshoe gripped his hand tighter and winced in pain as he pulled away.

"I told you he was a gunslinger," repeated Jamie.

"This is all your fault, Quentin. And I'm gonna make sure Granger and Penrose know about you, Ned Ames, and what you did to me. You can bet your life they'll be interested in learning that you're in cahoots with this widow woman."

Sadie turned away from the belligerent man. "I'd say you got what you deserved."

Handshoe's eyes glared at Sadie as she walked away.

"That's enough," cried Quentin before the injured man could utter another word! "I tried to tell you, didn't I. What's Mr. Granger gonna say about this when he finds out?"

"Just get me on my horse." He looked back at the gunslinger once more before mounting. "I thought you were dead for a long time, Ames. But now there's no secret. You can't keep hiding out behind this woman's skirt. We'll be coming to get you."

"Ben Granger knows I'm not dead and he has long stopped caring about me. I am sure he knows that I cannot lead him to what he is seeking to find."

"He cares about you all right," Handshoe growled. "I see your face on the wanted poster every day – the one he has laying on his desk."

Jamie assisted the wounded man on his horse; then bowed his head low to Sadie and Anton who were standing nearby. Anton had held Jamie's horse when the gun fired to keep her from bolting. He handed him the reins. "Penrose told us there was to be no trouble," Jamie apologized. "I only came out here to deliver those papers. Honestly. I didn't know..." Looking back to Evelina, he apologized again. "I'm sorry about all this."

The young woman held on to the Indian woman's arm. She realized her own hand was trembling something terrible and felt uncertain about how to respond to the handsome young man. *Maybe she didn't know Jamie after all,* she thought. *Maybe her mother was right about him running around with the wrong kind of people.* She felt her insides turn over just thinking about the whole shooting ordeal. *He did try to stop him,* she thought. *But he also delivered the thick roll of papers that might force them off their land.* Papers. Gold. The poor Indians. It was all confusing. She didn't know how to feel about him.

One thing was for sure – the handsome man she certainly took a liking to – was sitting in the saddle riding side by side with the wicked Caspar Handshoe, his work partner. It didn't make sense. Somebody in her family could have been killed. As she dwelt on all these things, she heard Jamie's final words to her mother.

"Mr. Penrose will be back here in a couple of days to follow up on the papers. He said to be sure to read them. Again, I'm very sorry."

Now, more than ever, she wanted to run away from Nebraska, from the prairie she hated so much, from every memory of her father and his land and his gold and, especially, away from her jumbled feelings about Jamie Quentin.

Jamie grabbed the reins of his wounded friend's horse. "Mr. Granger is gonna be madder at you than a nest of hornets when he hears what happened."

"Forget Granger," Handshoe moaned as he winced in pain. "I don't care what he thinks. What matters right now is my hand." He observed it briefly, wrapped his bandana around it, and tucked it under his good arm. "I ain't gonna forget this Ames. You're gonna pay." He fixed his threatening look on the brown-skinned man and broke his scowl only when the two horses sprinted away from the Williston farm.

SEVENTEEN

❀⟋

T wo days had passed since the confrontation with Handshoe. The family took a rest from the chores and gathered in the kitchen.

"The papers look legal," said Evelina. She pitched them on the table.

"How would you know?" asked Anton.

"I just know. Yes. He'll force us off the land."

"Legal or not," vowed her daring younger brother. "Nobody's gonna force us off our land. There's enough of us and we'll fight that Granger until we kill 'em all."

Sadie, standing near the window, placed her hands on both hips and eyed her son. "And how many of us will be killed?"

"This land sure isn't worth fighting for," said Evelina. "Why don't we just let them have it and move east?"

Sadie shifted her eyes to her daughter. "You're talking foolish. You're both talking foolish."

Her rebellious daughter seemed to sigh from boredom and lacked any restraint. "This land ain't worth our lives. I hate living here."

Anton didn't appreciate her attitude. "But this is Pa's land. We can't give up his land."

"It was Pa's land. He's dead."

"He's not dead."

"He's not coming back, brother. You'd better accept that."

Their mother intervened. "Children, you're both wrong. We're not leaving our farm. And we're not fighting for it – at least not with guns. We will lose the battle either way you two suggest. And we don't know if your father is dead or not. But there is another way we can fight – on legal terms."

Anton objected loudly. "You can't out lawyer him."

"Then we'll get our own lawyer. Not all of them are like Ben Granger. There are some who follow the Lord and with the good Lord on our side, we don't have to resort to shooting."

Anton calmed down. "This is our land and he has no right to it. That man is a crook if there ever was one and I won't stand by and let him just have it. I couldn't live with myself if I walked off and let him have it. I'd be better off killed."

"Killed!" Evelina questioned his reasoning. "Anton, will you think this through?"

"I have thought it through."

"No you haven't. Why, back east and in the cities there is jobs, and civilization, and justice, and dances, and parties, and theatres, and…"

"And boys," furthered Anton.

"I ain't interested in boys," she said convincingly. "I'm grown now and I'm interested in men, which they are scarce of out here; they are scarce of everything out here."

"Scarce of men? They're all over the place out here."

"Not civilized men."

"My goodness, daughter," Sadie coddled her, placing her worn fingers on her slender shoulder, "you make it sound like we're the children of Israel wandering around in the desert."

"No, Mama. We're still in Egypt."

The sound of rapt, pounding hoofs directed them outside where Lutie and Lillibet were playing. When they heard the snorting of the horse's nostrils and watched it rear up and stamp, they ran to their mother's brolly skirt. It was Jamie Quentin who sat astride his horse.

"What do you want?" asked Sadie, coming out into the yard. "We thought you gave us more time to decide."

"I'm not here to discuss Mr. Granger's business."

"Then, why are you here? To apologize again?"

"Well, I am truly sorry." The young man looked nervous and shifted in his saddle. "I sort of just came by today for a social call."

Sadie looked at Evelina. She observed again how Jamie Quentin's eyes fixed on her daughter's eyes, like a surprised rabbit, and did not even blink. "We don't have time for social calls Mr. Quentin."

"Yes, Ma'am, and please call me Jamie. I am sorry... sorry for the way my partner treated the Indian woman. I didn't plan on him doing that. But I know sorry doesn't change anything."

"Okay. You have apologized. She's all right, thanks to our friend."

"Ned Ames," he replied.

"Yes... Ned."

"I'm not here about Mr. Ames either. I know who he is and that the law has been after him for some time. Unfortunately, Mr. Penrose and Mr. Granger know him too and Handshoe told them what happened here the other day. He embellished the story much like a traveling salesman." Jamie's horse stomped and grunted as though he understood the conversation and he stroked his neck. "I have no argument with Ned Ames... or anybody."

"Then tell me, why have you really come here today? You want your hands on this land too?"

"No, ma'am." He planted his eyes back on Evelina. "I'm not like those fellows."

"How do I know you're not like them?"

"Well, the real reason I'm not like them is," the young man began explaining, "I had a mother back in Kansas and you remind me a whole lot of her. Reckon I had a Christian upbringing too."

"Fine and good to be raised a Christian," Sadie replied sternly. "But if you hang around with the wrong company and, if you associate with the wrong kind of men, you'll turn out to be just like them whether you 'spect to be or not."

"Mama," pleaded Evelina. "He's trying to be nice."

Sadie knew that her daughter's feelings changed like the wind. "Let me tell you a story, Mr. Quentin." She emphasized his sir name. "And you listen too, Evelina. My family had a big, brown dog when I was young. He was as friendly and loyal as a family dog could be. One day a pack of wild dogs came around tearing things up and killing some of the livestock. At first my dog growled at them and barked fiercely, but then he accepted them and started running around with them. He didn't kill any chickens or do any threatening himself, but when the farmers from other farms came around hunting them dogs, guess how they decided which ones to shoot?"

"How?" asked Evelina.

"That's the point."

"I understand, Mrs. Williston," the young man responded with a slight nod of his head. "They didn't decide."

"Do you really understand?" She continued. "I watched you the other day. You did try to stop that man from hurting the Indian woman. I could tell you had some decency about you the way you took up for her. Reckon it must have been your mama's Christian upbringing to make you do that. But if you hang around with corrupt men long enough, you will be corrupt too."

Jamie looked like a scolded child. "Yes, ma'am."

"So how did you get tied up with the likes Mr. Granger and Mr. Penrose anyway?"

His answer was simple and direct. "The war changes a person."

"Mama," pleaded Evelina. "The Christian thing to do is forgive him and to show hospitality to strangers. Isn't that so?"

Sadie groaned and placed her hand under her cheek as though she were thinking hard about it. "I know why you came here today."

"Ma'am?"

"To call on my daughter."

"Mama, he's trying awful hard to be nice."

Sadie pursed her lips at first; then smacked them open. She didn't know what to think of the young man. "Well… maybe you are swayed by your Christian upbringing or you wouldn't have come out here today to apologize. Get off your horse young man and you may visit a while."

He thanked the matron of the Williston farm and dismounted. Evelina beamed like a full moon and held his horse's reins. When Sadie went back inside with her children, she stopped and watched through from the tinged window pane while the young man and her daughter strolled towards the barn... much too close together for her liking. "Dear, Lord," she prayed, "I really don't know which one of those two needs prayer the most. So, would you just give them your wisdom and not let one corrupt the other."

For the next couple of weeks, the Williston clan saw a lot of Jamie. That he came only to see Evelina was obvious, but he was friendly with everyone. Sadie was glad, on one hand, that her daughter had a man to talk to – a man with a respectable upbringing, at least as far as she knew – instead of daydreaming about running off back east or flitting down to New Orleans; but on the other hand, she worried that the prodigal spirit in the young man was too strong for him to overcome. After all, why would a decent Christian man ever work for a dishonest lawyer like Ben Granger? Just like a bent horseshoe, the story didn't fit.

She made it a habit to keep a close eye on them, but it wasn't easy with all the work to be done. Jamie lent a strong hand to a little plowing and some other needed work around the farm. She noticed that the Indian squaw seemed to eye him like a hawk watching its prey. What was going through her mind? Perhaps she was just as confused by his outward good nature after witnessing him ride in the other day with the likes of Caspar Handshoe. The Indian woman wore a pouch around her waist, which she opened and, after extracting peculiar colored corn seed, planted them on a bare patch not far from the cemetery. She seemed to have no plans to leave.

Then, one afternoon Jamie rode out again, this time alongside Handshoe. She knew this was no social visit. Evelina must not have seen them as she was in the back of the house assisting the widow Lenora.

"Colonel Granger is a very gracious man." Handshoe did the talking, passing her a new folder of copious, yellow papers. "He is extending your time to leave his property." He grinned roguishly and then spit on the ground, wiping the tobacco sap at the corner of his mouth with the back of his hand. "You have until the end of the summer to vacate."

Sadie took the bulky bundle of papers and did not reply. "You spit more than any man I have ever known, Mr. Handshoe."

He grinned a wide, sooty grin.

"Yet, with all the spitting you don't seem to ever get the filth out of you."

The grin disappeared. Sadie moved her gaze towards Jamie, who turned his face away.

The impish gunslinger persisted. "If I was you, I'd be gone before the end of summer. That ain't long."

"But you're not me," answered Sadie.

"No." He smirked. "I believe you act a speck tougher and stubborner than me. But maybe you ain't as smart. Mr. Granger has some folks moving here on this property the end of August and he wants you gone by then. And if you don't make the deadline…well… I'm afraid it won't be too good for you and your offspring. Won't be too good for that outlaw neither. We might just have to collect on the reward money."

"How is your hand?" Sadie offered her own grin.

"Next time he won't be so lucky," he snarled.

"You've done your work," she growled. "Now, you may leave."

He laughed. "It's not your land to be putting people off of. Mr. Granger wants to let you stay here through the summer because… well… he has his reasons." He glanced at his silent partner.

Then a man's voice from the other side answered him. "I reckon Granger figures we might be some help in locating the buried treasure." The voice belonged to Preacher Pearsall who stood on the boardwalk outside his room holding onto a post. Handshoe took note of him and Abner Abercrombie, who stood by the minister with his arms crossed over his chest.

"Yes." Handshoe seemed to love hearing the sound of his own voice. He liked confrontation. It befitted a gunslinger. "I reckon my boss figures you might want to tell us about the treasure for the sake of all the folks living here on this property."

Jamie interrupted, "Let's go, Handshoe."

"Don't rush me."

"We've been through this once before. Remember your hand?"

Handshoe turned his eyes back to the sun baked face of Sadie Williston. "We were hoping Quentin here could have figured it out by now with all the time he's spent with your pretty little daughter. But he ain't got it out-a her yet."

"Handshoe!" barked Jamie.

For a second time Sadie's eyes fell back on the handsome young man still sitting on his horse, wearing a sheepish expression. She proffered him her most disheartened look. "I think you both had better leave. And don't come back here again. Neither one of you."

Jamie looked up as he jerked on the reigns. "I'm sorry, Mrs. Williston."

"You sure do apologize a lot, Mr. Quentin."

Handshoe bellowed as he pulled on the reigns. "You ain't sorry for nothin' – 'cept you ain't found that gold."

The two men pulled aside and rode off abreast of each other. As they and their rides grew smaller in the distance, Sadie prayed a quick prayer for strength. What were they going to do? She grasped the yellow papers tighter in her grip and scorched them with seething eyes. But her biggest problem right now, she decided, was what she was going to say to Evelina? How could she tell her that her handsome friend was merely a spy and that he had used her feelings only to seek to discover the missing gold. That is… if the preacher didn't tell her first. And all this drama for what? She wagged her head deliberately. There was no gold. Not on this land. *If there was gold here,* she thought, *she sure needed to find it soon in order to save her little farm from Ben Granger.* But the gold was as mythical as Jamie's affections. 'God, please help me,' she prayed silently. 'Help me to know what to do about our land and help me to know what to say to Evelina.'

EIGHTEEN

❦⁂

That evening Sadie gathered the entire household, including Ned Ames, around the supper table. The Pawnee woman and her child remained outside and sat somberly beside their little sod home as though they might have been attending another funeral. Evelina said she would take them a basket so they would not go hungry. Poor Evelina. Her daughter was heavy on her heart. Not only had she lost a father – whether he was dead or alive made little difference – but she had been deceived by the man she trusted with her heart.

Though losing her farm to ruthless men seemed like a giant problem compared to Evelina's emotions, the mother's heart inside her could not keep from dwelling on her daughter's disappointment when she would hear the shocking truth about the man she liked. She prayed for the right moment to approach her and the least distressing words in which to break it to her. Still, it would have to wait, she knew, until she unfolded Granger's ultimatum to the rest of the family on her homestead. They were gathering for her announcement, even as she thought about it. Sadie wanted to prepare a good supper before laying it out.

The younger girls helped her cook and set the table. In the late afternoon, they boiled and plucked the dead chickens. Later, they cut them up, battered them with flour and meal, gathered the wood for the iron stove, and sizzled the meat in a heavy skillet. Biscuits, however, were Sadie's specialty, made from scratch, and made with much time and love. Everyone loved her chicken and biscuits, but it was hard work. First, she had to stoke the stove and raise the heat. She lifted the heavy flour sack and placed it on the table. Then she washed her hands in the pan of water near the stove.

"Let me help roll it," Lutie eagerly volunteered.

"Ok. You and Lillibet wash your hands."

The girls helped their mother with the flour. They mixed it up into biscuit dough with the other make-do ingredients, coating their hands lily white while rolling the pin through it and flattening it like a pillow case. Again, their mother stoked the stove and washed her hands. Then the girls used the open top of a tin can to form the biscuits to the proper round size. Twice more she stoked the stove and washed her hands each time until the rusks were finally ready to bake. On top of the stove the beans were boiling, and the chicken was frying. The smell was as welcomed as if it were apple pie and sugar cookies baking.

"Let's sing Amazing Grace," she told the girls.

"Why?" asked the preacher.

"There are many verses in Amazing Grace," she explained. "When we finish singing all the verses, the biscuits will be done."

Evelina came in the kitchen with Lenora on her arm. When she heard the song request, she rolled her eyes. "That's Mama's time keeper for baking the biscuits."

"Good Heavens!" The cynical man of the cloth shook his head. "Why don't you simply count?"

"That's not as pleasurable," she replied. "Besides, Amazing Grace is a wonderful hymn. Singing is much better than counting."

He lolled his head side to side.

Lillibet looked up at the preacher and appeared to be reading his face. "Don't you like Amazing Grace?"

"Of course, I like it."

Lutie tried to figure out the bitter man. "Maybe he doesn't like to sing."

"Yes, I like to sing, girls, some of the time, just not as a timer. Both of you wipe your faces. You have flour all around your noses."

The girls giggled at the preacher's opossum face expression.

While they sang, the men and boys washed up and took their places at the table. Evelina lifted the coffee pot from the crowded stove top and poured a couple cups of coffee for Ned and Preacher Pearsall. Abner Abercrombie sat beside the widow Lenora just inside the doorway of the adjoining room and he held out his mug.

Evelina spoke aloud to no one in particular. "I wonder why Jamie hasn't come to visit me today. He said he might show up here for supper."

Sadie disregarded the matter.

"He might have become a bit tied up working in town," suggested Ned. "The coffee is very good."

"He doesn't work for Mr. Granger anymore," she replied.

"Where did you hear that?" her mother implored.

"Well, he told me he was going to make a change and look for some other kind of work. Your dog story must have gotten to him."

"Dog story?" several voices chimed in.

"Never mind that," she deflected their interest. "But that doesn't mean he has already quit. Work is hard to come by. I'd say he's still employed by the dishonest lawyer."

"You like him," said the preacher, sipping the hot coffee. "Don't you?"

"Yes. He's nice to me." Evelina stargazed. "I wish he had never started to work for that lawyer. That's not like him. He's nothing like those other men who work for Mr. Granger. Jamie's different."

"Do you know him well enough to say what he is like?" asked Ned. "You have not known him very long."

"Oh, yes. I can read his eyes like a poem." She paused a second. "He likes me too, I think."

"You know he likes you," bullied Anton. "You'd have to be blind not to notice it the way he walks with you so close you can't stick a greasy feather between the two of you."

"Oh, be quiet, Anton." The men and boys laughed.

He went on. "The way he watches your eyes so close he doesn't even look where's he going. Why he nearly tripped and fell last week…"

"Mama!" pleaded Evelina.

"That's enough, son. Don't tease your sister about Mr. Quentin."

Anton needed to have the last word. "He doesn't know her like I do."

Preacher Pearsall picked up where he left off. "Yes, it's obvious that you like him, and he likes you, but I advise you to steer far clear of him. He's not what he seems to be."

The girl set the coffee pot down hard on the stove. "What do you mean by that?"

"I mean nothing by it at all, except what I said plainly. He works for that evil lawyer and keeps company with his hoodlums. That should tell you something about the kind of man he is."

"But he's not like them at all."

"I know I may not have a right to say this since I'm not your father or your brother; but I don't want to see you get hurt. He's the kind of man who will disappoint a godly woman."

"I told you he said he won't work for Mr. Granger anymore. That says a lot for him." She turned and hurried to the window and looked past the curtains. "I believed him when he said he was sorry and that he's finding some different kind of work." Yet, the expression on her face indicated the prairie was empty.

"Of course he still works for that lawyer," the preacher argued. "And what's he sorry about? Why he rode out here earlier today on some business."

"That's enough discussion on this subject," ordered Sadie. "Let's sit down and eat before this ruins our meal."

"Mama? How did I not see him?"

She handed the preacher a scolding look. "I'll tell you about his visit after supper, honey. Let's eat now."

After the satisfying supper, everyone remained at the table when Sadie reminded them that she had something to tell them. "Mr. Handshoe and Jamie rode out here today and brought me some more legal papers." She lifted the yellow forms from her lap.

"Why didn't you tell me he was here?" roared Evelina. "I was looking for him all day."

"I'll get to that. Let me speak first. I have something important to tell you all." Turning her attention back to the papers, she continued. "Mr. Handshoe informed me today that Mr. Granger has given us until the end of August to get off his land."

"His land!" exclaimed Anton angrily. Other voices murmured.

"Would you all please be quiet until I am finished speaking. It's in these new papers. I haven't read them close all the way through yet, but it looks legal."

"Of course it does," remarked Ned. "He is a lawyer by trade and he wants your land."

"He wants Pa's hidden gold," cried Anton.

Sadie remained perfectly composed as though they might have been simply talking about attending a church social. "Mr. Handshoe says he has someone else moving here and he wants us off the farm by the end of August." She quieted down the chatter again. "Yes, Mr. Granger believes there is a lot of gold hidden here on this property. He certainly believes it exists to go to all this effort. William was known for hiding his money – but gold? Who knows? My dear husband and father of these children was a man of mystery and he, by his own confession, had his hands in things in the past so secretive he would never talk about them."

"What sort of things?" asked the preacher, seemingly surprised by the revelation.

"I say this to you all," explained Sadie, "and I want you to know that I loved that man…"

"Loved?" questioned Evelina.

"Okay – I still love that man. But I know he had invested in some shady deals, even some since we have been married."

"No, Mama," Anton pleaded.

"Your father was – is – a good man, Anton. Like most men, he had a weakness."

"Like what?" asked the preacher.

Sadie took a deep breath. "Money."

"Money!" young Amos seemed stumped by the answer.

"He couldn't get his hands on enough of it and he was known to do some mighty risky gambling. He told me so himself when he got back from New Orleans."

"Unfortunately, a lot of men gamble," stated Ned.

"Well, that's not all. William had a business head and was always investing in some new scheme, some that didn't turn out too well."

The preacher chuckled, but quickly stopped when he saw no one else was laughing. "I haven't considered investing money a sin, Mrs. Williston."

"No. But let me finish. I know for a fact that he went to Arkansas that final trip before he disappeared to meet with some men about the war."

Several voices started at once. "He didn't take a side." "Pa didn't own no slaves." "How do you know what he went for?" The voices began to run together. Sadie held up her hands bidding silence. "He usually didn't discuss his business with me, but before he left he told me that this trip would be the most dangerous and one that involved a lot of investing in the war effort."

"Which side?" Anton asked.

"He didn't talk about that?"

"The South, I'm sure," blurted the preacher.

"Why the South?" questioned Anton.

"Arkansas is in the South. It just makes sense."

Sadie called everyone's attention. "I don't know if he took a side or not. My point is that your pa had his hand in things that may not have been perfectly honest."

Anton loudly objected. "I don't see why you have to bring up Pa's past just because this crooked lawyer is trying to steal our land. If Pa is still alive he'd be awful hurt to hear we'd been talking about him this way; and if he is dead… you shouldn't…"

"He's not dead," barked Amos. "You been telling us that since he disappeared."

"I'm sorry, boys," Sadie responded leaning back in her chair and releasing a deep breath. "I don't say this to disgrace his name."

"Well, you are. My Pa has done nothing wrong."

Sadie rose and walked behind Anton's chair with the papers

clutched in her hands. "I didn't mean to say he did something wrong and I never want to disgrace William's name by any means. I am simply saying that this Granger may suspect that there is gold on our land because he knows something about your father's business dealings in the past. I hope I'm wrong. I don't even know. I just know that Mr. Granger for some reason believes awful strong that gold is buried here on this land. Why else would he draw up these papers? And Mr. Abercrombie heard William talking about some hidden gold."

Abercrombie nodded.

"Why would Daddy get involved in something like this? asked Evelina. "He never owned no slaves and he had no loyalty to the South. This makes no sense." Anton and Amos joined in.

"Do you all even hear what I am saying," Sadie asked, raising her pitch. "I'm only saying that Mr. Granger has some reason for believing gold is hidden here – reason enough to lie and cheat to get us off our land. He wouldn't go through all this trouble if he didn't know something about your pa."

Anton protested with fervor. "He's not running us off our land."

Sadie sat down and pushed far back in her chair. "Getting back to Mr. Granger and my news... he has pulled his legal strings to show that we owe some unpaid taxes and fees amounting to two thousand dollars from back when we came here before the Homestead Act..."

"What is he talking about?" Anton demanded.

"I'm not sure, son."

Amos joined in. "Lies. All lies. I'll fight with you, Anton."

"That's enough of that kind of talk," the matron put down her foot and raised her voice. "No one is going to fight anybody. I don't want that ever mentioned in my presence again. Do you hear me? That is not the Christian way. We do not return evil with evil. Understand?"

No one dared to move.

"That Granger has it all written up legal." She waved the rolled-up sheets like a paddle and smacked them on her open palm. "He says we have to come up with two thousand dollars or we have to get off the land. He intends to pay it himself and take over our property."

"Why is he going to wait 'till the summer's end?" asked Ned. "Why does he not take the land now?"

"Apparently, there is a legal waiting period."

"For what?" asked Evelina.

"For us to come up with the money."

"How will we ever be able to get that much money?" she asked again.

"Yeah," added Anton. "We couldn't come up with two thousand dollars if he gave us a hundred years."

Once again, she hushed the mutterings around the table.

In the silence that followed little Lillibet, her eyebrows drooping, asked, "Are we going to have to move away from our pretty farm?"

Sadie forgot all about the little ones listening within ear shot. "Not without a fight, child; and I don't mean with guns. I'm going to read this thing through word for word and try to find something that we can use to fight him with… or, at least, slow him down."

"The man is a devious lawyer," interjected Ned. "You cannot fight him in legal matters."

"Then we'll hire our own lawyer."

"With what?" asked the preacher. "If you had the money for a lawyer you could pay the money for the land. Do you know how much one would cost? Is there even another one around these parts?"

"Or one who would dare to stand up against Granger?" added Ned.

Sadie sighed, but quickly regained her tenacity. "I don't know the answers to any of those questions right now, but I won't just stand idly by and let him steal our land. I do have a few dollars stashed away…"

"And Ned here can rob a bank for us."

Ned cast a frown at the preacher.

"As I said," she continued. "I don't have any answers right now, but God will see us through this. He will not fail us. Wrong will not prevail. He will fight this battle for us. We need to pray and pray and pray some more."

Evelina spoke up. "Jamie won't let this happen. He likes our family."

"He likes you," interjected her oldest brother.

"Jamie won't be helping us," her mother confessed.

"But look how much he has already helped us with–"

Sadie cut her off. "I'm afraid honey that Mr. Quentin is in no position to help us."

"What do you mean? Even if he's not working for Mr. Granger anymore, he will still help us – even better that he's not working for him."

Sadie placed her hand on Evelina's forearm and squeezed it gently, but firmly. "I'm afraid that he still is working for Mr. Granger, honey. I didn't want to have to tell you this right now, but since you insist on bringing him up, I'm afraid that Jamie only helped us in pretense."

"What do you mean?"

"He was spending time here because he was spying for Mr. Granger."

"No. That's not true.

"He was spying on us to try to locate the gold. I hate to be so forthright, but he used you, sweetheart."

"No," she cried.

"You can't mean he was a spy?" asked Anton.

Amos agreed. "I can't believe it either."

"Yes."

Evelina protested. "That's not true. He wouldn't do that. He likes me."

Ned agreed with her. "Yes, I could certainly see that he likes Miss Evelina very much. I know people and I am not easily deceived."

"Like her or not…" She stopped in mid-sentence and turned to look her daughter in the eyes. "I know this is hard for you to accept and it is hurtful, but Mr. Handshoe told me today…"

"He was lying," she burst out.

"He told me that Jamie only wanted to get on our land to try to find the gold."

"He's lying! You can't believe a man like that, Mama."

Sadie swallowed hard and reached out both hands to her

daughter. "Darling girl, Jamie was right there and did not try to deny it. The truth is he told me to tell you he was sorry just as he and Mr. Handshoe rode off."

Evelina stiffened quickly. Her head and shoulders went back abruptly, her face reddened, and her eyes widened like the plains. She then burst into tears and ran from the room.

"Let her be," Sadie ordered before anyone could go after her. Lutie and Lillibet began to cry in sympathy. "Hush all the crying. Evelina will be alright. She's not hurt physically. Her heart is broken and that will heal. Oh, I didn't intend it to come out this way, but right now, we all must remain positive and determined to fight this evil man, Granger. He will not run us off our land."

"How can we do that?" asked Anton, dejectedly.

"I'll read the papers thoroughly like I said," she explained again, brushing the loose greying strands of hair back from her eyes. "You all can read them too. If we can find something in there that might help us or buy us some time... I don't exactly know how we can fight him; but God will show us the way. He will not fail us. He cannot fail us. He just cannot."

Ned shook his head.

"I know you don't share my faith, but that's ok. You are welcome to doubt and believe in whatever you like, but I know for myself that God has always been there for us when we needed him most. He will come through for us yet again. He has to. He is a miracle worker."

"I believe in miracles too," spoke the outlaw, looking around at each face at the table. "Remember how I nearly died. You all were my miracle. But I don't know if a miracle will come this time. Ben Granger is evil. Remember, he knows quite a few ways around the law. I believe a miracle will be the only answer that will save your little farm."

The preacher leaned forward and rested his elbows on the table. "Since you seem to know so much about that man, then I reckon that is what is needed for certain – a real, God wrought miracle, one right from the hand of God himself. We must pray for one at once."

"Yes." Sadie rounded the long wooden table. "Girls, start cleaning up the dishes. You boys can lend a hand too. Won't hurt us all to work together."

Anton and Amos began complaining that it was women's work when Preacher Pearsall spoke up and volunteered. "I'll help the girls," he said. "It's the least I can do seeing I'm not good for much else." His eyes followed Sadie as she stood and turned away from the table. "Where are you going?"

"To get started on these papers. There has to be a mistake or an oversight in these documents some place."

Ned shook his head again. "Not likely you will find an error in those papers, Mrs. Williston."

"How do you know that?"

"Ben Granger is a thorough lawyer. He makes no mistakes. But if he were to make a mistake, he has a reputation of being a cut throat dating back some years before the war. You are facing a steep cliff."

"Reputation or steep cliff," Sadie stated resolutely. "Ben Granger is still just a man. I'll find something with the help of God. I have to. It's our only hope."

NINETEEN

❀⤲

K ansas City persisted in being hot and parched. There had been no rain in more than a week obliging the ponds and streams to dry up and leaving the fish gasping. The door with the single glass pane at the top of the outside staircase opened into a large room that served as an office. Through the door walked a man, perhaps in his early thirties, with thick, wavy blonde hair, and soft, unblemished skin that had felt little of the Kansas sun. He closed the door soundlessly and removed his round hat. "Brodie!" he called out.

The door on the opposite side of the room opened and a man who could have nearly passed as his double entered. He was carrying a tray of leftover food and a long metal instrument and set them hurriedly on the desk between them. "What are you doing here, Browning? I told you to stay downstairs. I'm worried that too many people seeing us together might not be good."

"Who's going to see us up here? Besides, you're my brother. Why would that look suspicious?"

"What do you want?"

"I just came to check on him." His eyes locked on the object on the tray. "What is that?"

Brodie lifted the metal tube that was bell shaped on both ends. "It's called a stethophone. I use it to listen to a man's heart and lungs."

"I've never seen one before."

"It's new. I keep abreast of the latest developments back east."

"Well," Browning continued, "How is he?"

"No change, I'm afraid. He just ate a few morsels. He's still lying down."

"Is he talking?"

"No. He's shown no change at all." He hesitated a second. "I guess you could say he mumbles a little, but he doesn't say anything I can understand."

Browning stepped closer to the desk, his plump black hat rotating through his fingers nervously. "So, what are we going to do?"

"I don't know."

"You know they've already been in Glensbluff. Two of their moles are still here."

"I can't help that. That's one reason I don't want you coming up here and drawing their attention." He sighed. "Nothing I've done for him has worked so far."

Browning nodded towards the patient's door. "Is the German doctor in there with him?"

"No. And I'm afraid he won't be coming."

"What?"

"He can't leave New York," Brodie explained. "Something about some important medical procedures he's involved with at his institution."

"Fantastic. That was our only hope."

Brodie walked around the desk and stood face to face with his look-alike. "Not our only hope, dear brother. You seem to forget I'm a doctor too and I have been treating him ever since he was wounded."

"Yes. I'm aware of your skills, but you were hoping this particular doctor could make a significant breakthrough."

"Well, he's not coming." Brodie sounded disappointed, yet optimistic. "But I have studied some of Dr. Wilhelm's treatments. Since the war ended, he has done a great deal of research in this area – you can imagine why with all the head wounds and mind traumatizing resulting from human beings seeking to blow each other into eternity –"

"I know what you think about the conflict. Go on."

"I've been intending to try some of these treatments on him myself. As a matter of fact I've already started some."

"But this isn't your area of..."

"It's a new field in a lot of ways," the doctor answered his brother. "No one is an expert at this stage; not even Dr. Wilhelm. I have just as good a likelihood of getting something out of him as the German doctor does. What I've started with is what he refers to as *games of the mind.*"

"I hope it doesn't prove to be a waste of your time," Browning replied, twirling his bowler in his fingers faster.

"Then what do you suggest I do? Abandon the entire thing?"

"No, I suggest a new course of action."

Brodie exhaled. "Take him home?"

"Yes. I suggest we let his family help do the healing for us. No doubt the familiar surroundings of his home and family will quicken the healing – if it is possible – and make him whole again."

"We're not talking about his soul. You stick with preaching and I'll stick with doctoring."

"But Granger and Penrose are already there."

"I know."

"If anyone finds him here and gets word to Granger..."

"No one will find him."

"But the marshal passed through here and took Abercrombie with him."

"Abercrombie doesn't know he's here."

"Then why did he come to Smithsbluff?" asked Browning. "And why did the marshal take him with him?"

"Listen, brother. You know Abercrombie took good care of our patient and made him some promises. He's probably up there warning his family about Granger. He hasn't seen him since right after the war and probably doesn't even know if he's still alive. I've been careful with the whole matter."

"It's too coincidental, with the marshal showing up when he did."

Brodie pulled back the window curtain and peeked outside. "There's no coincidence. He's up north looking for Ned Ames, the one with the big price on his head."

"He's not interested in reward money," contended Browning.

"That's a handful of change compared to the gold. He knows Ames is wrapped up in this thing and that's the only reason he's after him. I'm worried, Brodie. I'm worried that there's too many players in this game and I don't know who's the good ones and who's the bad ones or who might end up getting hurt."

"I can agree with you on that point," replied the doctor. "When I first met my patient, I would have told you he was the bad apple; but now I'm not so sure. The more I look into this thing, from the robbery all the way up to Granger and his boys settling in to Glensbluff, I'm convinced there's more to it than we've been told."

Browning nodded fervently. "And I can certainly agree with you on that point. I'm beginning to think that the essential men in Washington don't even know what happened."

"Don't worry. I, likewise, may not know what happened back then, but I know what I'm doing now, and I'm going to get through to my patient." Brodie peeked through the curtains again. "Right now I'm worried more about people wondering why you're up here so long."

"For goodness sake. I'm your brother. Why did you ask me to come back down here then?"

Brodie smiled. "You're my brother."

"The real reason."

"You know the reason I requested you down here." Brodie stepped to the patient's door and opened it. "He looks like he's sleeping now. He didn't sleep much last night and I sat up with him for nothing. I was hoping maybe he would dream or talk in his sleep and I could learn something. But all he did was babble a bit. I can't sit up with him all night every night. I have other patients to see to and sometimes I have to ride out to their farms. You know I can't trust anyone else to do this. I wanted you here for when he wakes up – at night – when no one's watching or coming around my office. I'm going to teach you some of the simple techniques of Dr. Wilhelm, simple, but with the most potential, I understand; and you can come back up here and practice them on him."

"I don't know. It's accomplished little good since I arrived here."

Brodie closed the door. "We'll keep trying and trying. That's part of the treatment Dr. Wilhelm recommended. Stimulation. That's what he calls it. You come back later and... and stimulate him."

Browning seized his spinning hat with the other hand. "How do I stimulate him? Stick a hat pin in him?"

"No. Talk to him."

"I've done that."

"Talk some more. Keep talking."

"About what?"

"About everything in his life. His family. His work. His travels. The war. The missing gold. Anything. I have a list of questions and ways to ask them that I learned from Dr. Wilhelm. I had planned to stop by the house later to tell you all this, but it's not necessary now. You had better go home and get some rest before returning later tonight."

Browning placed his little round hat back on his head. "Mother and father keep asking about you."

"They know as much about this as I do. They're the only two I can trust." He smiled. "Besides you." He clapped his brother on the shoulder.

"I still say it may be a waste of time, but I'll come back tonight. At this point I'll try anything...again. Maybe I should talk mostly of the gold."

The doctor spun around and dropped in the chair beneath the oil lamp. "You exhaust me, brother. You need to leave before the moles get suspicious."

Browning opened the door to leave, but his brother called out to him. "Just be careful you don't say anything in such a manner that will lead him to believe you want to get your hands on the gold. We can't afford to cause him regression by having him go off in anger or clam up in panic. The plan all along is to bring him back to himself and find out where he hid that wagon load of gold."

"How do you hide a wagon load of yellow ore for years and nobody discover it?"

"That's what we hope to discover, Browning."

"I still say my plan is better."

"You may very well be right," said the doctor. "Sending him to his familiar surroundings might prove to stimulate his memory. But for now, keeping him here is safer."

"Keeping him safer hasn't yielded any results."

Brodie tightened his lips and nodded in agreement. "I pray his mind returns to him soon before Ben Granger and Siler Penrose cause too much trouble. If Dr. Wilhelm's treatments do not work in, say, in a couple more weeks, we just may have to put your plan into action."

TWENTY

❀~

When Preacher Pearsall, Anton, and Evelina went to town in the morning to pick up some goods, something the family had feared finally happened. Evelina gave them the slip and disappeared for hours, spoiling their early return. It was almost dark before they found her. The two worried escorts had split up and for hours searching every building in town, inquiring of every soul they met, but had no luck finding her. Yet, when they gave up the search and met up back where they started, there she sat on the wagon bench as though she had been good-naturedly waiting for them to return.

"Where have you been?" cried the preacher, feeling the most responsible for the wayward girl's safety, knowing he would have to give an account to her mother.

"Where have you two been?" was her modest reply. "I've been sittin' here waiting on you."

"Don't tell us no lie," argued her brother. "We have looked high and low for you. Where were you?"

"Let's go home," she said sulkily.

Anton climbed up on the seat beside her. "Let's go home! That's all you gotta say? We done missed a day's work huntin' around for you. Were you with that Quentin fellow?" Then he observed tears on both of her cheeks and the red, swollen eyes. He figured there was no use mentioning Jamie Quentin any more. The man either left town or told her he was through with her. So Anton roused the horses to life and drove home.

No one in the home had seen Evelina since she marched in that evening and went to straight to her room. Sadie figured that something must have happened in town between her daughter and Jamie Quentin. She had not stirred all night and took no supper. Sadie provided her daughter time to herself, keeping the younger girls in her room that night. She knew that Evelina, at such an impressionable age, probably thought it seemed like the end of the world. She would wait until the morning to talk with her.

The next morning when Sadie went to check on her, the covers were thrown aside, and the bed was empty. No one had seen her get up during the night or in the morning when the sun peeked over the plains. Evelina was usually up early anyway, thought Sadie. But where did she go? She wasn't in the house or out front on the porch or in the barn. The yard was empty except for a quartet of pecking chickens. Worry was etched all over the mother's face.

"I was out milking the cow at the crack of dawn," said Anton. "I saw her heading for the barn."

"She wasn't in there when I looked," said Amos.

Sadie lifted a lament. "Why does she have to be like this dear Lord? You made her with that defiant spirit, and I can't do anything with her. Help me know what to do. Reckon I'll check the barn again. That girl had better not be in there with tobacco." By this time, Sadie had slung open the shabby barn door. "Help her, Lord. Grow her up in her mind to match the way she's growing up in her body."

She called out and received no reply. She sucked in air through her nostrils. No scent of burning tobacco, at least. A quick look in the stalls revealed no sign of her. Back inside the house she saw Lenora rocking contentedly in her favorite chair and softly singing about the sweet by and by. Abner was by her side, but no Evelina.

"Evelina," her mother called. "Where could that girl be?" She caught Abner's eye. "You seen where that girl went?" Abner wagged his head and she hurried back on the porch.

Outside Anton and Amos were just circling the crude barn, one carrying a pick ax and the other a shovel.

"What are you boys up to?" she called.

"We're caught up with the chores for a while, Mama," Anton replied. "We're going down by the stream in the woods behind the house."

"For what?" She already knew.

"To look for Pa's hidden gold."

"Heaven's sake! We don't even know if your Pa hid gold on this property... or if there even is any gold. Right now I need your help looking for that sister of yours. She's still missing."

Anton protested. "Ma, Evelina is old enough to care for herself. She probably just went off someplace by herself to be away from all of us."

"Reckon you're right." Sadie pressed her lips together in thought. "She's so upset about... well... anyway, I reckon I can understand that. But she could have let me know."

Anton leaned on the farm tool. "If you could of seen the look on her face yesterday sitting there on the wagon seat lookin' like she'd been crying and all. I knew right then she'd been talking to that fellow she's sweet on."

Amos agreed. "Well, ain't that the whole reason she went to town in the first place? Girls. I can't figure them out."

Sadie told the boys to go on with their treasure hunt, though she had little faith they would find anything. "You boys keep an eye out for her, okay? If you see her send her home so I can wear her out for worrying me."

"Yes, ma'am," they answered together.

After the boys left, Preacher Pearsall rounded the corner of the barn.

"This sure is a busy corner today," she said.

The preacher stopped and looked Sadie face to face. "You seen my horse?"

"Which horse?"

"Matilda, the one with the white on her nose. She's the only one I ride since Gertrude hurt her leg in the Indian attack."

"Come to think of it, I didn't see her in the barn."

"You don't reckon..." the preacher didn't need to finish his question.

Sadie's eyes widened. "Evelina!" she exclaimed, spanning the open grassland. "That girl better not have gone into town by herself." A worried look immediately took over her angry face.

Lillibet and Lutie came running from the house crying out for their mama.

"What is it girls?"

"Evelina took her clothes with her," reported Lillibet. "Her dresses are gone; even the old one you mended and gave her."

Lutie was not to be out done. "And she took the biscuits on the stove from last night."

Just then, Ned rode in on his horse bareback and, hearing the report from the girls as he dismounted, immediately sensed the tension. "What's wrong?"

"Evelina is missing," she told him. "And one of the preacher's horses is gone."

"She is a daydreamer if there ever was one," said the preacher. "And acts before she thinks."

"Do you believe she left to meet with the man she took to from town?"

"It looks that way," the preacher answered Ned.

Sadie did not argue. She simply nodded her head anxiously. "I reckon she was more attached to that young fellow than I figured."

"Or hated this place more than you figured," added the preacher.

"She was so upset that I can't believe she'd go back after him. I should have never told her about the way he was using her."

"You did nothing wrong, Mrs. Williston," Ned consoled her. "She is young and thought she was in love with this man. But do you know that she went into town looking for him?"

"No, I don't know anything for certain. But Matilda is gone and, either way, she's gone too."

The gunslinger made his way across the small yard, past the well house where he stopped for a drink. The large yellow dog moseyed up to him and sat down to watch him. Ned poured some water into an old pan for the dog; then made his way over to the Indian home where he poked his head inside for a moment. When he came back to the front of Sadie's house she was waiting for him as though she was expecting some news.

"The Indian woman saw her ride away at dawn." He raised his arm and pointed to the land beyond the preacher's room. "But she rode that way."

"That's not towards town," Sadie objected. "Is she sure?"

"Yes, ma'am. She watched her until she was out of sight. Of course, she might have ridden in that direction to throw you off, if she didn't want you to know where she went; and then circle back to town."

"No. She wouldn't have thought of that while being so upset. And why would she want to throw me off?"

"She knows you would not approve of her going into town alone," said the preacher.

"I wouldn't have approved of her going anywhere by herself." Sadie stopped herself and groaned. "Oh no."

"What is it?"

"The girls said she took her clothes and some food with her. She rode off that way aiming to… to meet up with someone."

"Jamie Quentin," said Ned.

The preacher turned his eyes towards the plains. "What you mean is you think she has finally followed through with her threat and run away."

"Run away!" exclaimed Sadie. "After what happened, you think she'd run away with Jamie Quentin?"

"No, Sadie," replied the man of the cloth. "I figured her courtship with Jamie must have ended yesterday after she confronted him about spying on her. I'm afraid, in her state of mind, she has finally followed through on her threat to run away from the entire territory of Nebraska."

"Away from Nebraska… away from her family… by herself? No!"

"I'm only supposing," he explained. "But she did despise this place and always spoke about wanting to move to the big city."

"She's not that foolish, Preacher." As soon as she spoke the words, a look of fear lined her face. "Is she?"

"She did pack some clothes and some grub…"

"No. She wouldn't do something like that. Not even Evelina."

Ned was inclined to agree with the preacher. "Yes, ma'am, I believe she would. She apparently had a big disappointment dealt to her yesterday and may have become disillusioned."

Sadie ordered her younger girls back in the house – their ears far away from the conversation. "Go check on Miss Lenora," she said.

"But I can hear her singing, Ma," answered Lutie.

"You know Miss Lenora. She might be singing lying on the floor."

"But Mr. Abercrombie is with her."

"Mr. Abercrombie can't call for help."

The girls hurried inside, glancing back as though they realized they'd miss a good story.

Ned placed his hands on his hips and shifted his weight to one leg. "Try to determine where she might be heading, and I'll set out after her directly. She can't travel fast on that old horse."

Sadie offered a helpless shrug. "Poor Evelina. I hope she's all right." Then the realization set in. "Hostile Indians?

"I have thought of that possibility myself as well as other dangers facing a young woman."

"She spoke a lot about New Orleans," suggested Sadie. "Some folks put the notion in her head that her daddy is living down there." She gave a short laugh. "She wanted so much to believe he's still alive."

Ned excused himself and leaped aboard his horse. "I will do my best to find her."

Sadie stared at the horse and rider as they bolted off in the same direction the Indian woman had seen her daughter ride.

Preacher Pearsall place his arm around her shoulders. "Don't worry. Mr. Ames is an Indian and he knows how to follow tracks very well."

"I'm surprised you have anything good to say about an Indian, Preacher."

He lowered his eyes.

"I'm sorry. Will you forgive me for saying that cruel remark? It's just that I'm so upset about Evelina. How I wish William was still here."

Preacher Pearsall raised his head quickly. "I understand. Do you really believe she would ride off searching for her father?"

The prairie woman shook her head. "No, I don't. If she wanted to find her father, she would have run away long ago. I don't know what to believe any more."

"She's not thinking straight right now."

"She seldom thinks straight. I still say that Jamie Quentin is involved in this somehow." Sadie folded her arms across her bosom. "I knew he was no good from the start."

"Let's just hope and pray she just rode off to sulk a while."

"No. She packed for a trip." Sadie briskly walked to the southwest corner of the house that contained the preacher's room, braced herself on the siding boards, and stared off into the bleak, empty land. "If Ned doesn't find her, I'm afraid we might never see her again."

"I'll take my other horse into town to look for her," announced the preacher. "Just in case she did circle back... or to see if anyone knows anything about all this. My lame horse has been resting that leg and going to town won't be too much for her."

"That's not a good idea," Sadie disapproved. "Your horse is hurt." She brushed the wind swept hair from her eyes. "She packed for a trip. You know she won't be circling back."

"I'll go easy on Gertrude and I'll be praying for Evelina all the way into town. You think the Lord still hears a backslidden preacher's prayers?"

She smiled and squeezed his hand hard before releasing it. That was her answer. "It's hard not to worry about your missing daughter," she confessed. "But I'm also worried about Ned. Now he'll be out there in open country and he's got a price on his head."

"He can take care of himself."

Back in the house, the worried mother couldn't focus on her chores any more.

"I'm scared," said Lutie, cuddling up against her mother's dress. "You look so sad."

Lillibet, worried about her mother, also feared for her sister. "Is Evelina going to be all right, Mama?"

"Yes, honey," she answered. "Because right now we're going to pray for her."

Lenora hummed softly *When The Role Is Called Up Yonder*, unaware that anything was awry. Abner sat by her side swaying the rocker with his hand. From her chair, Lenora called out loudly. "Evelina! Come here and help me to the privy."

"Evelina isn't here right now," Sadie informed her. "I'll help you."

"Where is she?"

"I don't know. She's outside somewhere."

"Gracious me!" roared the widow woman. "Where is that girl when you want her?"

TWENTY-ONE

With no sign of Evelina or her whereabouts, life on the Williston farm had to go on. In Glensbluff, not too many miles away, Sheriff Potts questioned the people in town about the runaway girl. No one had seen her in town since the day she rode in with Anton and the preacher. He also interrogated Granger and Penrose; but they naturally denied knowing anything of her whereabouts. As peculiar as it felt to the sheriff, he believed them. He got the impression they were completely disinterested and had more important matters on their minds.

"What about that Quentin man she took a liking to?"

"What about him?" Granger deflected the question.

Sheriff Potts groaned and stroked his whiskers. "You know what about him. Where is he?"

Granger looked to his cohort. "What about him, Siler? Have you seen him around lately?"

Siler frowned. "Seeing as he don't work for you no more, I don't bother to keep up with him. But, no, I ain't laid eyes on the coddler for a few days."

Sheriff Potts glowered, then continued his search outside where he questioned Handshoe and Taylor who were hanging around the front of the saloon.

"Quentin is gone just like the girl," Handshoe informed him. "Must of run off with her. The fool!"

"Yeah. He rode out a couple days ago," said the tough hand,

Taylor. "And didn't come back. He was no use to us, anyway, falling for that Williston girl the way he did. He's too soft."

Sheriff Potts realized he had a mystery, if not a crime, on his hands. Quentin missing was no big conundrum. He could take care of himself. But he and the Williston girl both missing at the same time, seeing they had eyes for each other, could mean only the obvious. He heard that the girl always talked about running away from Nebraska anyway – and young Quentin was her free ticket. However, he knew that with Granger and Penrose involved, anything could have happened.

The sheriff felt his age while standing in the blazing sun. He was just too old to run around like he used to when he packed a lighter load and fewer years. He sent out some men to search the area – old shacks, boulders, any place that could make a good hideout. But hideout for what? Only if they were running from something. More likely, if they were in a place like that, they were being held against their will. But it made no sense either way. They had each been seen riding off on his own. In his professional law man's opinion, they had run off together to get married. Yes, that had to be it, he decided. There was no preacher in Glensbluff now, and no one had asked him to do any marrying.

He wired the marshal up in the Dakotas the next morning to make him aware of the situation. He knew Babb wouldn't make his way back to Nebraska Territory until he had caught his man or heard that he had slipped away in some new direction. Rumors had gotten back to town that Ned Ames was in Nebraska anyway, maybe even holding up, of all places, on the Williston place. He wired that to the marshal too, though he didn't expect him to change his plans based on new speculation. Sadie was too agreeable to turn anyone away from her farm, killer or not; so it could be true. Was the rumor worth checking on? He'd planned to ride out to the Williston farm soon anyway, since he knew he was going to face the unpleasant duty of evicting them from their own property. What would he do if he ran up face to face with the half Indian gunslinger?

Ben Granger met him on the boardwalk late in the morning

while he was still deep in thought about the matter, and commanded his audience. "Heard anything about your missing girl?"

"No. I haven't."

"I certainly hope she is safe out there with those marauding Sioux Indians about." He quickly changed the subject. "You do know, Sheriff, I plan to evict the Williston family by the end of summer."

"I'm well aware of your intentions."

"When the time comes, I want them off my land."

"Yes. Your land," Sheriff Potts answered somberly, cocking his nearly bald head, and shutting one eye tightly.

The burly man reached his hand into his coat pocket and withdrew a folded bundle of papers. "It's all right here, Sheriff, the updated copy. It's all according to the law. I had my men serve the final batch to Mrs. William Williston last week."

Potts looked hard at the papers but didn't attempt to take them. "I'm sure you have it written up all legal for Sadie's eyes."

"I do, Sheriff. It seems that William Williston left a few things undone when he came out this way to claim his land."

"I'm sure a lot of men did."

He chortled. "But I'm not worried about a lot of men. I'm just concerned about this one, William Williston and his farm."

Sheriff Potts looked across the street as a wagon rushed by. "So, why are you telling me this again? I know my job."

"I'm a business man and an attorney. I just want to make sure you are aware of the legal responsibilities."

"Ok. I'm aware." The sheriff stepped aside and started to pass by, but Granger blocked him.

"I expect your cooperation as a lawman. Everything is legal."

"If everything is legal and done the right way, you'll have my cooperation." He eyed the papers in Granger's grasp. "Now that I think about it, would you mind if I take them papers after all... and read them over?"

Granger smiled and looked pleased. "Didn't know you could read." He slipped a cigar between his teeth, biting and spitting out the tip onto the dusty street below. "This is your copy. That's why I stopped you. Take your time with them, sheriff; but you'll discover everything is in perfect order. The Williston family farm belongs to me now."

Jamie Quentin rode his horse hard across the open plain, but he wasn't alone. He glanced over at the rider and horse who were keeping pace with him. "I don't like being out in the open like this, especially with you riding on that old animal. We'll slow down when we reach those rocks up ahead. There's a water hole and some trees beyond it where we can all rest."

"She might be old, but she has spirit," said the woman. It was the voice of Evelina Williston.

"You still haven't told me exactly where we're going or what this is all about."

"Yes, I have. Kansas," he shouted above the rumble of horse hoofs. "I also told you why we're going."

"But I can hardly believe it."

Soon they reached the rocks and circled behind them. When they dismounted beneath a small cluster of trees and bushes, he scanned the plains.

"What are you looking for?" she asked him.

"To make sure we're alone."

She became aware of the sound of trickling water. "You mean you've seen some Indians?"

"No. I've not made out any signs of them being around. But I'm more concerned about seeing Granger's men. Maybe Ned Ames."

"I don't understand."

"You will soon."

"When?"

"Tomorrow, if we make good time. You have to trust me."

"But why would Ned Ames be after us?"

"To bring you back."

"Oh." The answer satisfied her. "But what would Mr. Granger want with us?"

"To follow us to Smithsbluff."

"But why?"

"You will understand everything better when we get there."

She wanted to question him some more, but his responses were always vague. He had told her back in Glensbluff that the trip would answer the questions everyone had about the missing gold. That alone didn't convince her to leave with him. Then he said that the trip would help her and her family to keep Granger from stealing their farm. She believed him but was still not persuaded to take off with him to Kansas. But when he told her the finest reason of all that she should trust him and head straight south with him, she needed no more coaxing. She would go with him anywhere. "So, my daddy really is alive?"

"I can't promise you anything. He was alive the last I saw him, but he was not well."

"When was that?"

"I've told you already. Sometime back."

"That doesn't tell me anything."

Jamie lifted the canteens from the horses and gave one to Evelina. Kneeling beside the tiny stream he took a drink.. "Four months, maybe a little more."

"I still can't believe it. It seems too true to be real. My daddy still alive! After so long."

"Don't get your hopes up too high. As I said, he's far from being himself."

"You mean his mind?"

"That's why I'm taking you there. The doctor has treated him unsuccessfully. It's just too dangerous to bring him to you, so I'm taking you to him. We hope your lovely face and sweet voice will bring him back."

"From where?"

"From the wasteland where his mind has been trapped."

Evelina finally paused to drink from the canteen. "I'm not sure if I can handle that."

"He needs you. We decided you were what he needed the most right now."

"We? But why?"

"My friend, the doctor. Because nothing else has worked."

She held onto her new wide brimmed hat as the wind gusted. "Who is this doctor you keep mentioning?"

Jamie planted his soft eyes on her and offered a weak smile. "I'll explain everything when we get there. Just trust me."

"You don't ask much of me, Jamie! This is a lot to take in. I trust you, though. I have to."

They led their horses to a small pool of water beneath a canopy of branches. Evelina began fanning herself with her hat and wiping the sweat from her cheeks with the hem of her dress. Then they stretched out in a shady spot beside a large boulder. "Why does Granger want his men to follow us?" She studied the terrain around her. Apprehension gripped her voice. "What do we have that they want?"

"I think Granger and Penrose were on to me. Ned Ames too."

"On to you about what?"

"My connection to the gold...and to your father."

"I don't understand you." A look of disbelief came across her face. "What are you trying to tell me?"

"Evelina, there is something about me that you don't know."

She wiped her forehead daintily with a handkerchief. "You're scaring me, Jamie. Maybe I shouldn't have come."

"You don't have to be afraid of me. I'm nothing like Penrose or Granger."

Evelina nodded, but with questioning eyes. "I know. But Mama was right about one thing. You don't belong with that bunch. You're different. You just aren't making sense right now."

His eyes swept across the plains once more. "You don't really know who I am."

"You're scaring me again."

"Evelina, I started looking for your father three years ago when he first disappeared."

She gasped. "Why were you looking for him back then? Did you know him?"

"I knew about him."

She looked even more perplexed.

"I work for the federal government. I'm an agent."

She caught her breath.

"I have been looking for your father and for the missing gold."

"Are you saying my father really did have something to do with that gold?

He nodded slowly.

She gasped; then drew in a deep breath, releasing it quickly. "I just can't believe all this. So there really is gold on our farm?'

"I don't know where the gold is hidden."

He stood up and walked past her, keeping a wide distance as he approached the grazing horses near the water. "I hope shortly you will come to understand that everything I have done was the right thing to do... and for your good."

"My good? How is all this for my good?"

He adjusted his hat and reached for the reins. Turning back around he peered into her curious eyes. "I'm taking you to your father after three years of you not knowing where he was. And I also hope eventually you will see that I truly do have strong feelings for you."

In the shade of the trees, Evelina seemed unable to move an inch. She wanted to believe him. She had felt something for him too. Her mind raced. Everything was coming at her too fast. *Why had he waited until they were on the journey to begin telling her so much?*

"Come on," he encouraged her. "We had better hurry and get across this open plain before night fall, if we can."

She curled her lips. "I'm not so sure now about going away with you. I miss my family already."

"You wanted to get away from that farm, didn't you? And you said you wanted the big city life. Smithsbluff is a big town with lots of dancing and fancy stores and shows."

"And my father?"

"I'm sure of it."

"Why is it too dangerous for my father to come back to the farm? Is it because of Ben Granger?"

Jamie looked as though he had a pebble in his mouth, swishing it around while tightening his lips. He was stalling – thinking of how to say it. "Granger is a concern, but your father isn't well. His mind is still an empty shell from the war. Traveling will be risky to his health."

"How do you know this? You said you haven't seen him."

"I have friends who are taking care of him," he answered caringly. "They have tried to reach through to him, but to no avail. We are hoping that seeing someone from his past that he dearly loves will trigger something, and he will come back to himself."

She seemed enticed by the proposal to see her father and persuaded by the tenderness in his voice that she turned and approached her horse. "Risky or not, I feel like a convict on the run. Seeing all his family would be better than just seeing me."

He helped her mount. "Yes. And if this doesn't work, that may be our next step. But it's probably not good for him to travel in his condition right now. Maybe soon. And it could also be dangerous for him to be seen."

Jamie mounted his horse and the young couple began to move away from the shadows of the small copse of trees. "Dangerous being seen by Ben Granger. He and his men have been looking for him too. They blame him for the gold missing all these years. They will stop at nothing to get that information out of him."

"Then, please tell me, what connection does my father have with this gold?"

Jamie stilled his horse. "That's what I'm hoping he will tell you. I'm hoping he will come to himself and explain a lot of things to you about the past three years."

Her eyes grew wider and her lips opened, but she couldn't think of what to say. Finally she said, "Then why are we dawdling?

TWENTY-TWO

❀ ∂ᴗ

Smithsbluff sat atop a wide terraced hummock on the Kansas plains, crowded together building against building with broad dirt streets in-between. As Jamie and Evelina rode in on the main thoroughfare, they smelled the smoke from the blacksmith's shop and felt the intense heat from the fire in the sky that bore down unobstructed on them. The horses slowed to an amble, their lengthy legs sluggish, their large eyes weary.

"Is this it?" Evelina questioned. "I thought it would be bigger than Glensbluff."

"It is bigger," he said, laughing. "We have two more buildings than Glensbluff."

Evelina took in the street scene and seemed disappointed.

"Don't worry," Jamie assured her. "The town is bigger and so is the populace."

Their first stop was the rain water trough in front of the mercantile store. They dismounted and watered the horses.

"I'm so sore," she complained as she panned the scenery again, resting her eyes on the grand hotel sign at the end of the dusty street. "I'm ready for a bath."

He followed her eyes. "You'll have your bath later. Right now I have to see someone."

"Who? My father?"

"No. Not yet. Come on and I'll show you who." He directed her down the street in the opposite direction from the hotel.

"I'm too tired and too dirty to meet anybody," Evelina complained. "Except my father. I want to get a room first."

"Smithsbluff is home for me, so you don't have to worry about getting a room in the hotel. I have family not far out of town. We'll take the horses to Simeon, the blacksmith, and also my cousin. Your old horse needs some rest. He'll check them over while we see the doctor."

"The doctor? The one who is taking care of my father?"

He nodded. Then he led the horses away, keeping them and Evelina to the far side of the street to avoid a wagon speeding through town. A couple passed by and greeted him.

"Do you know them?" she asked.

"Yes."

"Of course. This is your home. I must look a pretty embarrassing sight to your friends," she said, removing her hat and attempting to rake her hair down with her fingers.

"You look lovely as always."

"Now I know you can't tell the truth."

They left their horses with Simeon, who greeted Jamie with an embrace that indicated they hadn't seen each other in a long while. Then, they crossed the street and stepped up on the boardwalk. "How far are we going?" she asked.

He took her by the arm and drew her closer to the wall as two cowboys passed by on the outside. He stopped suddenly and held her back before she could take another step. "I was taking you up there," he answered her, nodding his head towards a long staircase that ran up the outside of a building to a red door on the top landing. "But we'll just wait right here."

"What's wrong?"

"Nothing's wrong. The doctor just isn't up there anymore."

The frustrated look was obvious on her face. "And how do you know that?"

"Because here he comes now."

A young and very handsome man approached them and stopped directly in front of them on the sidewalk. "Well, I see you made it back to Smithsbluff, Jamie." He nodded his head towards the lovely young woman with the frazzled hair. "You must be Evelina Williston. So good to meet you. I'm Doctor Smith."

Evelina carefully observed the man. He looked to be in his thirties and was dressed in dark pants, a white shirt, and a string tie. She paid special attention to his wavy blonde hair. "You look …" Her lips fell silent and she gaped at him, clamping her hand over her mouth.

"What's the matter?" the doctor asked.

"You… you look like… like somebody… I know," she answered in a stutter.

"Who?"

"Never mind. Somebody back in Nebraska Territory – I mean who used to live in Nebraska Territory. You just remind me so much of him."

"Well," said the familiar face, "My given name is Brodie." He reached for her hand.

She lightly touched his fingers and drew her hand back quickly. "Are you the one caring for my father? I must see him right away. It's been so long and I didn't even know he was still alive until Jamie told me. Is he all right? Where is he? I want to see him."

The doctor turned his eyes to Jamie and gave a half smile.

Evelina squeezed her eyes shut for a second, as though she were tired. "Forgive me for talking so much. I reckon I'm so rattle brained after the hard trip here." She stared at the doctor with inquisitive eyes. "I'm sorry. I must look a sight to you. But my father?"

The doctor turned his head and she followed his eyes up the stair case to his red door office. "That's where I have been looking after him, but he's not up there now. I moved him to a much more private place."

"Private? Why?"

"I'm his doctor. The treatments I'm using with him require a lot of his attention with little opportunity for distraction. But you will see him soon enough, I promise. That's why you're here."

"I still can't believe this is real," she responded, breathlessly.

Jamie placed his arm across Brodie's back. "It's real, Evelina. Don't be surprised when I tell you this too, but Brodie is another of my cousins. That's why I know your father is in good hands."

"Is everyone in this town your cousin, Mr. Quentin?"

"No. Just half of them."

"And Jamie is not a Quentin, stated the doctor. "He's a Smith too." She turned quickly to Jamie. "Is that true?"

He nodded. "I used the name, Quentin, when I was working as part of Granger's bunch."

"Why didn't you tell me this?" Evelina altered her glances back and forth between the two men. "What else about you haven't you told me?"

"I'll explain everything later." His eyes deepened and his voice grew solemn as he asked his cousin, "Is everything here the same?"

"Yes, it is. There's no significant improvement, I'm afraid..." he took a quick breath and exhaled deliberately. "Dr. Wilhelm's treatments have not been successful."

"I'm sorry to hear that."

Evelina was curious at the mention of the name. "Who is this Doctor Wilhelm?"

"He is an expert on your father's condition."

"Which is...?"

"Brain injuries," Dr. Smith replied. "Or, more specifically, war injuries that affect the mind. He has studied the effects of disease and trauma on the mind for decades in Europe. But his treatments have not helped your father, I'm afraid. I'm hoping that may change since you are here." He considered Evelina's reaction.

"Is my father really alive?"

"Yes. He is."

"I still can hardly believe it's true. It's like a dream." Her eyes widened. Will he even know me?"

"I'm counting on his seeing you and hearing your voice to prompt a miraculous transformation in him. You might say I have tried everything else and nothing has worked. But seeing you..."

Evelina seemed confused by all the talk of her father. "You mean to tell me that all this time, he's been right here in Smithsbluff?

Brodie glanced around to see if anyone might be able to hear him. Feeling it was safe, he explained. "No. During the war, I managed to move him to a small hospital. After the war ended, I kept him in a treatment facility where I began to study Dr. Wilhelm's techniques on mind restoration. Only recently did I move him here."

"How did this happen to my father's mind, Doctor?"

"Your father no doubt experienced some traumatic horrors during the war and when he was wounded, I believe infection from his shoulder may have gone to his brain."

"Oh, yes, his shoulder wound. Is his arm gone?"

"What?"

"Abner Abercrombie said he might have had his arm…"

"Oh, no," Brodie cut her off when he realized what she meant. "He still has both arms. It's his mind that seems to be lost. That's Dr. Wilhelm's area."

"Where is this Dr. Wilhelm? I'd like to meet him."

"I'm sorry, but Dr. Wilhelm isn't here. We have only corresponded about your father during the past year. I had hoped he would see your father when he crossed the ocean for a medical tour to teach his methods in America. But, unfortunately, his visit was cancelled due to some conflict with his teaching duties. He was our brightest hope for your father's condition."

Evelina was tired, yet the mention of her father's condition and Dr. Wilhelm's cancellation seemed to strike her interest anew. "Take me to see him. Right now."

"I will soon, " Jamie promised.

"Take me now. I haven't seen his face in three years."

"Not now. He's not even in town. First we're going to take you to Brodie's house and get you that bath you want."

"Who cares about a bath!"

Jamie offered a sympathetic smile. "Then after that we'll arrange for you to see him."

"Tonight?"

"If everything goes as planned."

"What does that mean?"

Jamie sighed and looked to the doctor for reassurance. "It's dangerous to keep your father in the same place for too long a time. We're not the only ones looking for him. Ben Granger has eyes down here in Kansas too." He turned his own eyes towards the street and the sidewalk beyond. Seeing nothing suspicious, he went on. "When it's dark, we'll ride out to the Smith home. It's just too risky now."

"Jamie, why don't you take her up to my office and let her tidy up a bit. There's fresh water in the bowl and a large mirror on the wall just above it. I have a patient to see right now."

"That sounds good." He looked to Evelina for her approval. "After you shine up a bit, we'll have a cup of coffee at the café, and when the sun gets low, we'll head out to Brodie's place."

She protested, but Jamie cut her off. "You must be patient if you want your father to be safe. Isn't that what you want?"

She nodded. "I'm trusting you, Jamie. You had better be truthful with me."

"I'm telling you the truth." He placed her arm through his. "Brodie is working hard to restore your father's memory to him. You're now the best chance he's had for success."

Brodie caught some movement out of the corner of his eye. "Right now I'm more concerned about keeping Granger away from him." He directed their eyes across the street where a burly cowboy wearing a grey hat stepped up on the boardwalk, spun around slowly, and propped his shoulder against the wall. He was chewing on a dry weed and intently looking their way.

"One of Granger's men?" asked Jamie.

"I don't know who he is," answered Brodie apprehensively. "But I do know he's not from around here and he hasn't taken his eyes off me since he came back into town a couple of days ago."

The brawny man spit out his weed and turned unhurriedly, his eyes staring down the trio until he disappeared inside the door of the telegraph office.

"Looks like he might be trouble," stated Jamie.

Evelina captured a quick breath and held it, upset by the strange man across the street. She pressed her fingers against her heart. "You mean Mr. Granger has thought all along that my father is alive and is here in Smithsbluff?"

"No," responded the doctor, glancing back at the telegraph office door. "I don't believe he necessarily thinks your father is alive. We have been diligent in keeping William hidden away. But he does think somebody here in Smithsbluff knows where the missing gold might be."

Jamie agreed. "Yes. After all Granger has kept his eyes on Abner Abercrombie for some time and he trailed him here to Smithsbluff. He knows that your father took Abner into his confidence and I suspect that he believes Abner might lead him to the gold. That has made him suspicious of everyone here with the name Smith."

"That seems to be most of the town, "she replied.

Dr. Brodie Smith checked the telegraph office door once more. Seeing no movement, he expected the worse. "I suspect that cowboy is in there wiring Granger as we speak."

"Wiring him what?" asked Evelina, her eyes wide with alarm.

"Ben Granger and Siler Penrose both know that the federal government has been trying to locate the stolen gold since it disappeared near the start of the war. And they know we're involved. Your father will never be safe as long as Ben Granger's bunch will stop at nothing to solve the mystery of the vanished gold and dig their greedy claws into it."

TWENTY-THREE

❧

"Time is running out!" bellowed Siler Penrose standing just inside the door of Mr. Granger's office with two of his cohorts, Handshoe and Taylor.

"Calm down," blasted the weighty boss, just as impatiently, scurrying around to the front of his desk where his men stood, and shutting the door quickly. "I don't need any hot heads right now. This must be done by legal means or we will complicate the whole matter."

Penrose heaved a noticeable sigh. "I'm tired of waiting. They're making no effort to vacate the property."

"They got no plans to leave at all," enjoined Handshoe.

Granger reassured them, "Everything is under control." He folded his arms across his stomach and rested his posterior on the edge of his desk. "I want this to go as smooth as molasses. What if we evict them today and we can't find the gold on the property? Yes, I'm taking this slowly. I'm counting on my threats to stir them up and cause them to panic and lead us right to the spot."

"What if they don't lead us to it?" Penrose complained. "What if they don't leave the property?"

"Don't you fellows fret." The lawyer grinned contentedly as he lifted a stack of papers from his desk and slid them in a large folder. He shook the folder at them like a teacher would shake his paddle at unruly students. "The Williston family will leave my property by my deadline."

"Or what?" yapped Penrose.

"Or the sheriff will legally evict them from the premises."

Handshoe chortled like a disgruntled schoolchild. "That sorry excuse for a lawman?"

"Exactly," answered the boss with a devious grin. "Because he is a sorry excuse for a lawman, he'll do exactly what I tell him to do. He's old and run down; and He knows I run this town now."

"Then, I say we go tell him right now," Penrose proposed, "Tell him to get busy planning the evicting. Tell him to ride out one more time and warn them that he means business and to start packing."

"Yeah," added Taylor, "and if he doesn't mean business, we do."

Granger chuckled. "I don't reckon the sheriff works that way."

Handshoe jerked his pistol out of his holster. "Then I don't mind evicting them myself."

The boss's demeanor changed instantly. "Ned Ames will cut you like a weed," he growled.

"Not this time he won't. We're tired of sittin' round and waiting on them. If you ain't gonna do something about 'em, we aim to."

"Put that gun up," ordered Granger. "I'm in charge here. You do it my way or the guns I control in this town will be cutting you down." His breathing quickened. His temples wriggled. His face turned a dark shade of red. "If you don't like the way I operate, there's the door. You can leave right now." His round, wobbly jaws flamed brighter. "Do you fellows think you can do this without my legal experience? The property is in my name now and if you can't follow my orders…" He spun around and slammed the stack of folders on his desk so hard they sounded like a gunshot. "You couldn't find sawdust, much less a wagon load of gold, without me."

The men's eyes widened, but Penrose crossed his arms and leaned against the door frame calmly. "I'm beginning to wonder if there's even any gold on that property. We ain't found a clue yet."

"Of course, you haven't found a clue," roared Granger. "Do you think he would hide a wagon load of gold in plain sight where anyone could just walk up on top of it? That's why we need that land – and we need it legally – so we can conduct a thorough and uninterrupted search for it. Mind you, it's a pretty big spread of land. The gold's there, all right. Where else could it be? And why do you think those two boys keep digging up the soil like gophers drunk on sugar beets? Why did Ames and Abercrombie make their way all the way up here to Nebraska territory?"

The men all nodded in agreement.

"Bezold is still watching the Williston place for any odd movement. At least he knows how to follow orders without bellyaching." Granger stopped talking and breathed one long and slow breath through his nose. He sat down and folded his hands. Looking up at his men, he moved his eyeballs back and forth from one to the other, then parted his wide lips. "I heard from my man down in Smithsbluff and its just as I suspected. Quentin and that Williston girl are in the town as we speak, and they met up with that doctor."

"Doctor?" questioned Handshoe.

Irritated again, Granger barked, "The one who took care of Williston when he got deathly sick from his shoulder wound."

Taylor had been silent up to this point, but he spoke up when he heard Williston's name. "You think he's still alive, boss?"

Granger dropped his head. "I'd be surprised if he was." Then he raised his chin again. "But I'll tell you what I do think. I think those Smiths know something about the whereabouts of that gold and aim to get their own share of it before the federal government gets any of it back."

"All his family thinks he's still alive," added Taylor.

"I'm not so sure all of them do." The big man rose anxiously and stood behind his desk, resting his arm on the back of his leather chair. "Let me give you two reasons I believe he can't still be alive since you asked. First, he was on death's door when I let that doctor take him away. You know I didn't let prisoners go just for being sick. I was hoping he could save him and find out where he hid the gold. But he was too far gone when the doctor got him. And second, if he was still alive, then where is he? My men can't find him. The federal troops can't locate him. And his own family hasn't laid eyes on him for three years. He can't be alive. If he were, he would have already dug up his gold and be living it up somewhere. We've hunted high and low over this green earth for him. No, I'm sure he's dead and in some hole in the ground now."

"Sure," mumbled Penrose.

"When it comes to this gold, I'm not so sure of much of anything right now. But I am pretty certain of this – somebody who's alive has got to know where that gold is hidden."

"Well, I'm sure of something too," roared Penrose. "It's gotta be on Williston's land somewhere. I covered every inch of the trail he traveled after we got separated. If it was there anywhere, me and my men would have found it. Not a single bar. Not even a wagon track. Yes, I'm sure its hidden on his place somewhere. We just gotta find it."

Granger returned to his desk chair once more, slid out the papers from the folder, and briefly looked them over. "I agree that our next step is to inform the sheriff that we do seriously aim to evict the Willistons from our land. That should make Sadie panic a bit. We will simply remind Potts of our intent and strongly suggest to him that he and his deputies ride out to the Williston ranch and give them notice again. Either pack up or get evicted and leave it all behind. Sadie Williston is a smart lady and she won't risk losing her possessions, including the gold. When she runs out of time, she'll get careless and go for the gold. All the better, her boys can dig it up for us."

"So, you think she knows where it is," said Taylor, "But won't tell her boys?"

"Maybe. It makes sense that she would keep it from them to try to protect them. They would have already dug it up if they knew where it was. Just figure, fellows, how could a wagon load of gold end up right under her nose and her not know anything about it. She knows alright and Ned Ames is helping her. The closer it gets to the deadline, the more nervous she'll be acting. But the sheriff will need a little nudging from time to time to put the pressure on her."

"Let's go then," said Handshoe, gripping his gun belt in front with both hands.

"I'll be the one who goes," decided Granger. "Do you think I want you hot heads around when I talk to the sheriff?" Then a sudden smirk appeared on his face. "Better yet, I think I will take you with me, Handshoe. Just don't talk. Not one word. I'll do all the talking. He knows you're a gunslinger and I want you there just to reassure him that we do mean business."

Sheriff Potts was sitting at his desk in the jail office when Granger and Handshoe opened the door and marched in. "I was expecting to see you gentlemen. I can guess why you're here."

"You've had a chance to read the papers I drew up?"

"No. I don't see too good. I couldn't read much when I did see good. But I had someone look at them. "And it's funny," said the sheriff, leaning back in his broken down old chair. "He said they were legal alright – but crooked at the same time. There's a lot of good men who didn't tie all the knots when they moved to Nebraska territory during the homesteading. Most of them couldn't even read."

"I'm not interested in a lot of good men who can't read, Sheriff. I'm interested in only one man who didn't settle all his territory fees and then let it get away from him. I am happy to pay the accumulated fees and claim the land myself. Unless Mrs. Williston wants to pay it off…"

Sheriff Potts frowned. "Yeah. Pay 'em to yourself. You know she ain't got that kind of money, though I hear some of the town folks are trying to raise the money for her."

"Why would they want to do that?"

"I reckon they'd pay anything to keep from having you as a neighbor."

Granger found the comment rather amusing. "I'm not worried about them raising money. I have everything under control, sheriff. I suggest you make a trip out to my place and give her fair warning – well in advance – so she will have time to pack up her possessions. Put the pressure on her. I don't want her to dawdle so long that she has to leave everything behind. I think that's a generous proposal."

"How very thoughtful of you. I didn't realize you were so kind. What makes you so sure that missing gold is on that land?"

"I'm not sure of anything. But that's none of your business." He made a point to observe Handshoe and his gun belt in a prolonged look. "Now, can we expect you to do your job?" As Granger spoke, Handshoe slid his fast hand down to the top of his white pistol handle. The sheriff's eyes followed his hand like a serpent crawling.

"Oh, I aim to ride out there," Sheriff Potts agreed, not showing the least bit of fear. "I may not like it, but it's my job." His eyes narrowed. "But I'll not be threatened with your timetable or your guns. I'll go next week and give them the deadline in writing, officially. That will give them a couple of weeks to pack up or sell off some of their things. Now, is that all?"

"Yes," replied Ben Granger without his wily smile. He wanted Sheriff Potts to know he meant business, if Handshoe's gun hand hadn't already convinced him. "You had better do it and do it right or I'll make sure you never do any sheriff-ing again."

"Are you threatening a lawman?"

"No, sir," he answered, wobbling his big jaws. "I just want to make sure you understand your public duty."

The old, grey-headed lawman stood up, strolled leisurely past the men, and opened the door. They turned to leave. "I will make an official threat to you, Granger," spoke the sheriff with strong intent as the barrister crossed the threshold. "We do this my way or no way. That means without any involvement from you or your hands."

The bulky lawyer turned back at the door to face the badge. "If you do your job, Sheriff, I won't have to take matters into my hands."

"I have some pretty good deputies – and I can scrounge up a few more," the lawman cautioned them again.

"Now, I wouldn't be too sure of that." The solicitor tightened his dress coat around his stomach and laughed heartily with Handshoe. "Come on, Handshoe I have a very important assignment for you." He spoke this loudly enough for Potts to hear him." Then they chortled some more.

When the sheriff's office door closed hard behind them, the two men stopped laughing.

"What you got in mind for me, boss?"

Granger pulled one of his cigars from his coat pocket and bit down on it. "I want you to snoop around and find out about this money the town is raising for Sadie Williston."

"What do you want me to do when I find out about it?"

The big man smiled with the cigar still between his teeth. "Stop it."

"How?"

"Anyway you want."

TWENTY-FOUR

❧

"Brodie's family doesn't live too far out of town," Jamie explained. "Hold on."

The breeze created by the moving wagon felt good. "When can I see my father?"

"You wanted a bath first, didn't you?"

"Yes, of course. But I can hardly bare to wait."

The two-storied white house sat just off the road. A picket fence could be seen in the generous moonlight, enclosing the lawn. Two towering, bleached pillars supported a balcony above the front entrance, furnished with two rattan chairs, a table, and a lofty flowering cactus. Jamie drew the horses to a stop and jumped down. He helped Evelina and took her handbag.

The captivated young woman drank in the beautiful structure surrounded by trees and shrubs and rows of florae. "Is this where Brodie lives?"

"He used to. This is where he grew up. My folks lived up the road a ways and we played together as boys."

"Do your parents still live there?"

"No. They died a few years back."

"I'm sorry."

The door flew open and Dr. Smith hurried out to greet them. The three walked inside, exchanging conversation about the house. An older couple sitting on the parlor sofa stood and welcomed their guest.

"My parents, Benjamin and Garnett," said the doctor.

The couple appeared to be in their sixties with greying hair and fitted conservative attire.

"This is Evelina Williston."

"Yes, I can tell," spoke the woman. "Have a seat."

Evelina offered a look with her eyes that asked, *what could she tell?*

"We'll talk later," Brodie said to his parents. "Evelina is tired from her long trip. She washed up in my office, but she wants a real bath and a change of clothes first."

"Yes, I would... if you don't mind. I must be an unwelcome sight."

"Of course we don't mind," answered Garnett. "And you are a sight most welcomed. With this dreadful drought in Kansas, everything is so dry and dusty. Come with me and I'll draw your bath and find you something to wear."

"I have clothes in my bag."

"But they will be flattened and wrinkled."

"There's someone I want you to see." Brodie called out after her.

"My father?"

"Well, yes, him especially. But there is someone else."

"When you're finished dressing," Garnett informed her, "we can get acquainted around the dinner table over a delicious meal." The ladies disappeared up the staircase.

"How about you, Jamie?" asked Benjamin. "Do you need to wash and change clothes?"

"Not now. I cleaned up a bit in town. I will wash my hands, though."

Later that evening Evelina descended the long staircase. She felt better now that she had bathed and removed the trail dust from her hair. She had piled her hair on top like a prairie mound to keep it from her face. Her dress was a dark cotton wrap that widened below the knees like a hoop. Her blouse was cream colored and had long sleeves, which she rolled up above her wrists. A large red bow had been embroidered on the material covering her heart.

"Don't you look lovely," said Jamie.

She smiled and took his arm as they walked into the dining room.

Brodie met them in the doorway. "I told you there was someone I wanted you to see."

"Who?"

"My brother."

Behind Brodie stood a handsome man with flaxen colored hair wearing a white shirt and string tie. He walked into the light and faced the attractive, young woman. "Hello, Evelina."

She instantly recognized that voice. When she saw his face she squealed with excitement. "Reverend Smythe! What are you doing here?"

"This is my home."

"Your home! I mean – I didn't expect to ever see you again. I thought you moved away to take another church." Her eyes widened larger than saucers when she remembered how Dr. Smith had introduced him. "Yes. You look just like him. You're Brodie's brother."

"Calm down. I know this is a surprise to you. And I do have a name. Browning, remember."

"But you're Reverend Smythe."

"Smith, actually," Jamie added. "And he's my cousin too."

"I don't know what to say. But how –?" She paused to catch her breath. "Don't tell me you're not really a minister."

He moved closer and took her by both hands. "I really am a minister. But I have been working with my brother and Jamie on this case for some time. Smythe was my work name."

"What's going on here?" she asked.

"Sit down," said Jamie. "We'll talk as we eat."

After the meal and many lengthy details, Benjamin led the group into the parlor, Jamie and Evelina, Brodie and Browning. They each took seats and Evelina followed up on the dinner conversation. "I just can't believe what I'm hearing."

Jamie noted her enthusiasm. "There are some good reasons we've had to keep all this from you, as you might imagine. The Smith family has worked with the United States government for three generations, starting with my grandfather and then my father and Uncle Benjamin here. They are what we call detectives. Now my cousins and I have continued the legacy. It's in our blood, you could say."

His uncle put in a good word for the Smith boys and their work. "My days of investigating are done, but the boys are carrying on the tradition."

"How did your family ever get involved in this kind of work?"

"That's a long story and meant for another day," Benjamin replied.

Evelina seemed to be mulling everything over in her mind. "It's hard to believe how all this has so much to do with our land and that detestable lawyer."

"Yes, but it does…very much," answered Jamie. "It has everything to do with him and the missing gold... and your father."

"I want to see him now. Is he here?"

"Yes, Garnett is upstairs preparing him for your visit."

The anxious young woman started to stand.

"In a moment she will call us," spoke Benjamin. "There is another woman sitting with him as well, someone we have known for years and trust. We hired her so your father would not be left alone at night. So, sit back down and get comfortable."

Evelina could not keep her eyes off the staircase. "Why can't I see him now?"

Benjamin looked to Jamie who took her by the hand. "Your father is not well, as you already know. We want to make sure you're ready to see him before you go in his room. He's lost a lot of weight and is feeble. He's not the same man you remember."

She gasped and placed her hand over her heart.

"We have to make sure you understand how important this visit is – not just for you – but for your family and Ben Granger and the government. For everyone involved. You see, we must learn what happened to the missing gold."

"Gold!" she exclaimed. "That's all anyone ever talks about. I just want to see my father. Why do you make me wait so unfairly?"

Browning leaned forward in his seat and spoke softly. "I'm sorry to make you wait, Evelina, but it is most important that we discover the whereabouts of the gold. Keeping your father's land may depend on it."

"I don't care about that land."

"I know you don't. But it is also important to find the missing gold before Ben Granger and Siler Penrose cause any more trouble. They will do anything to get their hands on it. That means your family in Nebraska is not safe as long as he has plans to take your farm and dig it up."

"It's all about this gold, isn't it? It's never been about me seeing my father. You all deceived me for your own gain."

"That isn't true," answered Jamie. "It was stolen gold and a lot of men have died because of it. If we don't locate it soon, more people are going to die. Ben Granger and Siler Penrose have made a pact with the devil to find that gold and they are motivated by hatred and greed. They have a personal vendetta against your father going back to the war. The only way to put a stop to their plan is for us to discover what happened to that gold and get it safely back to Colorado."

"Colorado?"

"Yes, there is more gold than you can imagine. It belongs to the federal government. We have investigated this for years, since the robbery, but we have come up completely empty – and so has Granger. We are convinced that your father is the only person alive who knows where it's hidden. That's a dangerous secret to be buried so deep inside his mind. If Ben Granger and his associates only knew your daddy was still alive and here in Smithsbluff, well… let's just say your father would be in greater danger than he is now."

The bewildered woman looked around from face to face making brief contact with each set of eyes in the circle. She looked more uncertain than ever, as though she were tasting a foreign food for the first time. "I don't think I completely understand how everything, including me, fits together in this wild tale," she confessed. "This gold… there's more to this gold story than I want to know. All this strange talk makes me awfully nervous about going upstairs to see him. I just don't understand why all the secrets."

"Let me try to explain," offered Jamie.

"No," Benjamin interrupted. "You all seem too close to the Willistons. Let me explain it to the young lady. About five years ago before my departure from the Pinkerton agency, I was involved in this case. I know it well." He clasped his hands together in his lap and scooted to the edge of his seat. "Your father, William Williston, was once a partner with Siler Penrose."

She gulped and swallowed hard. "No. That can't be."

"I'm sorry, but it is true. They were also partners with the half Indian gunslinger."

"Ned Ames?"

"Yes. At the start of the great rebellion they were part of a gang of eight to ten men who robbed several thousands of dollars' worth of gold from Denver, Colorado."

Evelina seemed to stop breathing. "No. I can't believe my daddy was a robber?"

The elder Smith went on with his explanation. "I'm still not absolutely sure of his motive behind the whole scheme, but there is no doubt of his role. It is a fact that he was suspected of being the mastermind behind the robbery. I'm sorry, young lady, but it is true. The federal government once had a high price on his head."

She turned suddenly towards Jamie. "Why didn't you tell me all this before we left?"

"I was afraid you wouldn't have come then."

"I wish I hadn't now," she cried. "Tell me it's not true, Jamie. My daddy can't be a wanted man. I know him – I mean knew him. I mean…"

"Evelina," he said pleadingly as he reached past Browning to take her hand in his. "He's not a wanted man any more. The gold was originally stolen to finance the war effort for the South. Jefferson Davis admitted to the fact himself. But the gold was never used for the war. It hasn't been used for anything; it would appear. There must be a reason he never delivered it to the South. No one seems to know where it is."

"Except your father," added Benjamin.

"Yes, so I have heard over and over again."

"After the robbery, the group got split up. First, the federal troops got after them and then there was some disagreement among themselves. We believe the gang fought over the gold."

"But why do you think my father knows where it is?"

Benjamin took a deep breath and let it out quickly. "Because all the remaining survivors of the gang are looking for it, all except your father."

She looked to Jamie again with eyes of despair. "But you said he was sick. You said his mind isn't right."

Dr. Smith rejoined the discussion at this point. "That's true. I have been working with him since right after he was shot near Vicksburg. We were hoping that you might be the very one to help him recover his mind so we can locate the gold. Ned and Siler are the only two of the ring left besides your father. They were separated from your father when the federal troops pursued them. Your father and a few other men went one direction with the gold wagon while Ned and Siler and a few others led the troops away. If they knew where the gold was, they would have attempted to retrieve it by now. It only goes to reason that your father must be the only one who knows where it is."

"No!" she said, looping her arm through Jamie's. "My daddy couldn't have done something like that. Could he? Maybe one of the other men hid it."

No one in the circle of faces responded.

"I don't think I can go upstairs and face him now – after hearing all this."

Finally, the minister, Browning, spoke up. "Evelina, dear. I know you love your father and he loves you very much, but what we've told you is true. You must put all that out of your mind and go up to see him when my mother calls. Finding that gold is the only thing that will put him and your family out of danger and the only way he can absolve himself of any wrongdoing."

The distraught girl seemed lost in deep thought. She sat silently and her hands trembled. "Why would my daddy steal for the South? He didn't even believe in slavery. He found his own gold, a lot of it, when he was in California."

Brodie stood when he saw his mother descend the staircase. "Mother is beckoning us to come now. He is ready."

Garnett brushed her dress with her hands and lifted the hem from the floor as she started back up the staircase. Brodie followed her. Jamie drew Evelina by the arm and followed them. Browning and Benjamin remained in the parlor offering each other pensive glances. At the top of the stairs, Garnett turned and led them to the end of the hall. She waited until they had all arrived at the threshold; then she slowly turned the handle and pushed the wide wooden door open.

When Garnett stepped aside, Evelina could see a large bed with the headboard against the back wall and closed curtains just above the bedposts. A plump, but small woman sat in a chair by the bed. There on the mattress lay the delicate body of a wafer-thin bearded man. A startled expression suddenly shaped across her face. "Oh!" she cried. "It can't be."

TWENTY-FIVE

❀⤳

With the vigor of a young colt, Sheriff Potts' steed galloped out to the Williston ranch. The sheriff wanted to prepare Sadie for what would happen soon – when she and her family would have to pack up and vacate the land they had called home for years. It's not that he looked forward to the conversation, but he didn't like leaving Ben Granger in his town unguarded for too long. He didn't trust him because he knew he was a manipulator, fraudster, and an egotistical greedy man. The sheriff had met men like him before, the kind of man who, wanting to impress people, would buy an expensive, hand-carved casket to bury his grandmother; but after the funeral would dump her in a pine box and return the casket for the money.

As the old sod barn came into view, he began to dread the discussion. He loathed Ben Granger like he did a callous on his foot inside a pair of untested boots. If it were up to him, he would lock him up in the far back cell, misplace the key, and forget all about him – at least long enough to determine if the man had a soul or not. Rounding the side of the barn he saw the Pawnee woman tending to a small patch of corn she had sown. She watched him carefully as he stopped and dismounted.

The front door opened, and Sadie walked out to greet him, folding her arms across her lap. "Hello, Sheriff. I can imagine why you've come all the way out here."

"Howdy," he answered, tipping his hat. "It isn't because I want to, for sure, unless it were a social visit."

"So, I reckon this ain't no social call."

He wagged his head slowly. "Ben Granger has drawn up his papers and I've had them checked out. They seem to be legal, although I don't know how he's ever been able to do anything legal in his whole life. I know he's dishonest, but I have no choice but to let you know in advance."

"Let me know what? That I have to get off my own land?"

"I'm sorry. But that's so. Seems your husband left some things undone and forgot to settle his accounts. Just hogwash, I know. Most men did it the same way he did and nobody would have ever tried to do a thing if Ben Granger hadn't of showed up and wanted your land so bad."

"Why don't you stop him?'

"I'm working on it."

Sadie unfolded her arms and shook the bangs from her eyes. She was hot and sweat formed on her face like dew drops. "I thought free land was free land. What fees could there have been?"

"I'm sorry to say this, but William purchased another portion of land adjoining your property and there is no record of having made the payment."

"I haven't heard about that before. Why would be do that?"

"It seems that the stream widened and gushed next to the property line and he bought that piece from another homesteader. Can you guess who owns that settler's property now?"

Sadie sighed deeply.

The sheriff wasn't done. "And that water well right there..." he nodded towards the heap of stones surrounding the hole. "Granger says he has proof that your husband never paid the men who dug it out for him."

"You know that's not true, Sheriff. He dug it himself with a couple of old horses."

"I don't know the truth, but I believe you. Still, he's got some more papers. Now, unless you have some record..."

"You know I don't."

The stocky man gently stroked his horse's neck and patted her;

then sat up straight in the saddle. "Me and Gracie here rode out the back way in town to see you and headed past the school. I stopped to see how Mrs. Porter was doing with raising the money for you. You know the town has been collecting money to help you out?"

"Yes."

"They collected a bit; but not enough to make much difference. Seems Granger's men put fear into the townspeople, and they stopped giving."

Sadie wagged her head and clasped her hands across her waist. "I figured as much. But we ain't ones to take charity much anyways."

"Mama!" cried Anton, walking purposely from the back side of the barn. "There's a wagon coming."

"A wagon?" She stepped past the sheriff and they both gleaned their eyes towards the trail across the plains.

Inside the house while feeding Lenora a bite of the apple pie left over from Sunday dinner, the preacher and Abner heard the cry. Preacher Pearsall rushed to the front window. He answered Abner's questioning eyes. "The sheriff is out there on his horse, but they all seem to be watching something. Somebody else might be coming. You stay with her and I'll see what's going on." He put on his hat and opened the door. "This sure is getting to be an awfully busy place."

Lillibet, though a small seven-year-old, was brushing the dirt yard near the boardwalk with the old straw broom whose handle stretched high above her head. She stopped sweeping and shooed away the cloud of dust in front of her face. "Somebody's coming in a wagon," she alerted the other youngsters. The sounds of the approaching horses and rumbling wagon soon attracted everyone's attention.

Sadie wiped her face with the hem of her smock. "I sure hope it's not another one of Granger's threatening visits. Maybe he's sent a wagon to load up our belongings."

The burley sheriff dismounted. "I reckon visit's too nice a word for it."

"It's a wagon team and three more horses," said Anton. "No one's riding on one horse. Who could they be?"

Amos came out of the barn carrying his rifle and stood beside his brother. "Can't tell," he answered, though the question was not directed to him. "More important, what do they want?"

"I reckon we'll find out," answered their anxious mother.

The horses with their riders reached the boundary of the small cemetery, passing near the low fence and gate that enclosed the graves and the assortment of colorful prairie flowers. Soon the rider's faces became clearer in the sultry sunlight.

"It's Evelina on the wagon!" shouted Amos. He kicked over a pail and galloped towards them, passing his mother and sheriff Potts. He stopped and turned his wide dancing eyes back to his mother. "I knew she would come home."

Sadie sighed. "I believe it is her. I didn't figure once she left she'd ever want to come back."

"Who's riding with her," asked Anton, concerned. "Is that Jamie Quentin?"

"I do believe it is."

"Who's the other man?"

"I don't know, but that's the preacher's horse."

"Maybe it's the law," he guessed. "Maybe they done caught her."

Sadie looked for the glint of a star on his chest. "No. I don't believe so." She found herself smiling with relief and uttered softly. "We'll know real soon, son."

The horses with their riders stopped. Amos stood tall like the man in charge and called out his sister's name. Sadie could see her daughter's tanned face and her long russet hair flowing beneath the brim of the open crown black hat she was wearing. Jamie looked the same, except for his need of a sharp razor, she thought. The man on the other horse looked somewhat familiar. Where had she seen him before?

"Evelina," she said. "I'm glad you're home."

The riders dismounted as her daughter bounded from the wooden carriage. Her words were a surprise. "I'm so happy to be home, Mama." She hugged all her family one by one as they made their way to her. "I missed you all."

"Where did you run off to?" asked her eldest brother.

"Yes," Her mother decided it was a good excuse for the question since Anton had brought it up so bluntly. "You and Jamie have some explaining to do."

Evelina looked at Jamie and their eyes communicated something to each other. "It's a long story," she said. "I'll tell it all to you when we get inside."

Sadie's eyes followed her daughter from hat to boots and took in the lovely new red skirt and cream blouse she was wearing. "Well, you look good to have been gone for so many days. Who is this other man with you?"

"Does he look familiar?"

"Yes, he does." She studied him, but couldn't place him. "I'm Sadie Williston," she greeted the man with the wide brim hat. "Welcome to our little farm."

Her wayfaring daughter introduced Doctor Brodie Smith to her clan. "He's Jamie's cousin. And if he looks like our former pastor Smythe, that's because he's his brother."

"Yes, I can see that now," said Sadie observing his face under the brim of his hat before he politely removed it and held it with his fingers. "You look just like him now that I recall. I didn't know that Pastor Smythe had a brother that looks so much like him. I remember when he left us to… anyway…what brings you here, Doctor? What brings all of you here together like this?"

Evelina took her mother by the arm. "I'll tell you the whole story later, Mama, but first…"

"Yes, first of all," replied Sadie, "Amos, Anton, you two unhitch that wagon and water the horses."

Amos took the reins to lead the horses to the water trough, but his sister stopped him. "Wait. There's someone else I want you to meet first."

She led them all to the back of the wagon where lay a man on a bed of scattered sun-bleached feed sacks and Indian blankets. He raised his head with what seemed like great effort and propped himself up with his left shoulder. His face appeared old and hollow with a scraggly beard and sunken eyes. The brim of his large brown Gus hat rested just above his untamed eye brows. Sheriff Potts walked around to the other side and watched.

"Is he hurt?" asked Sadie.

"He's been very sick for some time," answered the doctor.

"What is your name, sir?"

The strange man dropped his eyes and didn't respond.

"Can he speak?" asked the preacher, coming around to the back of the wagon.

"He doesn't talk much."

"Another Abner," the preacher said, turning away when he spotted his missing horse.

Sadie looked perplexed by the peculiar fellow and his odd position of lying on his side and twisting his neck around to view his audience. Before anyone could explain, she asked, "What's wrong with him?"

"He was hurt in the war," answered the doctor.

When the men gently helped him from the wagon to the ground, still holding cautiously on to him lest his legs give way and he fall, Abner Abercrombie left Miss Lenora on the porch and hobbled over to the man to stand face to face with him. They looked as though they could have been brothers too, both ancient and pathetic in appearance, though Abner had put on a bit of weight since arriving at the farm.

They led the bizarre visitor to the front of the wagon, everyone holding his breath anticipating a fall at any moment. Oddly, the Indian squaw appeared in the midst of them and moved quickly nose to nose with the man. She cradled his face between her palms and held it there while she seemed to look into his eyes. She chanted something briefly; then released her hold and walked back to her sod house. Abner moved up beside him, studying him. He peered beneath the sick man's wide brim, stroking his own scraggly beard as he studied the face. Since he wasn't able to utter a solitary syllable himself, Abner tottered away and reached for one of the hitched horses, placing one hand on the bridle and the other on the creature's long face. He began to stroke the animal on its nose gently.

Sadie now acquired a greater interest in the traveler. There was something... something familiar. She saw that the third button of his waistcoat was missing. The coat looked dirty and worn. She looked up under the shadow of his hat... closer. His cheek bones sunk in like gullies, his face pale and lifeless like a corpse – and his eye sockets sagged like wrinkles in the kitchen curtains. Deep pock marks and jagged lines scarred his complexion, his lips were barely parted and bone dry. He swallowed hard, tightening his lips, and licking them with the tip of his tongue.

Abner Abercrombie returned to the stranger and patted him softly on his chest, just over his heart. Yet, the man hardly seemed to notice that anyone had touched him. When Abner turned back around, tears were flowing down both cheeks. He hurried towards Sadie and seemed to want to speak, but only whispered moaning sounds escaped his lips.

Sadie seemed startled by everything. Her suspicions arose. "What is it, Mr. Abercrombie?" She watched his lips as he tried desperately to speak. Then she whirled about quickly to face her daughter. "Evelina. Tell me what's going on here. Who is this man?"

Evelina shifted her eyes from her mother to the peculiar man. She realized her mother was starting to recognize something. Sadie stepped closer and examined the tender eyes of the stranger. The eyes were there – inside those wilting sockets – but they were not moving, not looking at anything or anybody; just there... glazed over like dew on the grass. Suddenly there was something beyond familiarity, but something she could only sense and not understand. An awareness, like a dream you suddenly remember late in the day, having it the night before.

"Mama, look closer."

She almost didn't want to look again. She was afraid; yet she trained her eyes to see – meticulously. At once the impression struck her. Could it possibly be him? *No. Of course it couldn't be him*, she began to converse with herself. *Miracles do happen – sometimes – but this would be impossible. Wouldn't it?* She studied his face carefully. She thought for a second that he wasn't breathing at all; but he was.

His chest rose and fell ever so slightly. She reached out and positioned her hand on his chest just as Abner did. Could it really be him? He bore a slight resemblance to him. But this man couldn't be William. This man seemed barely alive. Her man was strong and built like a mountain. Or he had been – some years before. Could these last few years have made this kind of a change in him? Could he really be here right before her eyes? He couldn't be. Evelina told her to look again. There could be only one reason she said that, one reason she had run off with Jamie, one reason she had come back.

Sadie withdrew her eyes from the sunken and unshaven face and searched for her daughter's eyes. She wanted to say, 'yes, I can feel him, I can sense him.' Yet, she labored to even draw a breath with which to utter her astonishment.

"You recognize him, Mama, don't you?" Evelina implored, taking her mother's hand and squeezing it within the grasp of both of her hands. "I was the same way. But, you do know who this is, don't you?"

Instead of pleasure, the unusual gesture of trepidation emanated across Sadie's face. She pulled her hand away from her daughter's grip and again touched the familiar form of a man across the top of his shoulder, only with the tips of her fingers. She felt something so familiar, yet so uncanny, through the cloth – a presence she had known before, but oddly enough, ghostly and arresting. She sensed her own anxious spirit within her breast suddenly mesh with the wandering soul of the man she had loved. It just couldn't be. Unexpectedly she erupted with abandoned sobbing and emptied herself of the loneliness and uncertainty that she'd harbored in her mind for three long years. Warm, stale tears spilt from her eyes as she buried her face in William's chest.

The preacher stepped forward to comfort her but stopped and stood back. He observed the scene like a small child who was too young to understand. "Is this really..." He didn't need to finish the question.

"This is my daddy," said Evelina.

"William Williston himself," added Jamie Quentin. "Back home at last from the dead."

TWENTY-SIX

r. Brodie Smith being unable to awaken William's memory, now had the alternate plan in effect. But this final step of placing him in familiar surroundings, the Smiths realized, also put him in greater danger under the noses of Granger and Penrose, who would stop at nothing to get the facts out of the sickly man.

Oddly enough, Brodie left his patient not long after bringing him back home to Nebraska. After spending all those months trying to restore his mind, he headed straight east early one morning. Why did he leave the Williston farm so soon? Jamie could offer one explanation. He said the doctor had simply done all he was able to do. Now, living back among his family, William was down to his last opportunity to recover. If his mind didn't come back soon, it probably never would. Protection was an even greater concern. The evil lawyer would discover he was alive... and back. The Williston's couldn't keep the secret for long. Word would escape like steam. For Granger, it would enhance his plan of finding the gold immensely.

Jamie determined the best thing to do was go directly to Ben Granger and tell the whole story, and warn him to stay away from the sickly man. They must convince him that William could not be of any help to him. Since Jamie Quentin was no longer safe himself in Glensbluff, and seeing that the land and gold dispute was her problem, Sadie took advantage of her next trip to town to face the lawyer like she would the devil himself. Evelina, Anton, and the preacher accompanied her; but she didn't tell them she was intending to confront Granger when she got there. Evelina stayed with her mother while the men left to take care of business at the mercantile.

The determined prairie woman intended to march straight into Granger's office and demand an extension of time to come up with the money to pay off the debt and keep her land. She was certain that he had heard about her husband's return. With his men spying constantly, they were bound to have seen him. "This is our own land, after all," she spoke for Evelina's ears only. "We deserve more time."

Her daughter wore an expression of disbelief. "You're not going to go right in and talk with that awful man, are you?"

"That's why I came to town."

"But he might suspect something."

"He already knows your daddy is back, I'm certain. He misses nothing." She walked briskly, determined. "I'm going to tell him that we need more time to come up with the money. But the real reason is we need more time to get through to your daddy's mind. If we find the gold first, we'll have the money to pay the crooked fees. Are you going with me?"

Evelina gazed in disdain. "Why didn't you tell me all this before we came to town?"

"Would it have mattered? I want to tell that man what I'm thinking right to his wobbly face."

Evelina sighed. "But, with Daddy back now, we have a good chance to keep our land. You know Ben Granger knows that Daddy got this land legally. Maybe he'll back down now."

Sadie stopped on the sidewalk and simply gawked at her daughter as though what she said was the most ridiculous thing she had ever heard. "How do you suppose that increases our chances to keep our land? If anything, he'll discover that your daddy can't remember a thing." She began walking again and her daughter caught up with her. "The evidence is on Granger's side – lies or not. That's why I'm going to talk to him." She wore her unwavering look. "I want to let him know a few things on my mind."

"A few things? Like what?"

"First of all, your father is off limits to him. With his poor condition, he doesn't need anyone interrogating him. Jamie said I should make that perfectly clear. Second, I'll demand more time. There's a lot about your daddy that even I don't know and I want time to try to figure it out."

"Like what?"

"Like where's he been and what happened to him. And how on this green earth did he join up with the rebel army. Oh, never you mind now. But you do know that your daddy loved chasing after the dollar and was known for throwing his money on the table in a poker game."

The young woman scoffed. "What's that got to do with anything? Besides, he surely hasn't been able to gamble in years. You know that lowdown lawyer isn't going to give you more time. There's not a good bone in his whole body."

"Everybody has at least one good bone," said Sadie, "and I'm going to try to tickle his. I've been praying hard that the Lord will soften up his heart just a bit. You want to know what his gambling has to do with it? If your daddy was careless with money, then maybe he got careless with the gold."

"That's not likely, Mama. Besides, Ben Granger won't believe that Daddy simply misplaced all those bars of gold."

"I reckon I don't care what he believes. I just want more time now that he's back home; and I want those men to stay away from your daddy."

They neared the law office and stopped a few feet away from the door to gather their courage. "What else are you going to tell him?" Evelina asked. "You said, 'a few things'."

"That depends on how he answers me."

"What do you mean?"

"I might beg him to show some mercy."

Evelina placed her hands on her hips defiantly. "I wouldn't beg that man for anything."

"I'm getting desperate enough try anything to keep your father's hard-earned land in his name," she replied. "And to keep his family on it. I might have to resort to Ned Ames's plan."

"What's that?"

"To tell him that William remembered where he hid the gold and to send them some place far away, like Arkansas, on a wild goose chase."

Evelina cackled. "He would deserve that, but he'd never fall for it. Even if he did, when he got back, he'd be mad enough to shoot us all."

"Well, I doubt I'd ever resort to Ned's plan. But at least it will give us some more time to try to restore your daddy's mind. I don't want to leave our home. Besides, we have nowhere else to go. That's where we live."

"But what if Daddy's mind never heals?"

The Williston matron eyed the looming door to the office without answering the question. She knew that this was a matter she had to handle. She simply couldn't give up her land without a fight, no matter if William remembered anything or not. She swallowed hard and uttered a quick prayer before entering the room.

Inside Evelina spread out her dress and sat down on a high back chair in front of the impressive desk. Sadie chose to remain standing behind her, facing the double chinned man in the thick suit as he positioned himself comfortably behind the ligneous table. Siler Penrose was seated beside him, as usual, on a small, uncomfortable looking pew of which the seat and back had been quilted with vomit green padding. Both men chewed on fat cigars.

"Glensbluff is a nice, quiet little town," Granger spoke, taking the cigar away from his lips. "We have a very cooperative sheriff and some generous townspeople. Of course, we don't have a preacher at the church on the far end of town; but that's because he up and left."

What does he know about that, thought Sadie? *Does he know about the Smiths?*

Sadie gripped the spindles on the back of Evelina's chair so hard she felt her knuckles turning white. She released her grip and extended her fingers to restore the blood flow to them. "You and I both know the sort of lawyer you are, but I believe there is some good inside that heart of yours, albeit very deep inside. Now, the reason we are here."

"I am sure I know why you have come to see me," answered the corpulent man. "We are aware that your lost husband had returned. I have eyes all around your little farm. Where was he hiding all this time?"

"He wasn't hiding and he didn't return on his own. He is sick, very sick. Evelina went and got him and brought him home. Are you surprised he's alive?"

"Actually, not in the least. I knew he was hiding all along and, perhaps, gambling away his money and keeping the company of strange women in New Orleans, but I am surprised he left all that behind to come back to this."

"Maybe," explained Evelina, knowing he was lying. "There are somethings more valuable than gold or strange women on his property."

"I can't imagine what?" said Penrose, conjecturing. "Why would you bring him back to his land in Nebraska unless there is gold buried on the property?"

Sadie's voice sounded like cold steel. "That's where we disagree, Mr. Penrose. If there is some gold my husband took and hid, I assure you it's not on our land. I don't know where it is, but it's not here. And you will make yourself look pretty foolish if you run us off this land and then it turns out there never was any gold buried there."

Granger harumphed. "So, what do you want to talk to me about, Mrs. Williston?"

"I have come up with an idea that might even satisfy you."

Penrose chuckled. "It's a might strange that the women come here to talk to us about the land, but all the men stay in hiding."

Sadie glared at him. "Preacher Pearsall and my oldest son, Anton, are in town with us."

"Yes, I know. But they're not here in my office." Granger readjusted in his chair and crossed his legs behind the desk. "I'm surprised that you would leave only your little children on the farm. Aren't you worried about them?"

"Why should I be?" Sadie grinned this time. "All the evil men are in town today."

The two men considered her joke and laughed. "I can't promise you that I will even consider it, but what is your proposal?"

Sadie stepped up to the side of Evelina's chair and laid her open palms upon the back. "You are a smart man, and I know you don't really believe the gold is on our land. It's all flat. Where could he have hidden it?"

"Go on."

"If there really is any gold, then William is the one who knows where it is. But his mind is lost and wandering in some world of darkness. Evelina brought him home in hopes that his memory can be restored. Give him some time with us and his familiar surroundings and we may be able to restore his mind. Then he may be able to tell you where he hid the gold. Otherwise, you may never be able to locate it."

"That seems like a very good plan," answered the solicitor without taking a second to consider it. Evelina and Siler both looked surprised at his response... and suspicious. But he went on. "What does your man say about the gold?"

"Nothing. He'll speak about it when he's ready."

"But he's not wanted to tell you where he hid the gold?"

"Right now he mostly mumbles. I told you, his mind is... gone."

"So, what you propose, if he really can't remember anything – which I highly doubt – and if his mind really can be restored, may take years."

Sadie seized her moment and heightened the pitch of her voice. "I would not lie to you about William's mind. I'm a Christian woman. Since he's home with his family and back around all the things he knows and loves, he..."

Granger spit aside a speck of the cigar. "Then he may or may not ever get his mind back."

"I believe he will."

Penrose seemed weary of the conversation. "I'm not interested in him getting his mind back. I'm interested only in getting my gold back."

"If there ever was any gold," Sadie replied. "I never saw it or heard about it before your men showed up."

"Oh, there is gold," Penrose argued. "I saw it. I touched them cold bars. I rode beside it. Abercrombie believes it. So does the gunslinger. And your husband was the last soul on earth to be seen with it."

"Where did you see it?"

"Arkansas. But it ain't there now. We searched every place along the road and off the beaten path and there was no sign of it. Not even a track. Every sign points to Nebraska."

Evelina spoke up before Granger could clear the cigar from his lips. "There is no gold on our land, I assure you. If there was, don't you think we would have used it for ourselves a long time ago?"

"Maybe he never bothered to tell you where he hid it."

Sadie walked a pace or two away from the chair and stood at the front of the desk. "I saw the gold he brought back from California – at least some of it. There were no bars, only nuggets. But he turned that in for money and that's how we had been living. He might still have a little stashed away some place. I don't know. But I assure you there is no gold the likes of the kind you claim he has."

"I'm sorry to disagree with you, but I know there is. Siler is telling the truth. Before the war ended, both of our governments were searching for it."

"Whatever may have been during the war," Evelina bellowed. "I'm telling you there is no hidden gold on our property?"

"Then why did he come back? Why didn't he go get it wherever it was hidden?"

"You obviously haven't heard a word we said. I told you he didn't come back," cried Sadie. "He was brought back."

"Then let me talk with him."

"No!" Sadie's response sounded final. "His health is poor, and he gets agitated easily."

Penrose interrupted. "I'd be agitated too if someone was looking for my gold."

Granger waited for his partner to stop mocking. "Oh, he remembers, alright. That kind of thing a man doesn't forget."

"But he was shot, and it has affected his memory."

"Let me decide that when I talk to him," demanded Granger.

"Otherwise I will not accept your plan, and you will have to be off my land in just over a week." There was silence while Sadie calculated the risk of him talking to her husband. He returned to his lawyer-like speech. "Are you aware of the robbery of gold. In Colorado? At the start of the war?"

"Yes. I am."

"Well, your husband was right there in Colorado in charge of the whole thing."

"I was there too," barked Penrose. "We stole it together."

Granger calmly advised her. "You can even ask someone else who was there. Someone you can trust."

"Who would that be?"

"Ned Ames."

Evelina rose from her chair and joined her mother at the desk. "We know all about the robbery and my father's part in it. But you will be wasting your time trying to talk to him. I tell you; he is not well enough for your kind of questioning. He can't help you now."

"If he would of helped us then," shouted Penrose, "instead of stealing it, Jeff Davis would have won the war for the South."

"No doubt he is right," agreed Granger, rocking back in his comfortably padded seat. "Whichever side would have found it first would have had the upper hand. But that is neither here nor there. I want to talk with your husband, or you will be forced off my land, Mrs. Williston, and the whole lot with you. That is my mandate. Take it or leave it."

"Did you not hear what I said?" Sadie stressed. "He cannot talk. This will only make him worse."

The crafty lawyer leaned forward and folded his hands together on the desk. "Mrs. Williston, there are only three members of the gold heist gang left, Penrose here, Ned Ames, and your husband. He is the only one who could possibly know where it is. We have looked everywhere he could have possibly disposed of it. If I cannot talk with your husband, then our business is done here today."

Sadie sighed, feeling defeat. "Why would my William want to steal a wagon load of gold? He found his own. No. You are wrong about him."

"One last time, let me talk to him or…"

She dropped her head and took a deep breath, obviously her mind in turmoil as she contemplated her option. "What if he really doesn't remember? Will you leave us alone then?"

"I want the land and I will take it."

"And if he does remember and tells you where it is?"

"Then I will be satisfied – after we find it – to allow you to keep your land. That's a promise."

"Like your promises mean something."

"Take it or leave it."

Back at the Williston farm later that afternoon, Ben Granger and Siler Penrose stood beside the boardwalk William had laid himself years before to the front of his house. Preacher Pearsall assisted Evelina and Sadie in bringing him out on the porch and seating him in a rocking chair. To the two visitors, William appeared much older than his years in the prison camp, a little thinner, and as pale as a summer cloud. His face structure seemed skeletal and his dark eye sockets as wide as canyons.

"I've explained to you the condition of his mind," reminded Sadie.

Siler Penrose blurted out, "Yes, you have, and don't you think we know this could be a tricky way to try to fool us so he could keep from having to return the gold."

"Take one look at the man," cried the preacher. "Do you really think they made him up to look this way?"

Penrose started to speak.

"Hold on, Siler," Granger spoke in a soft, faint tone of voice, one that neither Sadie nor Siler had ever heard coming from the large man's throat before. They both turned to look in disbelief when they heard the somber expression. Sadie stared the longest. *Was Ben Granger moved by what he saw?*

"I can see for myself that he is not the same man I knew." *Did Sadie hear a break in his voice?* "Hello, William," the syllables escaped unhurriedly from his lips. "I am Ben Granger, your prison commander during the war. Do you remember me? I remember you."

Sadie raised up and drew her head back slowly. She could hardly believe what she saw. *Is that a tear in his eye?* She wondered. She could also not believe what she heard. It sounded as though Granger was talking as if he were addressing a little child.

William squinted his eyes and studied the large face, slightly nodding as though he understood the question but didn't know how to answer.

"Do you remember me, William?" he repeated.

The frail man raised his eyes a little and seemed to be looking directly at the wide forehead and thinning hair.

Siler, impatient with his partner, spoke up loudly. "Well, you remember me, I know. Tell me where you hid the stolen gold?"

William nodded his head slowly again.

"Good, good," spoke Granger. "Now tell me what you did with it."

The sad eyes drooped. They looked tired.

"Can you at least write it down for me?" He turned to Siler who patted his pockets looking for something to write on. "Somebody get him a pencil."

Granger sighed and pushed his partner aside with his arm. "You can tell me, William. It will go much easier for you and your family if you tell me."

"Tell us where you hid it," yapped Siler.

"Don't shout at him," demanded Sadie. "Can you answer them, William, dear. Can you tell Mr. Granger where you hid the wagon of gold?"

Only silence followed. The sickly man made no attempt to talk. His eyes moved back down to the lawyer's smooth-shaven face and then dropped to the boards of the sidewalk below as though he were peering into an empty bowl.

"That's enough," said the preacher. "You can see he can't talk. He's a sick man."

"Sick or not," roared Siler, "You're the only one who knows where that gold is and you're going to tell us one way or another."

"Leave him alone," ordered his wife.

"Give me a sign – or anything. Give me something – so I can know where it is!"

Sadie jumped between her husband and Penrose. "I said you could speak to him; but not like this."

"That's my gold and I want it. Let me ask him about it another way."

"No. You will be wasting your time. I am his wife and I should know."

Ben Granger stepped away from the rocking chair and seemed to compose himself. "I'm sorry to see William like this, Mrs. Williston. I really am. He doesn't appear to be pretending."

This time Siler sighed heavily, stepped away briskly, and complained raucously.

Granger noted him briefly, then turned to face Sadie, "We know there is gold and we know William is the only one who can tell us where it is. That's why we have to take this land and search it diligently."

"There is no gold here. Why can't you accept that?"

"Did your husband not bury something before he left for Arkansas in 1863?"

"Yes. But –"

"Did he not tell someone in his confidence where it is hidden?"

"Well, he usually told someone."

"Are not your two sons, who still believe that their father hid some valuable resource on your land, still continually digging for it?"

"Well... yes... you know they have been."

"Then do not tell me there is no gold on your property." The lawyer turned back towards the man in the chair who was staring off into the distant prairie. "I am convinced he is sick and that he has irrecoverably lost his mind. I will not bother him again."

"Just like that?" shouted Siler, removing his gray hat and pacing back and forth. "Is that it?"

"No, that's not it," answered the lawyer as if he were threatening a witness on the stand. "If he doesn't suddenly remember who he is and where he buried that gold, we will come back with the sheriff and have you evicted. Then we will tear the land apart until we find it."

William began rocking in his chair, mumbling something incoherent, his legs and arms quivering. "That's enough," ordered

Sadie. "You're upsetting him. He doesn't understand what's happening and it's frightening him."

"I am going to be extremely lenient with you, Mrs. Williston. I am giving you two more weeks in August to restore his memory or leave this property."

"Why do you keep giving them more time?" Siler questioned angrily. "Next it'll be Christmas. Let's take this land right now. It's ours, ain't it?"

"I have my reasons," Granger replied.

"You've lost your mind – or your guts!"

"I'm about to lose you."

"He's gotten to you, Ben. You've gone soft."

The big man's eyes returned to the frail frame of the former prisoner. "We will come back with Sheriff Potts and his deputies. That way it will be done legally, and no one will get hurt. Just remember that date. If you aren't ready to leave by then, you will forfeit your possessions. Make good use of the time you have to pack up."

"Yeah," added the slithering Siler, "make good use of the time and find my gold since we sure ain't gonna find it." He turned away ranting and slinging his arms.

"Middle of August," warned Granger one final time.

"Why do you keep giving them more time?" Penrose shouted out again. "I can't figure you."

The two rogues mounted their horses and left behind a puff of dust as they scampered away.

Sadie watched them ride off. Then she bent down and looked into William's hollow eyes. "Can you understand any of this, my dear husband?" When he did not respond, even with his eyes, she leaned in closer until only inches apart. "Dear William, do you know what is happening to us? If you can't remember where you hid that gold… or your money…or something…real soon, you are going to lose your hard-gained land and we are all going to have to leave our home for good." She released an exasperated breath and his gray hair blew over his eyes. "Try hard to remember. Your body has come home, but we need your mind to come home too."

TWENTY-SEVEN

❀⤐

"I'm sorry, Mrs. Williston," spoke the preacher. "I'm sorry this didn't go well for you. Life just isn't fair." He dropped his head. "God isn't fair."

"Thank you for your compassion, Preacher," the prairie woman responded, "but God is fair, It's Ben Granger and Siler Penrose who are not fair."

The Indian woman, as if she sensed the cloud of gloom drifting over the front porch of the Williston home, approached the pitiful white man in the rocking chair and squatted by his side. She held one of his arms with both hands, closed her eyes as she lifted her head towards the sky, and began to quietly chant her sad dirge.

Sadie looked touched by her concern. "That sounds an awful lot like the one she sang for the dying old man."

"He must make her think of the old Indian man."

Then the woman reached with both of her gnarly hands and touched William's head, gently, but firmly in a grip, as though she were steadying him. Instantly she made unbroken eye contact with him and began chanting a different tune in Indian phrases that made no sense to anyone else. But William seemed to understand her. She captured his complete attention, it seemed. Finally, she pressed her fingertips lightly on his eyelids. He appeared calm and soon began to breathe rhythmically like a sleeping baby.

"What is she doing?" asked the preacher.

"It seems peculiar," answered Sadie, "But I'm guessing she is trying to awaken his mind – in her own way."

"Or put him to sleep."

When the Indian woman finished, the preacher took her place and spoke his own lament in a loud whisper into the ears of the shell of a man. They all could understand his words. "It must be a terrible shock to you, Mr. Williston, to finally come back home from the dead only to find that your land is being taken out from under you. You do know that don't you? You must come to yourself and be strong for your family. They need you. The Lord is the Great Physician and I am believing that he will heal you. Can you come back? Back to your family?" The preacher stood up straight and laid his hand on the weak shoulder. "Poor fellow, you haven't the faintest idea that anything is even happening."

"We're not giving up, Preacher."

"Well, I admire your faith."

"You and the Indian woman have helped him, I'm sure."

"Do you really think so?"

"I saw the way he listened to you and watched you... both. We have to keep trying to bring him back... to set free his mind. It's in there somewhere. Something has to unlock the prison inside his head and let him out."

"Or someone."

"Yes."

By this time, all the family had come outside, even the old widow, Lenora, and Abner. Jamie and Evelina had been walking and just then strolled from the side of the house. They all gathered around William, except the Indian woman, who stood at a distance by the well and watched. The Williston children and the little Indian boy played in the yard; yet they seemed immensely aware that something significant was taking place on the porch. Anton and Amos soon abandoned their chores and joined the others sitting in old rockers and benches, or standing beside the prodigal father. Miss Lenora began humming her own Christian hymn, a pleasant tune that brought comfort to everyone.

"We've got to find out where he hid that gold," said Amos frustrated. "I don't want to lose this land."

"There is no gold here," said his mother.

Anton wasn't convinced that there was a wagon load of gold buried on that land, but he agreed with his brother that something was there. "We know Pa buried something the night before he left. That's a fact. He even wrote a letter and took it to the preacher in town."

"Maybe you ought to dig up your old minister," Preacher Pearsall told him with a sneer. "If you find the letter, you find the gold."

"You aren't digging up nobody," his mother halted that idea. "We don't even know if the note was buried with him. He could have dropped it or misplaced it anywhere."

"Or it was stolen," suggested Jamie.

"By who? If Ben Granger had the letter he wouldn't be bothering us."

Both boys nodded as though they understood, but Anton was quick to add, "There's something buried on this land, something important enough for those men to come after it. Why do you think me and Amos's been diggin' all over this farm land for three years? We know something is hid here somewhere."

Silence followed for a moment. "Maybe a picnic will help restore his memory," suggested Evelina, smiling proudly at her own idea. "You know how he always liked picnics."

"What a wonderful idea," remarked her mother with a new glimmer in her eyes that had not been seen in a long time. "It just might be the thing to work."

Evelina leaned forward and closely examined her father's vacant eyes, but they now simply stared blankly past her. "It can't hurt anything," she explained. "We might just find out where the gold is hidden before we lose everything." She caressed his aged hand. "Would you like to go on a picnic, Daddy?" She could have sworn she saw the semblance of a smile.

Sadie watched the Indian woman disappear inside her home, her work completed. She shifted her weight, touching William's other rugged hand, patting it firmly, hoping to stir a response; but got none. "William, can you hear me? I'm Sadie, your wife." She dropped her head and rested it on his boney shoulder. "I hope and pray that He will come up with something to save our land."

Evelina's mind was racing. "Back to the picnic, we'll have to plan this quickly so we can work around our chores. The crops need work and the animals need tending to. Let's make it a big day with lots of food and games and fishing. Is tomorrow too soon?"

"No, tomorrow is not soon enough," answered her mother, her mind churning with thoughts. "Boys, you and the men folk need to work extra-long tonight. Preacher and Jamie, tell Ned about it. Mr. Abercrombie – where is he?"

"He went inside to lay down, I think. He's not too well either," explained Evelina.

Just then the door opened, and Abner walked out with a pencil and notepad. He began to write and then handed the tablet to Sadie. She read his scribble aloud. "Ned rode off early. Saw him leave."

"Where did he go?"

He took the pad and wrote back. "Don't know. Towards town."

Evelina shook her head. "Ned wouldn't go into town. Maybe he snuck off, something to do with this gold mystery."

"I'm certain it has something to do with the gold and our land," Sadie thought aloud. "Everything is all about that. Maybe he decided to have it out with Ben Granger."

"Let's hope not," said Jamie. "Ned doesn't seem the kind of man who goes after trouble."

"It doesn't matter," spoke Evelina, impatiently. "It's our family that needs to go on the picnic. That's who always went on picnics with Daddy before. I believe this will cause him to remember. I can't wait to get started getting everything ready. We got to make things look just the way they used to be. Oh, just some sweet memory or some gay word or some pleasant scene down by the stream. It has to work."

"Don't set your hopes too high. It's a wonderful idea, but he might not ever come back to us."

"I know, Mama. But I feel like it will work. It just has to."

Sadie seemed to be rooted in thought and it was only after a long moment that she spoke. "I suppose the worst thing that could come out of this if he doesn't get his mind back is that he won't know his land was stolen right out from under him. The poor thing."

"If it doesn't work, there ain't no reason to keep working so hard on this land?" grumbled the preacher. "If you lose your land, Granger and his men will be the only ones eating good. I say we stop working the crops until we know for sure we're still gonna be here."

"No," said Sadie, shaking her head. "We're not gonna stop. Don't you see that's like giving up? We have to trust God and keep on living like this land will be ours for the rest of our lives."

Evelina nodded, inspired again as she sprung up on the porch walk. "Then, let's plan the picnic for tomorrow. We'll leave early, and we can go down to his favorite spot, under the trees by the stream." Her eyes beamed as she moved her hand to her father's shoulder. He didn't respond to her touch, but she smiled at him anyway. "That spot will ease his mind, Mama. He loved to rest by the water after a long, hot day in the sun. Didn't you Daddy?"

Sadie didn't expect an answer. "He liked the spot further down the stream, the spot near the McConnell's property. The water was backed up there and it became his favorite fishing hole."

"We'll take the poles then, and some chairs to sit on, and the old table in the barn."

"That should stir his memory," imagined her mother with confidence. "I'll fix fried chicken and biscuits. It will be like going back to the days long gone, to the sweeter days, the days before the… before Arkansas."

The next morning early, the boys had loaded the wagon and hitched the horses in their positions. Ned had returned last night after supper but didn't tell anyone where he had been. His face read something. Worry? Anger? Everyone could see in his eyes that something was going on in his mind. Jamie talked with him, but all he would tell him was that it was a wasted trip. Had he confronted Ben Granger? Sadie had to dismiss it for a more important matter and her family all climbed aboard the wagon.

"We men folk will take care of Miss Lenora," Jamie said while holding the horses' reins. He looked up into the lovely eyes of the young woman on the wagon seat. "I'm praying that this will awaken your daddy's memory – not just for the sake of finding the gold – but that you will have your daddy back home again."

Evelina smiled and tugged her hair back behind her ears.

Preacher Pearsall stood at the side of the wagon and waved. "Don't worry about the widow woman. Me and Abner will look out for the squaw and her boy."

Anton, who sat up front with his father and his sister, holding the reins, quickly beckoned the horses into a fast trot.

"Let's talk to him all along the way," suggested Evelina. "Talk to him like it is still before the war and he hasn't left for Arkansas yet."

"Tell me again how much money we need to get rid of Granger," requested Amos from the back of the buck board.

"I'd say near two-thousand dollars."

"Two-thousand dollars!"

"Yes, son," His mother reached down and patted his shoulder. "Mr. Granger no doubt has his own way of adding up numbers. Don't you get too excited. That's not a big sum to the Lord."

"But how can we owe two-thousand dollars on our own land?"

The day grew sultry hot, but the shade beneath the rich foliage felt reviving; and the fish were ravenous. The stream looked as clear as well water, rushing over rocks and pausing at the small dam, as though to rest, in a deep pool. The country picnic of chicken, biscuits, homemade jams, and rhubarb pie tasted as good as it ever tasted back when William was himself.

"What do you think, Daddy?" asked Evelina expectantly. "Isn't this the best spot to have a picnic?"

Anton tried too. "What about these fish? You just gotta toss your worm out there and they jump right on the line. Do you remember fishing right here on this spot, Pa?"

"William, dear," said Sadie, looping her arm through his as they sat on the grass together. "Do you remember us all being here before? This is your favorite place to come to fish and to just rest. Does it look familiar to you? Say it does. Say something. Please say something to me."

The afternoon passed pleasurably, but anxiously. It was a mixture of happiness and hope, but William did not come back to himself. He looked without seeing and he listened without hearing. The familiar surroundings and voices of his loved ones were not enough to overcome the damage caused by the angry bullet in his shoulder and the fever in his head. It seemed as though an iron gate had closed over his memory and rusted in place. William was trapped inside like a prisoner with a life sentence. The picnic lunch was just like old times; but that was the only thing that was just like old times. The fragile man appeared as pale and as lifeless as a ghost, merely staring blankly across the stream at the weeds and shrubberies with an empty expression on his face as if he were blind to the colors of life around him. His memory was sadly gone... forever?

"What are we going to do, William?" Sadie asked. She raised her eyes to watch the children scamper across the meadow as they played a game. They laughed and cried out with joy, unaware of the one-sided conversation taking place near the wagon wheels under the trees. "Do you see those children? They are your children. Evelina, Anton, Amos, Lutie, Lillibet... do you remember them? Can you hear them laughing? Listen. Do their voices sound familiar?"

William sat with one leg bent and resting his elbow on one knee. He seemed weary. His head hung low and he took slow, steady breaths. Hardly a morsel of food did he taste, turning away from the hand that fed him. At times, he didn't flinch a muscle, except to raise his eyes to Sadie and then look back down at the grass. She petted his hair and brushed it back with her worn fingers. She gently lifted his chin with just her fingertips and tried to see something inside his hollow eyes, but they seemed glazed over.

"Oh, dear William, try to remember who you are. You are William Williston. I am your wife, Sadie. Speak my name? I am your Little Butterfly Weed. This is your land in Nebraska territory. Don't you remember riding off to Arkansas? What happened to you then? Do you remember joining the rebel army? Do you remember being shot? You were in a prison hospital. Abner Abercrombie was there with you? Try to remember who you are."

But William Williston did not remember. He seemed not to hear her or understand her. She may as well have been talking to the fish. He bowed his head slightly to the right and slowly turned it back again, like a sick horse that was down and refused to try to stand up.

"William," she spoke his name solemnly. "What will happen to us if you don't come back? Did you bury some gold on this land? If you did, please try to remember where you hid it. Can you just point to it? Can you just show me the way? If you can't remember where you hid it we will lose everything you worked so hard for. Poor William." She petted his forehead. "What has become of you? I was so happy that you finally came back home to us. But you didn't really come back at all, did you?"

On the ride back to the smiling face house, with suffering disappointment, Sadie surmised on what she was going to do now. Would they lose their land? Were the days remaining enough time to come up with anything to stop Granger and his men? How could they possibly come up with that kind of money? Where would they go once they were evicted? Questions flooded her mind, questions that included no answers. God, help us, she prayed softly. Anton was still holding the reins. Evelina was petting her daddy and wiping tears from her eyes. The others were lying down and sleeping. The bold sun had drained them. Sadie was drained too, but not because of the sun.

Nothing could have prepared Sadie for what she saw when they rode out from the canopy of trees at the picnic sight and came into view of their home from a distance. Smoke was billowing from their farm in three different columns.

TWENTY-EIGHT

❀⟋

"No!" she exclaimed. She could see as they got closer to the house that smoke was rising from the barn and that the sod structure looked different somehow, like it was missing part of its walls. Anton saw it too. He jostled the reins, cried out a command; and the horses broke into a hasty stride.

"What is it?" asked Evelina, sitting up. The other children raised their heads too and murmurings could be heard from the back of the wagon. "What's happened?"

Anton stopped the horses short of the smoldering barn. The sod didn't burn, but everything that could burn, everything else inside the barn, was near ashes. He jumped down.

"Wait, son," called Sadie. "They might still be…" She didn't finish her sentence as he circled the corral. They all knew that someone had been there. Maybe hostile Indians, she thought. Maybe Granger's men. They were gone, whoever they were. There was no movement – not even a frightened chicken.

Amos had leaped off behind his brother and ran to the smoking entrance. Sadie stood up on the wagon. She was speechless. Her eyes took in the shocking devastation. The earthen barn lay in heaps, the Indian woman's home, smoldering like a smoke house, and debris lay scattered across the yard. Thank God her smiling face house was standing and seemingly unharmed, but smoke rose from the field beyond the wing where Preacher Pearsall stayed, one of the fields of corn. She ordered Evelina to keep the younger children in the wagon, and then scanned the ground all around the front of her home. What she saw sickened her.

The body of the Indian woman lay on its side near the well house, motionless. Beyond her, closer to the porch, lay another body, a man. She could only imagine that it was Preacher Pearsall... or even Jamie... dead. She could not see his face. Could it be Ned? Was he the one they – whoever they were – came for? She leaped down from the wagon and ran toward the Indian. The crumpled figure was bloodied and dirty. Her thick black hair lay plastered with sweat and grime across her face. Sadie brushed it back and saw the deep gash on her forehead. She rested her hand on the woman's chest. She was still breathing.

Amos approached while she was kneeling to the ground. He held the rein attached to an unfamiliar horse. "Is she dead?'

She noticed the strange horse but made no comment. "No, son. But she's been hit on her head. She's dazed."

"Who did it?"

"I don't know. Someone who owns that horse, I'd say. Who is the man over there?"

"I can't tell," he answered. "I'll have a look." Amos turned his eyes towards the form lying in the dust near the front boardwalk. "Do you think he's dead?"

"I don't know. Just go on and see."

While Amos paced carefully to the body, Anton met his mother at the well with pails in his hands. Sadie hurried to the well and lifted a pail of water. She returned to the woman and dipped the hem of her dress in the water and began squeezing it out over the sickening wound. Red water washed down her cheeks. The Indian woman groaned and tried to sit up, holding her head, and began jabbering in her own language.

"Who would have done such a thing?" Sadie lamented. She feared for the others who were home while she was at the picnic. She dreaded the thought of looking inside and around the smiling face house.

Amos had stopped over the still figure and studied it like an ancient explorer. He squinted his eyes; then turned back to his mother again. He suddenly felt full of fear as the reality of what happened set in. "He's not one of us. This horse must belong to him. It was just standing beyond the barn – I mean what's left of the barn."

Sadie felt relief that the man on the ground wasn't one of theirs, but still didn't want anybody to be killed. The horror seemed to hang over the house like a dark rain cloud. Were the others dead or did they flee? It sounded too quiet. "Is he dead?" she asked about the stranger.

Amos cocked his head sideways took another step closer. "No. I don't think so. His back is moving up and down like he's breathing."

Anton fixed his eyes on the front door of the house. He saw shards of glass lying on the porch. He thought about rushing to the door, but the thought that the perpetrators might be lying in wait kept his feet anchored. His eyes fell upon the Indian woman, now sitting up, and his mother washing her face with water from her cupped hand. "What about the boy?" he asked.

"He's not here."

"Maybe he's inside. Maybe they're all inside," Anton speculated, panning the scene behind him. Suddenly he realized the obvious. "There's no other horses here. Whoever did this must be gone."

"Don't be too certain. They could still be here. But I'm more afraid that our men folks and Miss Lenora may be…" She stopped mid-sentence, unable to finish. Then she looked around the yard and towards the wagon where Evelina was keeping William and the younger children, pausing to catch a breath. "Have you looked in there?" She directed Anton with her eyes towards the burnt sod house. He immediately rushed to the ruins and stooped over to better look into the crumpled heap. "I don't see anyone."

His mother squeezed her eyes tightly, sighing. "If anyone's in there, he can't be alive."

Suddenly a noise! Anton and Amos jumped at the same time. Sadie looked up anxiously as the front door of the smiling house opened and a shadowed figure stepped onto the porch, a rifle in his hand.

"Jamie," cried Evelina from the wagon as she recognized him when he came into the bright sunlight. She and the children climbed down. She ran towards him and flung herself in his arms. "Thank God you are alive."

Jamie embraced her with his free arm and raised his eyes to Sadie. It appeared as though her expression was begging for an answer. "It was Granger's men," he told her.

"Granger!" Despite her suspicions she could not believe what she heard. "Could Mr. Granger do something like this?"

"Not a doubt." He nodded towards the motionless man. "He's one of Granger's. Pete Bezold."

She began moving towards him. "Let's see how bad he is."

Jamie cut her off. "Don't bother helping him after what he's done to us."

"You don't mean to just let him die?"

"Why not? I shot him… and I shot to kill."

She stared at Jamie briefly; then continued towards Pete Bezold. "That's not how we do things around here. We do not return evil for evil."

"Where's the preacher?" questioned Evelina.

Before he could answer, the door to Preacher Pearsall's room opened and he and Ned Ames walked out onto the wrap around boardwalk. "We're all right. We were out back trying to put out the fire. They set the crops on fire."

"Oh dear," cried Sadie. She knelt over Pete's body to check his wound.

"Where's William?" questioned Ned.

"O my goodness," declared Evelina. "I left him in the wagon."

Preacher Pearsall hurried towards the wagon and patted on the heads the distraught children as he passed by them.

"And the boy?" Sadie asked, raising her eyes from the wounded man.

Ned moved towards the door and held out his arm, draping it around the Indian boy as he ambled out. "He's ok."

When the boy saw the Indian woman, he broke into a run and

fell on her, holding her like he would never let go. *He was strong to be so young,* thought Sadie. Evelina released Jamie and hurried towards the boy and his mother.

"And Miss Lenora?"

Jamie answered first. "She's in the house. Abner is with her, but…"

Before she could respond, Anton approached his mother from behind and gestured at the motionless man on the ground. "What are we going to do with him?'

She looked down at Bezold. "We need to get him inside," she said and turned to see that Anton's face was streaked with soot like war paint.

"All the animals got out alive," he reported.

"That's good, son."

"The Indian woman got them out," said Jamie. "She sent the boy to us, but she stayed to defend her place and the animals, even though bullets were flying all around her. Somebody hit her and knocked her down."

"Wicked men," commented Sadie. "Father, forgive them for they know not what they do."

"What did you say?" asked the preacher.

"Nothing." Then she met his questioning eyes. "I said, let's get him inside."

Ned and the preacher didn't bother to argue and, with the help of the boys, carried him inside. He was still unresponsive. They saw that blood stained the soil where he lay and the right side of his vest. Sadie approached the porch cautiously because of the shattered shards of glass beneath the window. She looked dubiously to Jamie.

"They shot through the window when they rode up and I knocked the rest of it out to shoot back."

"How many were there?"

"Six or seven, I reckon. It was impossible to see them all from the window. They scattered."

Anton fumed. "Was Granger one of them?"

Jamie shook his head.

"Coward," said Anton. "Wait 'till I find him."

"You'll do nothing of the sort," his mother said. "That won't satisfy anything, except to get you shot too."

"Your mother's right," agreed Jamie. He moved carefully towards the porch post to brace himself. Grabbing it with both hands, he grimaced with pain.

"Jamie!" cried Evelina, rushing to him. "You're shot. There's blood on your shirt." Sadie rushed to his other side to balance him.

"It's just a graze and some broken glass. I'll live."

"It looks worse than a graze to me." She replied. "We'll get you inside and take a look."

"No. It's not bad."

Sadie examined his blood stain. "We need to fetch the doctor for all of you. Amos!"

Jamie shook his head. "I wouldn't send anybody to town with Granger's gang out there."

A few moments later, Preacher Pearsall joined them on the porch with William on his arm. William's face, already sickly pale, had now turned a ghostly white. *Was he somehow understanding what had happened to his home?* Sadie wondered.

She looked from the shards of glass on the porch to the jagged window panes. "I'm sure Miss Lenora is frightened half to death. Poor thing couldn't have understood what happened. She must be terrified right now with all that shooting and commotion going on. Miss Lenora!" she called out. "I need to check on her. Miss Lenora!"

Sadie realized right away that the men's eyes averted away from her and that no one was saying anything. At that instant, the door swung open again and Abner stepped out rather timidly. Her eyes studied his eyes closely and quickly realized that words were not necessary.

"Miss Lenora?"

Preacher Pearsall turned to face her and nodded. "I'm afraid she's dead."

"Oh no!" Evelina and Sadie cried out at the same time.

"They shot that old widow woman?" screamed Evelina.

Jamie stepped closer, still grimacing, and took her hands in his, drawing her closer to his chest. He was holding on to her, but she was giving him the stability to stand. He explained. "The bullets were crashing through the window and striking everything in their path. But she didn't seem to notice anything. She was humming all through the gun blasts and the shattering glass. Abner was with her and had her lying under the table. She even started singing a hymn. She was singing about Heaven and, while she was singing about Heaven, she was suddenly there."

"I pray she didn't suffer," said Sadie. "I pray she never knew what had happened."

With Evelina's help Jamie eased himself into a chair. "The old widow wasn't shot. No bullet came near her, thanks to Abner."

"She wasn't shot? Then how…"

"I reckon she just died while she was singing."

"But how?"

"I don't know. It was just her time to go."

"I can't believe that."

"But I checked her." He looked up at Sadie. "Me and Abner both checked her over good." Abner nodded his head in agreement. "Miss Lenora wasn't hit by a single bullet anywhere. Maybe with all the commotion… It was just her time to go."

Tears filled Sadie's eyes like little fairy pools. "Oh, heaven have mercy. Poor Miss Lenora."

"I wouldn't worry about her," added Jamie. "She died peacefully in her own little world. I don't think she had a fear at all when she died. She looked like she was smiling the whole time and just kept singing that same song over and over."

"What song was she singing?" asked the preacher.

"When the roll is called up yonder, I'll be there."

Preacher Pearsall smiled. "Well, I reckon its roll call up yonder right now for Miss Lenora."

"You didn't see her die?" Sadie asked the minister.

"No. Ned and me were outside when they rode in. We ran to the side wing. After they rode off, I went inside and saw her lying there, so still."

Jamie added his version. "I had already just gone inside when they rode up shooting. Abner got her on the floor. I tell you, she couldn't have been any happier when she died."

When she composed herself completely, the prairie matron got back to business quickly. "The injured man – what are we going to do with him?"

"Ned's inside with him. I reckon we'll have to look him over and decide."

"So much is happening so fast. I have no idea what we should do with him." She took a deep breath and released it all at once. "I don't know what to do about anything right now."

Jamie held his side and leaned forward in the chair. "Just slow down. Thank God everyone else is okay."

"Yes. Thank the Good Lord. Somebody has to go fetch a doctor, danger or no danger."

"I wouldn't worry about fetching a doctor for him," Jamie groused.

"Not just for him, Jamie." Sadie turned to face the smoldering barn and sod house and was sickened by the horrific scene of destruction. We need him to examine the Indian woman, if she'll let him, and take a look at you, too."

As she spoke the words, Jamie winced and slumped down in the chair.

TWENTY-NINE

he funeral service for the widow Lenora was brief. There was little time to mourn with all the work that had to be done to the devastated farm. Jamie insisted that he ride out after the burial to fetch the doctor, despite the bullet that had grazed both his arm and chest. Thankfully, it passed under his arm, barely scathing the flesh, and brushed his side near his ribs, leaving an open and tender gash. He knew he was lucky. He might have been laid out next to the widow and would have no need of a doctor. But he would not be deterred from heading into town, despite the protests, because his underlying motive was to confront Ben Granger face to face.

Preacher Pearsall, just as determined, rode with him a nose behind the horses tail, struggling to keep up. Sadie had asked him to go with Jamie since she knew there could be trouble. "What would I be able to do?" he had questioned, exasperated. "I'm not a gunfighter."

"You know Ned can't afford to be seen in public and I refuse to let my boys have any part of it. Somebody needs to go with him to keep him in line."

"Sure," he scoffed. "I can do that. And don't worry about the preacher getting killed."

"You're a man of peace. Your presence just might keep everyone calm."

"He's got no business riding out after being shot and with his good arm side all sore. He doesn't even need a doctor now. But you can't tell him nothing."

"He says he's fetching the doctor, but I'm worried that he might head straight for Granger's office. Watch out for him, will you?"

"For which one?"

Later, the preacher found himself trailing Jamie to the doctor's house, rolling his eyes with disbelief. Fortunately, Jamie had the sense to head straight to Sheriff Potts after telling the doctor about Pete Bezold and the squaw. He didn't even mention his own injury. Sheriff Potts and his two deputies, three feet behind Jamie Quentin and trying to keep up with him, followed him into the sinister lawyer's office. The preacher slipped in a few seconds behind, keeping a cagey eye open.

Granger sat at his desk in his high cushioned leather chair. He greeted Jamie with a crooked grin and with a soggy cigar using the same pair of thick lips for both. "Well, Jamie Quentin," he greeted him like they were old friends. "I didn't expect to see you in my office again."

Siler Penrose, standing with his back turned at a table across the room, swung around and stood rigid when he saw his former colleague. He snarled and remained bull faced as he fixed his eyes on the young man like an owl sizing up his prey. His glaring eyes seemed to radiate malice like a wood stove puts off heat. Sheriff Potts had assigned his two deputies outside the door and they stood there like bank guards at the threshold to the office. He halted his own bulky frame abruptly in front of the massive desk. His pot belly sagged over his belt and his pistol dangled from the holster against his wide leg. He made sure he talked before Jamie could lick his lips. "Is it true, Granger?" He growled, not the least bit intimidated.

"Is what true, Sheriff?"

Jamie snapped like a turtle. "Don't act like you don't know what he's talking about. I was there, remember?"

Potts waved a back hand at him. "Let me handle this."

Granger removed the unlit cigar from his lips and smacked them as if he were savoring the flavor. He leaned back comfortably in his chair, gave a quick upward glance to his partner and returned the cigar to his mouth. Speaking with the stogie between his teeth, he gave the impression that he might be smiling. "Suppose you tell me what you're talking about."

"Yeah," added Siler Penrose, tucking the thumb of one hand inside his belt and shifting his weight contentedly to one hip. "Suppose you do that."

"A gang of men shot up the Williston place and started some fires that destroyed the barn. The Indian woman was hurt pretty bad and the old widow woman who lived with them died right in the middle of all the commotion – not to mention the crop that was burned and the livestock that run off. A pretty low down thing."

"Livestock!" chortled Penrose. "They ain't got nothing but some chickens and a couple of ugly horses. Well, maybe a dry milk cow."

Granger beckoned him to be quiet with his stogy in his hand. "What makes you think I had anything to do with it?"

"Two reasons, Ben. One, I know you. The second, one of your men was left there with a bullet hole through him."

He shot his eyes to Jamie. "Is that what happened?"

"Yeah. I was the one who put the bullet in him. It's Bezold."

"Bezold? I don't remember a Bezold ever working for me."

Penrose chuckled.

Jamie's face hardened like granite. "He's part of your mob and you know he works for you. Tell the truth for once in your life."

Granger grinned. "Do I have to raise my right hand and swear on the Bible?" The smile quickly disappeared as though an invisible hand wiped it right off his mug. "I can't help what Bezold does in his spare time, sheriff."

Potts sounded angrier than two wild cats in a brawl. "Don't lie to me. They were your men. You got some explaining to do – you and Penrose."

The heavy-set attorney turned his head. "What do you know about this, Siler?"

Penrose pressed his lips together grimly and his eyes narrowed. His gun hand slowly dropped to his side. "I don't like being accused of something I didn't do."

"You don't like being accused of something you did do," followed Jamie.

Penrose's expression didn't change. "Maybe our boys did ride out to Williston place to see how the packing up and moving out was coming along. I mean our land. But that's all they did."

Granger turned towards the preacher standing against the wall. "What do you have to say about all this, Preacher?"

Preacher Pearsall swallowed hard.

"What's the matter? Weren't you there when this happened? Were they my men or not?"

"They weren't Indians," he answered.

"I can't help what this Bezold fellow does in his free time. But not being Indians doesn't make them my men? Speak up, Preacher. I reckon I'm on trial right here. Are you certain they were my men?"

As every eye went to the minister, he moved away from the wall and stepped closer. A sudden surge of courage seemed to shoot through him. He thought about Sadie and the widow woman, Lenora, and then the Indian woman and her boy. Their faces emboldened him. "I'm certain they were your men, Mr. Granger. They all bore a distinct resemblance to you and Mr. Penrose here."

The Sheriff cocked him head. "How do you mean, Reverend?"

"They all had horns and sharp, pointy tails."

Penrose tightened his fingers on his belt and started forward.

"Hold up," Sheriff Potts stopped him.

Penrose let out a stored-up breath. "Ben, I think you should ask the sheriff and his friends to leave."

"I won't ask them. I'll tell them."

"I'll leave when I'm good and ready," shouted Potts. "I've got two deputies outside the door with double barrels and I told them to come in a shootin' if they heard your big mouth flapping."

"I wouldn't be too sure about counting on your deputies," said Penrose.

"I'm not interested in hearing from your sidekick, Granger. I want to hear it straight from you. Did you send your boys out to the Williston place?"

The huge man leaned forward and propped both elbows on the desk, discarding his cigar in a silver tray. He fidgeted with his string tie before answering. "You won't believe me no matter what I say. But I'm certain I had nothing to do with that horrible disaster at the Williston place. I did not leave the office all, except to go to the saloon and eat lunch."

"The same here," added Penrose.

"I didn't ask you anything," barked an angry sheriff. "Boys!" The two stout deputies entered the room and held the barrels chest high. "If he opens his trap again, fix him."

Penrose grinned as wide as the Mississippi. He folded his arms comfortably across his mid-section and leaned against the wall with his feet crossed. Granger stood up. "I don't appreciate the way you come busting in here, Potts."

"I didn't expect to get anything out of you," the lawman explained, tugging at his belt. "I'll be riding out to the Williston's place to check this out myself. If your man, Bezold, lives and opens his mouth, I'm going to come back after you. This town has had just about enough of you."

The lawyer offered a flagrant grin, eased back in his chair, and returned the cigar to his lips. "I'm not worried too much about you, Sheriff. You're old and slow and you no longer have the support of this town to come in here barking up my tree."

"Yeah, I know I'm old and slowed down quite a bit. But I aim to turn in this badge on my own terms without running scared. My law keeping days may be nearly over and all that waits me is a rocking chair; so you might can see why a bullet in the back doesn't scare me."

Granger sat up business-like. "You must know that I am backed by the federal government in Washington to find out what happened to that shipment of gold."

"Federal government, my foot," cried Jamie.

"And you must know that everything I have done has been done legally. Here are the papers to prove it."

The sheriff turned to leave but halted abruptly and turned back around. "What happened out there wasn't legal and I aim to find out exactly what did happened. If you were involved in that attack, I will hold you responsible for that old widow's death."

"Good day, gentlemen," Granger dismissed his guests icily.

"You won't get away with this," warned Jamie.

"You have no proof I was involved in that fiasco. I can't help what this Bezold fellow does."

"You will pay, and you too, Penrose," warned Jamie a second time, wrapping one hand around his fist on the other hand. "Now I'm giving you good warning right here and now. If you set foot on that farm again, I'll shoot you myself."

"Then I reckon we had better come armed," replied the big lawyer, "because the next time we do come out that way, we'll come with the law on our side and every Williston and all their squatters will be evicted. Isn't that right, Sheriff Potts? You still have a job to do."

"We will see," answered the Sheriff. "If you had anything to do with killing that woman, you won't set a foot on that land. In my business, murder trumps legal papers."

After the sheriff and his cohorts departed, Ben Granger donned the face of the grim reaper. His lips barely parted as he whispered to his associate, who leaned closer and placed his ear beside the hefty man's jaw. "What went wrong?"

Siler whined like a rabid dog. "How could we know that Ames, would be there? And Jamie too? Next time I see him them I'm gonna shoot first..."

"Stop raving. What about Bezold? Will he talk?"

"No chance of that."

"How do you know?"

"I fought alongside him. He won't turn on me and that weak legged sheriff don't know how to get anything out of nobody anyhow."

Granger stood up and walked to the window just in time to see the visitors riding off. "Why did you have them kill the widow woman?"

"They didn't kill no woman. I reckon she just caught a stray bullet. Why they never even saw no woman, except that injun. We figured they'd all be gone."

"Don't worry about it." He flapped his hand. "They can't prove anything on us. You and I weren't there. But I don't want to give that marshal no cause to come back down here." He walked back to his desk and stood face to face with his partner. "Our plan will still work. I want them off that property by the deadline. It is all legal and written up to any judge's satisfaction. Maybe that little shaking up will give them a mind to clear off my land ahead of schedule."

"You keep giving them more time, remember? What if they don't leave?"

"I have legal papers, so they don't have a choice. I had hoped they would lead us to the gold."

"What if the gold ain't there?"

"Where else could it be? No. It's there and I aim to have it."

Penrose leaned closer in with his unshaven face. "But, like I said, what if they won't leave?"

Granger chewed on the old stub while he seemed to be giving it some thought. Then he pulled it out of his mouth and replied. "Siler, I think you already know the answer to that."

THIRTY

❀⤳

iss Lenora's grave looked fresh covered with overturned soft
brown Nebraska soil. Around her grave in the little cemetery on
the knoll lively prairie flowers, recently transplanted, bloomed
and waved with every breeze. They seemed unwilted by the strong sun.
Sadie watched the injured Indian woman and her boy sift through the
ruins of the sod house and then make their way to the nearby grave
knoll. The boy just stood there and watched as the woman rocked
back and forth on her knees and groaned with grief. Ned Ames sat
with Sadie and her family on the porch observing the ritual.

"Another grave," lamented Sadie, wiping the sweat from her
brow with the hem of her apron. "How many more will be there on
our land in my lifetime?"

"I'm afraid not any," replied the preacher, standing against the
porch post. "Not if you have to leave this land for good."

She looked at the preacher as if considering what he said. "I
reckon you're right." She turned back towards the cemetery. "What
is she doing?"

Ned watched the Indian woman and shook his head. "I can't say
that I know. I believe she is grieving."

"For her man still?"

"Not that kind of grieving. I believe her spirit has been broken by
all that has happened to her and the boy." He observed the woman
with squinting eyes. "She appears to have lost heart. She refuses to
eat and wills herself to die."

"No."

"She feels old and lost from her people. The blow to her head may have affected her mind."

The preacher recalled what Sadie had said a moment before. "She may be the last one you bury there before you leave your land."

"Then we'll have to find some of her people who will take her in."

"It's not as simple as that," responded Ned in his near perfect English, allowing his words to gradually trail off to give everyone a clear moment to reflect on what he said.

The younger girls played nearby. They were intrigued by the hushed voices. Lillibet seemed distraught as she listened, and hurried to the rocking chair, leaning on her mother's arm and looking up into her weary eyes. "Mama, will we have to leave Laura and Alfonso and little Ammon in the ground here all by themselves?"

"And the baby?" added her little sister.

"Let's pray not, dear children."

Lillibet implored with dew in her eyes. "I don't want to leave them. They will be so lonely without us. Who will plant the flowers on their graves?"

Anton, lingering nearby, took a deep breath as he stood up to head back to work. "Don't you worry, Lillibet. Ain't nobody kicking us off our land." He looked at his poor father sitting in the straight spindle back chair brought out for him. The sight of the man who had once held his family together tugged at his heart. Now he was able to do nothing. William drooped over, shoulders slumping, like a wilted flower, and stared mindlessly at the lovely purple flowers blooming below his shoes. "If I thought we'd walk away from our own land, I wouldn't bother to do any more work," Anton finished his thought. "Why would I? No evil lawyer is going to run me off my pa's property without a fight."

The young man intentionally avoided his mother's eyes. But his anger subsided somewhat when he turned back to the sight of the broken man he called *Pa*. He bit his tongue, though he had plenty more he wanted to say. When he did glance back at his mother, her eyes cast a gentle rebuke. Sadie knew her son wanted to make a rash vow to fight to the death to keep Lillibet from having to leave her siblings behind in their graves. Anton drew a quick cooling breath and succumbed. "God will make a way for us to keep our land." It was what his mother would want him to say to the little ones, he knew.

"But how?" Lillibet inquired with a little child's innocence.

Anton had no convincing answer just then. His plan all along had been to take up his gun and shoot the invaders if they came around the homeplace to seize his father's rightful land. But now he was the man of the family. He wished more than anything that his father possessed even an inkling of awareness of what was happening to them, and still enjoyed his former robust health, and could leap right up and swear to defend those little graves with his life. But William simply stared at the flowers without ever raising his brows. He mumbled a few sounds. So, Anton knew it was up to him to figure out a realistic plan to save their farm. "Well, I am still thinking on it, but I'll come up with something."

"What your brother means," Sadie tried to explain, "is that God will provide a way for us and will take care of us whatever happens. You know Lillibet – and you too Lutie – that your sisters and brothers aren't really in that ground."

"Yes 'm," they answered in unison.

"They are in Heaven with Jesus." She turned aside to get a nod of approval from the preacher, but he wasn't there. She spotted him near the cemetery with Ned and the squaw and her boy. Preacher Pearsall had his hand on the boy's shoulder.

"I thought he didn't like Indians, Mama," commented Amos, pulling the straps of his overalls with his thumbs.

"I believe God has changed his heart, son." She permitted a comforting smile. "Preacher Pearsall went through a very rough time in his life, children. He was hurtin' and mad at everything. We gave him room to grieve over his loss and now he has finally found some healing. God truly can do anything in His time."

"Will He have the time to save us?" asked Lillibet.

"I pray so."

Suddenly a cloud of dust kicked up on the trail coming towards them from the direction of town. Anton quickly retrieved his shotgun. "It's Sheriff Potts," he announced. "And a couple of riders with him. One of 'em is Doc Goodwin."

"Doctor Goodwin?" Sadie repeated. "He's back so soon."

The three horses pulled up to a slow stop, the red Palomino, stomping his front foot on the ground and nickering.

"Might be his shoe," they heard the lean deputy, Cogney, say as he looked down at his mount's leg from the saddle.

Sadie looked at the horse's leg. "My boys will check it out. Howdy, Sheriff, Doctor, and you Mr. Cogney."

"Good day, Mrs. Williston." Potts tipped his hat. "Sorry to hear about Widow Lenora. She was a good woman."

Lillibet held her mother's hand and gazed up at the heavy man on the horse. "Are you here to run us off our land?"

"No, honey blossom, I'm not," grimaced the old sheriff as he dismounted. "I'm here to see the man who was hurt. Mr. Bezold. You been taking good care of him?"

"No, sir. Mamma told us not to get near him."

He smiled at the girl and redirected his eyes to the weary matron. "I brought the doc back so he can see if Bezold is up to talking."

"Evelina," Sadie called to her daughter who was standing beside the chair where her father rested. "Will you take these men inside?"

She made no reply. She looked down at her father who seemed to be following the three men with his glazy eyes as they approached. Was he remembering something? *Maybe it was the sun*, she thought. *Or perhaps he saw something familiar about them.* Sadie had almost expected him to jump up and greet the sheriff like old times. Could this be the inspiration she was waiting for? She was hoping, praying. But poor William's eyes dimmed and fell back towards the cruel, dry earth, and he didn't look back up, even when the men spoke to him.

Evelina opened the door. "He's in the back bedroom."

Sadie directed the boys to look at the horse's leg. Lillibet and Lutie carried a small straw basket to the side of the fresh grave and began removing clumps of butterfly weed and blue asters, and other colorful stems to sow in the prairie soil. They were grateful for Ned pulling up the plants for them earlier that morning so they could decorate Miss Lenora's grave.

Sadie scanned the horizon. Would this be one of the last times she would see this simple and peaceful view of her land? Her eyes returned to Preacher Pearsall and Ned as they led the Indian woman and boy back to their recently patched up sod home. The Pawnee guests made no attempt to go inside, and simply sat on the ground by the door. The preacher returned to her side.

"So, what are you thinking?" he asked.

Sadie sighed heavily and then smiled. "I was thinking how good it was for me to see you comforting the Indian woman and her boy."

He removed his hat and wiped his forehead with the back of his arm. "Well," he started slowly, as though unsure what to say. "With everything going on around this place, I reckon I realize that the woman and her child had nothing to do with what happened to my wife and baby. It doesn't make it any easier to go on without them, but those Indians are about as helpless as I was before I came here. God hasn't finished with me yet." He took a deep breath and released it quickly. "But, you have something grave on your mind. I can see it in your eyes."

The prairie woman turned and scanned the open plain again just as a light wind scattered her skirt at her side. "I'm sure you know what I'm thinking. I was just wondering if God is going to allow me and my family to stay on this land. The truth is, if he doesn't do something soon, I don't know where we'll go. What about you?"

"You mean, where will I go? I'm not sure. But I'd like to start preaching again."

"Glensbluff needs a preacher."

He smiled. "If they would even want me! But I'm not sure if I'm ready to start shepherding a flock just yet, though God does move in mysterious ways."

She looked back at William on the porch. "Sometimes I can't make sense out of His ways. Will we have to leave this land we worked so hard for and leave everything behind, including my precious little babies in the soil there." She paused for a long moment. "I'm still trying to figure all this out and make sense of it. But it makes no sense at all. If only William had never gone to Arkansas, if he hadn't got shot, and if he hadn't got taken in to robbing that gold shipment."

"That's a lot of *ifs*."

"I pray that my faith will remain strong. It's all I have to hold on to. But I'm getting weaker with every day that passes."

"God is still in control," he assured her. "Even when it doesn't seem like it."

"What it seems like is that my William, bless his confused mind, brought all this trouble on us. What was he doing? Why was he robbing gold out in Colorado? Be sure your sin will find you out. How could he?" Her voice cracked and both girls, with their dirty fingers wrapped around long, green stems, raised their eyes toward her. "My whole life has fallen apart."

"Sadie, no matter how bad things seem to get, you know it's not over unless the Lord says so. There's still some time left for God to work to help you figure something out."

His words brought little comfort. She felt looming darkness. She was exhausted. "Time is running out and there is no way under Heaven we can ever come up with that kind of money."

"Perhaps there is no way, under Heaven. But Heaven can still have a way."

The visit inside with the injured man didn't last long. When the sheriff and his party came back on the porch, Sadie and the preacher joined them beside Evelina and Jamie next to William's chair. Jamie inquired about the wounded man.

"As we figured," said Potts. "|He ain't talking."

Sadie volleyed her eyes from the sheriff to the doctor. "Well, how is he?"

"Not the best of health, I'm afraid. He's got a fever. He could still die."

The sheriff barked. "He's too ornery to die."

"But if he does," Evelina asked. "What do we do with him?"

"What does it matter?" scoffed the lawman. When he saw that

no one seemed satisfied, he offered a cordial suggestion. "We'll just have to let Granger and Penrose know. The boy must have family somewhere." He put his hat back on his balding head and secured it above his eyes. "Course, he'd be better off dead. If he lives he's going to go to prison for a long time... or hang."

"No one shot the widow woman, Sheriff," Jamie volunteered.

"So I hear." He stroked his whiskers. "In my book, they still caused her to die."

Jamie reminded him that Granger denied any involvement in the attack.

The sheriff nodded. "Yeah. Unlikely story. But we'll need proof."

"What about my horse?" asked Cogney.

He asked as Anton just then arrived at the end of the porch leading another horse by the reins. "I can't tell what's wrong with him, but I don't think it's good to ride him until he's looked at better. It might be his shoe. Here's that man's horse, the one you just saw. You can ride this one and come back when you find someone to look at your horse."

"Let me take a look at the lame horse," suggested the doctor. "I know something about them."

"No," snapped Potts. "We've got to get back. I don't like leaving Granger alone in my town for too long. Take Bezold's horse, Cogney. He's got no more use for him anyways. Like the boy said, you can come back with the blacksmith later."

The three men reached for the horses. The sheriff hesitated before mounting. "Sadie, as much as I don't like to even speak of this, if you can't come up with that money in a couple more days, you and your family will have to get off this land. I'm sorry, but he's got the papers, legal and all and, unless you can afford a sharp Yankee lawyer, I'll have to do my job."

"You know we can't afford any lawyer," objected Evelina, grasping her father's shoulder firmly. "How are we supposed to get it?'

"I don't know," he answered somberly. "Reckon just pray for a miracle."

"We don't blame you," Sadie said to the old Sheriff. "We have been praying and we aim to keep on praying. That's all we've got now."

"That's a good thing to have, Mrs. Williston. Praying for your man's mind to come back or praying for the money. Either way it'll take a miracle. You don't just need a miracle. You need one of them big Bible miracles. It will take that to save your farm now."

THIRTY-ONE

✿～◞

adie hurried from the fixed-up barn with a few eggs in her basket.
The sun had just risen above the horizon near the final day
of August startling the chickens with its sudden brilliance and
compelling the old rooster to give his everyday warning. Warning!
Sadie thought. It was a warning all right. Today is the day, she knew
quite well, that Ben Granger advised her to be off their land. She
gazed restlessly across the prairie, expecting to see them at any
moment galloping up in a stirring of dust.

Jamie caught up with her as she entered the kitchen. "Ned has
found a home for the Indian woman and her boy."

"What?"

"He has some Pawnee friends and they have arranged to take
the woman and boy."

"Where is this?"

"I don't know for sure. Somewhere further up north."

"Will it be safe?"

Jamie merely shrugged. "We have to do what we have to do."

She set the eggs on the table and grimaced. "And because no
one except Granger will be here after today? Does the woman want
to go?"

"Ned says she is willing." Jamie paused. "They are her people.
I think she would have a much better life there with her own tribe.
Don't you?"

She nodded. "When will they leave?"

"Ned arranged for his friends to take them up there today. He plans to ride with them."

"Oh," The thought that Ned would be going with them disconcerted her. "That's awfully soon. Will he be safe out there in the open?"

"It's a dangerous journey for all of them; so I've decided to go with them, me and a couple of men from the town church. We're leaving soon."

Sadie remained quiet for a moment and seemed to be lost in thought.

Jamie now sounded practically apologetic. "I'm afraid Abner is leaving too. He's riding with us a ways and then he's turning south."

Sadie still seemed transposed, her eyes fixed and rarely blinking. "What is it, Mrs. Williston?"

"Oh, I was just thinking how this is the day we're supposed to leave our land, but you and Ned and Abner and the poor Indians will be the first to go. It's already happening so fast. I reckon I'm still not ready for it." She went to the sink and poured water from a pitcher over her hands. "I'll fix you all some grub to take with you."

"Thank you. But, you haven't packed any food for yourself, have you? You haven't packed anything at all."

She exhaled sluggishly and drew in a new breath. "No. I reckon we'll just pick up what we can and leave the rest. We have no way of taking it all with us in one wagon anyway." She sounded exasperated. "Why doesn't the sheriff stop them?"

"Granger has the sheriff outnumbered ten to one." He nodded sympathetically. "You're still holding out for a miracle, aren't you – even to the very last minute?"

Sadie stopped and looked directly at Jamie. He was chiseled and handsome, and seemed so considerate. No wonder her daughter was drawn to him. "The last minute would truly make it a miracle, wouldn't it?" She chuckled. "Maybe Mr. Granger and the sheriff won't come today."

"You don't really believe that do you?"

She smiled. "I'll have your food ready soon. I want to say good-bye to 'em all before you leave."

ROBERT ANTHONY BROWN, SR.

As Jamie turned away, Sadie called him. "Jamie, if you ever come back to this place, we probably won't be here. So take what you want with you."

"No, thank-you, Mrs. Williston. I have a home in Kansas. But where will you go?"

"I reckon back east," she replied. "With just my children and a few animals and whatever we can haul in that old wagon."

"Do you think Granger will give you time to pack anything up?"

"I can't say there's really anything I want to take with me." She paused and swallowed to choke back tears. "Sheriff Potts said he would make sure we had the time. But I can't blame him if he didn't. We had fare warning. I just can't make myself..." Her voice trailed off in tears and Jamie took her hands in his.

After breakfast, when normally Sadie would be finishing her morning chores, she said good-bye to the Indian woman and hugged the little boy. She told Abner she would be praying for him. Then she asked Ned and Jamie to be careful. "I'll feel lost without you men being around. Your being here gave me heap of peace of mind. I'll never forget how you came here, Ned, all shot up and barely alive. But I'm glad you did. Without you, I feel afraid."

"I am glad I came here too, Mrs. Williston, because I would not be alive now without you."

With her basket of goods in their wagon, they rode off to the east in an old, half broken down contraption that Ned's Pawnee friend was driving. The little Indian boy lifted his hand and waved. Slowly, but eventually they disappeared over the horizon.

Instead of rushing back in to pack the things she knew she should, Sadie chose to sit on the porch alongside her reticent husband in their usual rocking motions. She prayed again, with a little less hope, that he would come back to himself. His physical presence wasn't missing, but he was not there beside her. His mind was already dead and buried.

The smaller children were carrying personal items across the yard while Anton and Amos attended to the animals and readied the wagon for traveling. She had persuaded them that a fight would only put all their lives in danger. As she thought more about Ned and Jamie being gone, she was glad they weren't there. Their presence would only heighten the tension when Ben Granger and his men showed up. Besides, there was nothing to fight about anymore. The land legally – or illegally – belonged to Ben Granger now.

Then she stopped rocking and leaned over, resting her elbows in her lap and clasping her fingers on both hands firmly together like a knot. She peered into her man's hollow brown eyes. William's mind seemed as empty as vast underground caves and her words seemed to echo off the walls. "My dear William," she began imploringly. "I sure do wish you would talk to me." His eyes did not move. He seemed to be watching the children scampering by the well, but for all she knew, he was gazing into a silent and vacant realm. "Do you know what day it is?" She sighed at his incognizance. "Today is the day we are to be put off our land."

She paused, hoping the thought would soak into his mind like an easy rain. But nothing could penetrate the hardness. She exhaled slowly and sucked in the warm air. "We're going to lose this land you worked so hard for. Can you understand what I'm telling you?"

Sadie sighed heavily again, leaned back in her idle rocker, and laid her forearms on the wooden rests. "I reckon you don't," she said. She looked away and then quickly turned back when William so deliberately turned his head towards her, his eyes narrowing into slits.

This spurred her to sit square up. "Did you hear me? Did you understand what I said?" She had hope – even if only a flicker of it. *Yes, he heard.* He turned his head and seemed to actually see her. *Could she be breaking through the barrier around his mind?* "Try, William. Try to understand what I'm saying. This is your farm. You are home now…back in Nebraska. They are taking your land away from you. Your land. You bought it. You worked it." She touched his hand and squeezed his crooked, boney fingers determinedly. "You are our only hope now. Do you remember the gold? They say it is stolen. Did you take it? Did you hide it somewhere? Where did you hide it? Is there any gold buried on this property? Tell me. Oh,

William, try hard to remember. Come back to me. We need you now more than ever. Help us."

But William still did not respond. His eyes sagged again and his chest sunk as though he had lost his best hunting dog. Then he looked back up, only to be looking through her at the pine panels on the wall he had brought from Kansas eight years ago. "Oh, my William." Her expression showed disappointment. "We stand to lose everything if you can't remember. Dear God, make him remember."

Then she heard it. A prickly little tune.

"Well, I'll be," she declared. "I believe that is Dixie you're humming." She laid her hand upon his slumped shoulder and listened. "At least you haven't forgotten everything."

Suddenly Anton's voice interrupted the pleasant scene. "They're comin', Mama." He sounded so official, absent of feeling. They both looked out beyond the rubble of the barn and saw the dust in the distance. "It's them. They really are coming."

Sadie stood. "It looks like a pack of 'em."

Amos came running from behind the horse corral, rounded the charred posts and clumps of sward, carrying his hoe. "What do we do? Should we fetch our guns?"

Sadie answered softly, "No."

Both boys looked at her with imploring expressions.

"I'll tell you what we'll do, son. We're gonna stay right here and wait on 'em. First, you and Amos take the girls inside. No. Better yet, you take them inside and stay there with 'em."

"But Mama!"

"No buts from you, Anton. This is your daddy's battle."

"But he ain't –"

"Don't you say it! I know he ain't." She wrung her hands and wiped them on her dress as though she were wiping away all hesitation. "That's why I'll be right here speaking for him. I need you to take care of the girls for me. For us. They're too little to be out here when those men arrive. Now you take them in the house."

Anton continued to protest. "But I'm the man of the house now."

"No, you ain't. Your father is sitting right here on his porch and we'll be greeting his old friends together."

"I'm getting my gun. I'm the law here now."

"You're talking like a foolish little boy who will get us all killed. Sheriff Potts is the law. Now, if you really think you're the man of the house ...well ... then you ought to be in your house ... looking after things."

"That's not what I mean. It could be perilous out here." Anton begged his mother to reconsider. "We can't just give up our home. It can't end like this."

"Girls!" she called out. "We got company. Your brothers are going to take you inside."

"But, Mama," her eldest son refused to give up. "We haven't even packed. You can't let them run us off today and just leave everything behind."

"I'm aware of that and I'm not letting them do anything."

"Then what are you going to do?"

"I'm going to sit right here and wait on 'em."

"Is that all?"

"No. I'm still praying for that miracle." She stood by William's rocking chair and looked upward into the blazing blue sky, moving her lips rapidly, but soundlessly. Then she turned and called back to Anton. "Get going. And you are right, boys. It will pay to be cautious, just in case. I mean just in case things go bad, you two stand behind those windows with your loaded shotguns. I don't expect them to, but we can't let nothing happen to the children."

Their faces indicated shock. That was what they were wanting to hear. "Yes ma'am."

"Now I really don't expect any trouble," she called out to them as they escorted the smaller children inside. "So don't get twitching fingers. Don't even think about shooting unless something goes awfully wrong."

"Like what?"

"You'll know. And tell the preacher to come out here. I'm hoping we can talk things out."

He shook his head skeptically. "They're done talking."

"And Anton –"

"Yes, Mama."

"Tell the preacher to bring Mr. Bezold out here. He's well enough to walk."

Preacher Pearsall soon appeared at the door with the injured man. He pushed Bezold ahead and then hopped off the boardwalk. The man was wearing his shirt bloused open and his unlatched suspenders flopping by his legs. He walked as though he were still in pain. "Looks like the sheriff brought a bunch with him," observed the preacher.

"Good. I just hope nobody loses his head."

A cluster of horses rounded the sod barn, thundering their hooves and scattering some lazy chickens into brief flight. Sadie checked to make sure the door to the house was closed; and she could glimpse Anton at his post through the partially closed curtains.

"Mr. Williston," she addressed her man who was still sitting idly in his rocking chair and humming his song. "It's time now for you to come to yourself. This is your moment to shine. There will be no tomorrow if you don't, at least not here on this land. If we don't come up with a miracle now, we'll never decorate those graves with lovely, prairie flowers again." She turned around and stood bravely to face the riders. "Dear God," she breathed. "Don't let this happen."

Sadie Williston, the prairie farm matron in her colorless dress and dark shoes, seemed to blend into the drab surroundings. To Granger and Siler Penrose, she may as well have been just a wild shrub that needed a scythe taken to it. The two men sat high in their saddles. A few more of their men drew up behind them. Sheriff Potts and two of his deputies made up the rest of the party. She recognized Mr. Cogney on Bezold's horse. The young Roark was the other one.

"I'm sorry to have to do this, Mrs. Williston," began the leathery faced sheriff. "But if you haven't come up with the money to save your property, well... then Mr. Granger here already has it as good as paid for and the land is his."

"No. I don't have the money."

"Then you will have to vacate the property, ma'am. I'm awfully sorry to do this to you. But that is the law and, as much as I don't want to have to enforce it, I am here to see it done."

The matron felt dreadfully lonely, even with the preacher standing by her side. She licked her cracked lips and pursed them into a frown. "We are obliged to ask for a little more time, Sheriff," she deliberately drew out the hopeless request.

"Times up," snapped Granger. "I've given you the whole summer and more."

Sadie pleaded. "Considering my poor husband just returned home after all these years with his feeble mind, I am sure you can be considerate enough..."

"I have been very considerate all summer, Mrs. Williston. And patient. I cannot wait a day longer to take my land."

Siler Penrose grinned and removed his hat, revealing snaky eyes and a weasely mouth. "We won't wait a minute longer," he squealed. "My men and I will see to that. Now get off our land."

"Unless..." began Granger.

Preacher Pearsall gruffly cut him off. "She told you she doesn't have the money."

"As I was saying... unless you can tell me where the gold is hidden."

"If I had the gold, don't you think I would have used it to pay you?"

Granger looked around at the men behind him. "Okay fellows, round them all up."

As they started to dismount a gunshot echoed across the plain. Sadie turned quickly towards the broken window behind her husband and prayed she didn't have to call her boys down. She gathered her breath when she saw movement at the end of the porch. Ned Ames stepped out halfway from behind the smiling house.

"Ned! I thought you had gone."

"And leave you here with these uncouth men? No. I returned to make sure things will be handled properly."

"Don't be an idiot, Ames," barked Granger. "You're outnumbered."

"Yes, but there are two more guns aimed at you as we speak, and we will drop most of you before you could clear your holsters."

Granger growled. "Sheriff."

Potts looked a might anxious – and irritated. "Ned Ames drop your gun. You are interfering with the law."

"I do not intend to interfere with the law. I just intend to help you do this without harm to anyone."

Penrose raised his scrawny frame in the saddle and protested. "Potts, that's Ned Ames, you know. He is a wanted man. Now do your duty and arrest him."

The burly sheriff snapped back. "I know it's him. Stop telling me how to do my job or I'll have you arrested."

Penrose's lips instantly transformed into a huge grin. He eyed the figure of the man barely visible behind the wall. "I wouldn't ordinarily be so mad at you, half-breed, if you'd only stolen the gold intending to use it to help the South."

The sheriff bit at Penrose like a snake. "You didn't care one way or the other about the South or North. Neither did you, Granger. All you two wanted was to get your hands on that gold."

The skinny man laughed. "Reckon you're right, sheriff. I was on Siler Penrose's side during the war after I learnt the gold was stole out from under me." His grin quickly vanished. "The war is over, and I want what's mine – now!" He placed his fingers near the white handle of his gun.

"Sit tight!" ordered his big boss. Granger targeted Ned Ames with just his eyes. "We can do this peacefully. Mrs. Williston, I will give you time to gather up your little chicks and whatever they can carry and leave my property – if you will do it right now. That's fair, isn't it sheriff?"

"I told her I would make sure she had time to pack up a few things. We can even help her."

"Help her?" Penrose cried. "We've given her all summer. I ain't helping one bit. You heard what he said. Start moving right now, lady."

"She needs more time," Ned insisted. "Give us until this evening. When you come back, we'll all be gone."

Granger seemed to be listening and contemplating the proposal.

Then suddenly, he laughed aloud. "No more delay. Time's up sheriff. Arrest them."

But Ned went on. "There's your man. There's a horse here that belongs to Cogney. They can switch horses before you leave the property."

Granger adjusted himself in the saddle. "If you know where the gold is hid, Ned, tell me, and we'll give you all the time you want to pack while we dig it up."

"Williston double crossed the rest of us after the robbery," Penrose growled. "It won't happen a second time."

Ned quickly countered, "That's because he knew you wanted it all for yourself."

"I stole it back then for the South, but the South never saw a nugget of it and lost the war."

"Will you two please be quiet," ordered Granger. "Forget what happened back then. That makes no difference to me. I just want that gold and I want it now."

"You want it alright," said Ned. "Enough that you killed off the rest of the men as soon as you found out that Williston was the one who knew where it was. You even tried to kill me. You couldn't afford to kill Williston because you knew he was the one who hid it." As soon as Ned mentioned the name, every eye quickly turned and glued to the old man in the chair on the porch.

"There's the man who caused all this," announced Granger. "There's the brain behind stealing the gold. He stole it twice, once from the government and then from his gang. He hid it and he knows right where it is. The answer is still somewhere inside that mind."

"I'm sure he would rather not have lost all his memory," said Sadie.

"Conveniently lost it, wouldn't you say," stated Siler Penrose. "So he won't have to tell us."

"I'm inclined to agree with Siler," spoke Granger. "How convenient to lose the gold and then lose your memory."

"Look at him," said an angry woman. "He looks like he's aged a hundred years and has wasted away almost to nothing. Does he look like a man who is pretending?"

"No." Granger replied, grasping the saddle horn and pulling himself up tall in the saddle. "He looks more like a dead man. But maybe now is the time to put him to the ultimate test."

"How do you propose to do that?" asked the sheriff.

"It's quite simple. We'll just have to make him choose."

Potts cocked his head. "Choose what?"

"Choose between his gold or his woman."

THIRTY-TWO

ranger dismounted but told the others to stay on their horses.

"What are you up to?" questioned the sheriff.

"I might be able to save a lot of people a lot of trouble," the large man replied. "Give me one last opportunity to talk to Williston."

"You've had your chance," objected Sadie. "So have we all. He can't remember anything."

"She's right," said Potts.

"Just one more opportunity. I think I can get through to him now."

"How?" asked Sadie. "What makes this time any different?"

"You'll see."

"No. You'll only disturb him more. Hasn't he suffered enough?"

"I won't hurt him," argued Granger. "You will be right here as witnesses. Just let me try one more time. If he remembers where he hid it, we'll not need to take your land. If he doesn't, you're no worse off than you are now."

Sadie looked to the preacher, her eyes asking for his opinion.

"Let him try," he said; then whispered to her, "Who knows if this might be the way God will work to bring him back to you?"

"You're right. It could be. Okay, then," she agreed. "But you must be gentle."

"Remember that I'm right here," Ned reminded Granger. "With you in my sights."

Granger rolled his bulging eyes. "For goodness sakes, I only want to talk to him." He took several steps past Sadie and Preacher Pearsall and stopped directly in front of the infirm man. He set his right foot on the boardwalk and leaned forward casually, resting his arm on his knee. "William, do you remember me? I'm Colonel Ben Granger."

William eased his head slightly to the side and seemed to be taking in the image of his old prison camp commander.

"Of course you remember me." He patted his leg and spoke cordially. "Now, my friend, we don't want to force your family off your land. All we want is the gold you took and hid somewhere. If you can tell me where the gold is and we find it, we'll let you and all your clan live the rest of your lives here. I don't want your land. I just want the gold."

The weary man's eyes closed and reopened as though he were attempting to focus in on the moon-faced lawyer.

"You have the stolen gold up here on your land, don't you? That's what we figured. You had to have brought it up this way in the wagon and buried it on this property. Is that about how it happened William?

The sickly man seemed to recognize his own name each time the lawyer spoke it and appeared to be trying to move his mouth. He swallowed hard and licked his cracked lips.

"That's right, William. Tell me. You know where it is. If you can't talk, then point that way." Then he smiled and whispered, "I'll even split it with you. Show me where you buried the gold."

"This isn't anything different than you did before," remarked Sadie.

"I'm not finished."

Immediately, the man in the rocking chair appeared to lose interest and turned his eyes away.

"William. Do you understand me, William? I said tell me!" shouted Granger.

"You're wasting your time," Penrose yelled from his mount.

Ned and the preacher, at the same time, warned Granger to cease his interrogation.

But Ben Granger took one more step closer and now stood on

the walkway beside William. "I'm sorry. I didn't mean to raise my voice." Then he bent forward and placed his lips beside William's ear, speaking something. Sadie could see his jaws moving but couldn't hear what he was saying. When he stood back up and stepped off the walk, she could see alarm in her husband's eyes. His hands and his lips were trembling.

"Leave him alone," cried Sadie. "That is enough." She stepped between her man and Granger. "What did you say to him?"

"Nothing, dear lady. Nothing."

"You said something to him that really upset him."

"I simply put him to the test. It doesn't matter, though. I can see he has failed. There's no use trying anymore."

"What test?" questioned the minister.

Ben Granger turned around and started towards the sheriff. "That's all. It's time to do your duty, Potts. Get these people off my land."

"Don't tell me what to do. I'll do what I have to when I'm finished talking to Mrs. Williston."

"We've had enough talking, Sheriff. My gold is somewhere on this land. Do your job."

Sadie had enough too. "Sheriff, are you going to sit there and let these men run right over you? You're a lawman. You know that gold, even if it is on this land, is stolen from the federal government and doesn't belong to them. They have no right to it either way."

Granger sneered. "I'm afraid the sheriff doesn't have much of a choice in the matter."

"You forget I have two deputies here and Ned Ames on my side. If you want trouble, we can sure give it to you."

"I'm sorry, Sheriff," said Granger. He turned to face Sadie. "You see, Mrs. Williston, his two deputies here... let's just say they aren't on his payroll anymore."

"Mr. Cogney!" Sadie exclaimed when she realized exactly what the lawyer meant. "I can't believe you... or you, Mr. Roark."

Sheriff Potts craned his neck back at his deputies with a look of shock. "What is this?"

Cogney pressed his lips together forcefully before answering. "I'm sorry, but I gotta take care of myself too."

"But why?" Potts demanded, casting his eyes back and forth between his two men. But he didn't wait for an answer. "You vermin."

Penrose had enough. "Give up on all the talking. I'm tired of waiting. Now Ames, are you going to shoot all of us? Drop your gun or these folks here are gonna get caught by all the stray bullets. You want them dead?"

Penrose hastily drew out his pistol and the others followed his action. "Ames, we have no reason to keep you or any of these folks alive."

Bezold bolted to the side and ran towards the horses. "Give me a gun," he yelled.

Sadie heard movement and turned to see their friend step forward. He returned his gun to his holster. Their eyes met. "I'm afraid he is right. I cannot have you and Mr. Williston and the preacher getting shot. And all your brood inside. With no deputies, it looks like you have no choice but to leave. Land is not everything. Your lives are more important."

For a long second all eyes were on the gunslinger and every mouth fastened as tight as a dead man's lips. Penrose and his men quickly dismounted, including the two deputies.

Sheriff Potts looked uncertain about moving off his horse, shaking his head as he finally stepped down. "I'm sorry, Mrs. Williston," he said. "I thought I could give you time to gather some of your things and safely pack up, but now I don't know. I didn't count on these two traders."

The matronly woman spoke softly as she knelt beside her husband. "It's not your fault, sheriff. We don't want you to get killed either."

"Forget my life. I'd rather die than tuck tail and run from these hoodlums."

William was quivering something awful now. His right leg twitched like he was keeping time with barn dance music. She clamped her hand on his knee and spoke in the tone of a child."

Penrose cried out again. "I've had enough of all this. Let's get that gold." He cocked his gun.

Granger snapped at him. "Stop! First, we get this woman and her children off the land."

The front door opened, and a rifle barrel appeared, sending alarm to the men.

"No, Anton!" Sadie cried out. "Not yet."

"It looks pretty bad to me, Mama."

Penrose growled, his hand twitching on the trigger. "Drop that gun, boy, or I'll shoot your mama first."

Anton, after meeting his mother's panicked eyes, set the gun down on its wooden butt.

"All of you," ordered Granger. "All of you come outside now. We got a heap of guns aimed right at your Ma and Pa."

Sadie nodded to her eldest son and he led the children outside. Evelina had her arms around both girls.

"All right," the lawyer barked, eyeing Sadie, "Get your family and your things in that wagon and get out of here. Sheriff Potts will see you back to town or wherever you aim to go. I don't care where, just get off this land."

When Ben Granger's breath settled from his last words, time on the Williston farm stood as still as a dead tree stump. A gust of wind swept across the dry soil kicking up a swirling cloud of dust as though by magic, settling it back down to the earth like sprinkled sugar. Suddenly, with great effort and, yet amazing surprise to everyone, William Williston placed his boney hands on the armrests of the rocker and forced himself up. He steadied himself with the shoulder of his bewildered wife and stepped precariously off the boardwalk. Sadie wrapped her arm around his thin waist and supported his weight with all her effort.

Granger raised his eyebrows and smiled. "Are you ready to talk? Maybe you have passed the test."

"I'm sick and tired of talking," Penrose loudly complained.

"I told you to be quiet. I'm in charge here. What have you decided William – your family or your gold?"

Siler, his gun still drawn at his waist, raised the barrel. He paced efficiently, like a soldier on guard duty, towards William.

"Leave him to me," commanded Granger.

Penrose cocked his revolver.

"Back away, I said. He's gonna tell us where he hid the gold."

Miraculously, like a ghost just ascended, William Williston drew in a full breath, expanding his chest as if it might burst; then freed it all at once. He ambled forward like a dead man walking, forcing his wife's supporting arm away, and staggered resolutely until he stood nose to nose with the cumbersome lawyer. He seemed half his size. The air felt heavy to everyone. Tense. A deathly quiet shrouded the scene. No one dared to move or breathe. Even the horses seemed arrested in time and unable to produce even a snort.

Every expectant eye felt captured by the solemn face of William Williston, like they were bound by iron chains, as he stared down his heavy opponent. Sadie hurried to catch up with his tottering frame, but he obstinately waved her aside. For the first time since he had been brought home to his family, he opened his swollen, cracked lips and spoke sensible words. Though he was hard to understand at first, the listless and drawn out syllables were clearly recognized by all. "Get... off... my... land."

Granger was speechless.

Siler Penrose, who stood under his spell like everyone else, broke free and madly rushed the few quick steps forward until he stood between his boss and the fragile man.

William focused on the eyes of the rebel soldier. "Get off my land."

His white eyes bulging, Penrose looked like he had seen a ghost and heard the prince of death himself speaking to him.

William's family broke into chatter and smiles. At first Siler swallowed hard, then composed himself. "So you can talk, old man. Tell me where you hid our gold."

"Tell us, William," followed Granger, stepping away from Siler's back. "Tell us where you hid the gold and we'll be good to your family."

The revived man pursed his lips, but his wife pleaded with him to tell them. Ned Ames joined in. "William," he began in his usual formal manner. "You can tell them. It is okay. You must think of your family now."

William turned his head towards Ned's voice and, appearing to lose his balance, stumbled. Ned rushed forward and caught him against his chest; but when he stood the old man back up, alarm filled Ned's eyes. William was holding a pistol in his hand. He couldn't react in time. William had it aimed at the chest of Siler Penrose.

"No William!" shouted Sadie, aghast.

A single gunshot sounded. Smoke poured from the barrel of the gun in Sheriff Potts's hand. He had fired into the sky. Siler Penrose's took advantage of the distraction, took one step forward, and knocked the weapon from William's hand. In one continuous motion he swung his balled fist and catapulted the delicate old man backwards. William fell to the hard ground with a sickening sound. Sadie cried out and a cacophony of noise rose from the children. Sadie fell at her man's side. Ned and the preacher attended the slumped figure, lifting his torso and gently laying his head in Ned's arms.

"You killed him," said the preacher.

"No," said the gunman. "He is still alive. He is breathing, at least."

Sheriff Potts took control of the situation, jumping in between Penrose and the fallen man.

"He had a gun on me," Penrose whined. "I had to defend myself."

While the group of men chattered and debated in the background, Ned bent his ear to William's lips. Sadie was crying. He told her to be quiet because her husband was trying to say something. The old man's eyes were open and his lips were moving. Preacher Pearsall placed his arm on Sadie's shoulder and leaned in. But with all the crying and arguing in the background, they couldn't hear what he was saying. Ned was straining to catch each syllable that escaped, his ear now almost resting on William's mouth.

In a few seconds, the figure of the outlaw slowly rose and faced the scrawny man with the rebel hat and Ben Granger by his side. Sheriff Potts still had his gun drawn and Ned followed, whipping it like lightening. Amos and Anton stood on the porch, their shot guns raised level.

"That's enough for today," Ned demanded. "We have to get him inside now or he'll die."

"Let him die," said Penrose, his fingers clenched tightly around his gun handle. "We didn't ask him to be a hero."

"Ames is right," shouted the sheriff. "You're done here today."

"We're not done here," Granger barked. "Today is the deadline and we want them off this land right now."

Cogney agreed with the sheriff. "I'm done with this. I didn't come here to kill anybody."

Roark slipped his gun back in the holster. "I've had enough of this too."

The sheriff was glad to have them back him up, but was in no forgiving mood. "I've had enough of everything about this whole matter. We'll come back when William is better."

Penrose protested. "But it's our land now."

"Would you please let me handle this," Granger insisted.

The sheriff was riding his emotions. "The marshal will be back this way any day now and I'll let him sort all this out, seeing that you took all my authority away and stole Cogney and Roark away. Sounds pretty underhanded to me. There's too many folks here, including these youngins, for me to handle this safely."

"He's right," said Granger.

Penrose blared, "I'm not going anywhere until I get that gold."

Ben Granger stepped out on his left foot and slapped the gun out of Siler's hand. "I said we'll come back." Then he muttered to Penrose, "He told Ames something just now. He told him where he buried the gold."

"How do you know?"

"He whispered something in his ear. What else do you think he told him? Ned Ames knows now. We've got work to do." He looked back to the sheriff. "Tomorrow."

"Not until Williston's able to travel – if he ever is – thanks to your idiot partner."

"Listen Potts, I'm trying to be cooperative, but Siler is right. This is my land now. I'll be willing to give you two days, but that's all. Marshal or no marshal, I'll be back in two days, and this time I want everyone off this land before we get here. I have been extremely patient. If these people are still here in two days, no more talking, no more stalling. It will be entirely on your head what happens to them youngins."

The preacher assisted the two boys in carrying their father in the house. The sheriff watched them until they disappeared inside. He spoke to Granger as he was mounting his horse. "I can't argue with you, Granger. I don't think you have a right to this land, but you have all the papers and the money to take it legally. But if you won't come back 'til the third day I will make sure this time that they are off the land before you get here."

Granger agreed. Siler cursed loudly. "What's happened to the tough prison colonel I used to know? You've gone soft as one of those delicate flowers yonder. Why don't you give 'em 'till next year? I've a mind to come back without you and get this thing done right."

"You come back without me and I'll make you sorry." He grinned wide at his partner and looked around at the rest of his men. "You boys remember who pays you. Trust me. You'll get your share if you do what I say."

Granger and his men and the deputies rode off in a blaze.

"Sadie," the sheriff spoke to her. "Those men are up to something no good again. They left way too happy. So, after three days are up, I want you to be off this land when the sun gets straight up in the sky. I'm not going to have a lot of innocent people getting killed when I come back with Granger. His men are hot headed and I'm taking no more chances. If the marshal doesn't show up by then, you and your family have to be off this property. If not, I'm going to have to arrest every one of you. I'm sorry, but your miracle ain't nowhere in sight."

THIRTY-THREE

❀ ∂❧

mid the sobs from Lutie and Lillibet, the men folk carried William's body into his back bedroom and laid him on his bed. Wrapped in a blanket, he seemed to waft between awakening and sleeping. Mostly he looked worn-out, his clothes soiled from the fall, and barely clinging to life. Evelina sat by his side and tended to him. Her father had not spoken since the blow. Tears stained her puffy cheeks.

When Sadie entered the room, she announced angrily. "They are really going to kill everybody over some yellow colored rocks? I've seen men at their worst."

Preacher Pearsall followed her in. "Right now forget about them and spend time with your husband. He needs you. He doesn't look good."

"I can't forget about them. And he hasn't looked good since he came home."

"What I mean is he looks like..."

"I know what you mean."

She approached the bed and stopped beside Evelina. "If he was sickly and feeble before this, the hand of Siler Penrose has nearly lowered him in the grave." She bent over, brushing back his hair and wiping his brow with her open palm. "Thank you, William. You did not let us down. You rest, my brave man."

"I can't believe he actually spoke," said Evelina. "There's your miracle."

"Not the whole miracle we were hoping for," her mother said. "But I knew he would come back to us and take his place as man of the house again. I knew he wouldn't just sit there and let those evil men steal his land right out from beneath him."

Preacher Pearsall took an unassuming position on the other side of the bed and clasped his hands in prayer. "You really believed in a miracle, didn't you?"

"I did. God would not let us down."

"But they'll be back in three days."

"Still, it was a miracle, whatever happens now."

"Yes, it was a miracle," the preacher heartily agreed. "And I know for certain that God answers prayer. But, if you don't come up with the gold – or the money – to pay off the fees, what good will having a miracle do in keeping your land. I don't see it."

Sadie didn't raise her eyes. She weighed what the preacher said but made no response. Then she told Lutie and Lillibet to fetch a wet cloth so she could wipe the sweat and dirt from their daddy's face."

Just then Anton, Amos, and Ned entered the crowded little room. "Is he going to be all right?" Amos asked.

She laid her open hand on her husband's chest. "He wasn't doing well even before Siler Penrose struck him. Now I'm awfully worried about him. His heart feels like it is pounding and his breathing sounds shallow and fast. It was too much for him."

"What did he say out there?" Evelina asked.

Her youngest brother answered proudly. "He said *GET OFF MY LAND*."

"I heard that part, but I'm talking about what he said after he fell."

Everyone looked to Ned. When the girls returned with the wet cloth, no one noticed them. Ned saw that every ear awaited a response. "He said something about the missing gold."

"What did he say about it?" Amos asked.

Ned stroked his chin wistfully and broke the news that everyone had been longing to hear. "He told me where the stolen gold is hidden."

"Is it here? On our land?" Anton blurted out excitedly.

"No, I'm afraid not. He was so weak and it was hard to understand him clearly at first. I didn't want to say anything with Granger and his gang standing around…"

"Did he tell you where it is?"

"Yes, Anton. He did tell me… in a whisper."

Every breath was arrested in great suspense. "Well, where is it?"

Ned spoke in his near perfect English. "He told me that the wagon of gold is hidden in the Lost Indian Cave."

"And where might that be?" asked Evelina.

"It is a cave near his childhood home in Arkansas."

"Do you know where it is?"

"I suppose that is why they call it lost. I'm hoping he'll be able to tell us when he comes to."

Sadie took the washcloth and wiped William's face. "I'm not sure he will ever come to, Ned. But I know where the Lost Indian Cave is."

The children cheered and squealed with excitement.

"Be quiet!" Sadie cried out. "Your father is sick. I've heard him talk about that cave years ago. Once he took me by it and told me the story about the Indian boy who got lost in it and was never seen again."

"Did you go in?" asked Amos.

"No. Of course not. It was deep and winding and, besides, there were signs up warning folks to keep away."

Amos seemed thrilled to hear the news. "Good. Pa can take us there when he's better and we can get the gold."

She caressed his face and patted it fondly. "I don't believe your father will ever get back to Arkansas, Amos. I fear he will never again get out of this bed."

"No, Mama," cried Evelina. "Is he that bad?"

"I'll kill that Siler Penrose if I see him again," swore Anton.

Sadie's voice was somber. "As much as I don't care for Siler Penrose, son, I can't put all the blame on him."

"What!"

"Your father was getting worse every day since he's been here. This was coming."

"You are the most forgiving woman I have ever met," said the preacher.

"I'm not saying I don't blame Siler for putting him here in this bed, but the war and getting shot and the prison camp – well – you know what I'm saying."

"So," Anton went back to the previous conversation, "Since Pa can't take us to the cave, you can show us, Mama. Pa would want that."

"Would he?"

"You know he wouldn't want us to lose our land."

"No, boys," explained their mother with words that splashed like water on a fire. It doesn't do us any good. That gold belongs to the government."

"Your mother is right," agreed Ned.

"But couldn't we take just a couple of bars to pay off the debt and redeem our land?"

"You know we can't do that, son," replied his weary mother. "That would be stealing."

Amos joined in. "But Pa stole it in the first place, didn't he?"

"Your Pa didn't steal it," Ned answered and began to enlighten everyone in the room. "Your father and I were involved in the robbery for a different reason. We knew about the plot to steal the gold to aid the South in the war effort. Your father and I both were against secession and human slavery. He was involved with the robbery only to prevent that gold from falling into the hands of the southern army."

The looks on the faces around the room indicated they could not believe what they just heard.

"It is true," Ned continued. "But what we did not anticipate was Siler Penrose forcing your father into the rebel army. He threatened to harm his family in Arkansas if he didn't. They literally took him by force. That happened quite often in the war, I am sorry to say. Siler never intended for him to be in battle and get wounded, but they were ambushed in a thicket. When he grew ill from the infection, they were not able to discover what happened to the gold shipment.

He, and only he, knew where it was hidden. It has been a mystery all this time and the federal government did everything they could to get the truth out of him. It took all this ruckus today to finally bring his memory back and enable him to talk."

Sadie placed the cloth in Evelina's hand and stood up. "So, all this time Ben Granger has been chasing the wind. The gold never was on this land."

"I'm afraid that is so."

"If we only had the letter Daddy wrote for Preacher Arder?" said Evelina.

"Yeah," added Anton. "Telling Pa's secret hiding place?"

"We don't know what was in that letter," his mother replied. "Prisca didn't even know what it was all about. If we want to know what it says we'll have to dig up Reverend Arder's body."

"That will not help," Ned explained. "The night I rode off and did not tell you where I had gone…"

"You dug up his grave?" cried Evelina.

"The letter was not in the box or in his clothes."

At first no one moved or said anything as they tried to process what Ned had just told them. Then, Evelina went back to swabbing her father's face. "You tried to tell somebody, didn't you Daddy? But then you weren't able to tell anybody anything – until today."

Anton exhaled heavily, like a man who had just finished a hard day's work. "Well, it really was all for nothing. All that digging and there never was anything buried here." He stared at his father's motionless body for a few seconds. "So, I reckon I'll go pack up a few things and get everything ready for leaving. Your miracle never came, Mama." Anton left the room.

Later that night, with Sadie and Evelina still waiting by his side, William's breathing slowed. His chest barely rose and fell. A fresh stain of tears donned both cheeks on his daughter's face.

"Don't leave us, Daddy," she pleaded. "We waited so long for you to come back. You can't die now."

"He's just too weak and worn out," spoke Sadie.

"No, Mama."

"He's getting weaker by the minute." She caressed his sunken cheek. "It's time you go rest, my dear William."

"But why does he have to die? We're losing our home and our land with all the babies graves on it and now my daddy. What purpose could God have in all this happening?"

"I don't know, my daughter," Sadie answered, placing her hand on Evelina's. "But God has a time and a purpose for everything under the sun."

In the early hours of the still morning, everyone except the younger girls were standing at his bedside watching William's chest rise and fall slower and slower each time.

"I don't care if we lose this forsaken land," said Evelina, squeezing one hand while her mother clasped the other. "But I don't want to lose my daddy again."

At half past three o'clock in the morning, William Williston breathed his last breath on earth. Sadie had done all her weeping before the sun rose. She was no longer worried about her farm. It was hard to grieve over William since he had been gone from their lives for such a long time and she had already grieved over him for three years. He wasn't even the same William she once knew. He had been just the shell of the man she had loved and married. But she thanked God that he came back to himself one last time and stood up to defend his family as the man he had been. She rose from the kitchen table with her coffee cup in her hand and sipped the cold, black liquid as she looked out the window. She could see Anton and Amos standing at the little family cemetery looking things over as they were preparing to dig yet another grave.

"So, what now, Lord?" she prayed aloud. "In a couple of days the sheriff and, maybe even the marshal, not to mention that wicked lawyer will be back, and we will have to give up our land, despite all we have done to try to keep it. Nothing's changed, except one more hole will be dug in the ground. I reckon I have looked like a fool. There is no gold buried on this land. There never was. Anton did all that digging for nothing. I suppose I should have given Ben Granger every acre on this property when he wanted it. Maybe William and Lenora would still be alive."

"No, Sadie," Ned interrupted her prayer coming through the open doorway. "None of this is your fault. I think your Lord would agree. Ben Granger and Siler Penrose are evil, greedy, and thoughtless men."

"Well, it doesn't matter now. We'll be evicted from our home when the sheriff shows up. We have to be gone before he shows up. With no money, we can't redeem this land." She faced Ned as he sat at the table. "And you had better take off before the marshal comes. You are still wanted, aren't you?"

"The Smith brothers will exonerate me concerning the stolen gold. And about the cavalry boys, they instigated it by harassing me. I was only defending myself. I'm willing to take my chances with a judge and a trial, if it comes to that."

Sadie turned back to the window. "Good. I don't want you to spend your days running away from something you've done or haven't done. That's no life for any man." She glanced back out the window. "Ned, would you mind running outside to tell the boys to wait until the morning before they did their daddy's grave."

"Yes, ma'am, if that's what you want. I think they had planned to begin when the sun gets lower in the sky. It is so hot out there anyway." He smiled and nodded at her.

"The sun has nothing to do with it. I'm just not quite ready to see another grave dug. Besides, I need some time to get William's body ready. Preacher Pearsall said he would help me wash him and shave him and get some nice clothes on him before we put him in the ground."

THIRTY-FOUR

❀ ➴

arly the next morning, Anton and Amos plunged their shovels into the brittle earth. The number of graves had grown from two to six. Preacher Pearsall and Ned began to fashion a solid pine casket from some of the timbers William himself had transported to the plains from Arkansas. They worked diligently on the project and didn't speak unless they had to. On the third day, their final day, they carried the completed casket into the house to the back bedroom where lay the body of William garbed in his Sunday best clothes. They didn't fit his shrunken frame anymore, swallowing him up like a blanket. They stuffed his clothes with rags and carefully lowered the body inside the coffer. With the help of the boys they carried him outside.

The sun already felt scorching hot. The two courageous sons, after they took note of how wide and long the coffin looked, grabbed their tools and commenced digging the hole deeper and wider. Inside Sadie dressed in her normal black calico dress and bonnet. She helped the girls with their clothes and brushed out their hair. Her mind drifted beyond the funeral service to the afternoon when they would leave. They would leave after the morning funeral. Their wagon was loaded and rested by the old barn. The chickens had been caged and the animals hitched and tied.

She felt bewildered. She was more confused about her own thoughts than about all that was happening. In a way she felt relief, relief that she didn't have to worry about William any more. For three years, that was all she thought about. Now, she found herself grieving more for her farm than for her husband. Was this not wrong? She chastised herself. Why were there no tears left for William? Why was she more preoccupied with the days still to come than the very day of her husband's funeral? Was she losing her mind? Would she ever be the same again?

She and the girls had cooked and packed some food for their journey while the boys had harvested what they could of the last crops. Corn from the Indian woman's late garden and dried shuckey beans completed the stores. The boys had labored so hard filling some large containers with water and making the small wire cages. Sadie also chose a couple items of furniture they might be able to haul if they stacked them high enough on the wagon. The boys would ride horses. The cow and the dogs could tag along. The animals probably wouldn't survive the heat and barrenness of the plains anyway, she knew.

Sadie also supervised the selecting of clothing and the personal affects that had the most meaning to them. They could not take everything. Now was the season to abandon what wasn't essential. How dreadful the very contemplation. Preacher Pearsall fashioned a small cart to pull behind him that would hold some of his books and clothes. She wondered about Ned. What would he do? Where would he go? Would he turn himself in to face a trial back down south?

As she prepared to go outside, hoping to take a long look at her smiling face home, she suddenly became aware of a lengthy scream, followed by a boisterous raucous like the cadence of an Indian dance. *What was all the commotion?* She wondered. It sounded like someone who had just discovered a wagon load of gold bars. It's not Ben Granger already, she heard herself say beneath her breath. They hadn't even held William's funeral yet.

When she opened the front door of the smiling face house and stepped onto William's homemade boardwalk, she quickly scanned the yard to see if there were new horses on her land, expecting to see Granger sitting on his large stallion and the marshal's badge glimmering in the bright sun. But all she saw were her two sons kneeling on the grave bluff and Ned and the preacher leaning over them. Once again, she heard a shout as a war cry coming from the cemetery. The girls pushed past her racing out the door.

"What is it, Mama?" asked Lutie, stopping when she saw nothing alarming and looking back to her mother.

"I don't know, honey." Sadie watched Anton throw his shovel high into the blue sky and let it fall to the ground. Amos tossed his pickaxe aside and embraced his brother. They danced arm in arm in a circle. A cacophony of voices sounded at once and every living soul on the farm rushed to the tiny graveyard on the miniature bluff.

"What in the world is wrong?" she called out.

"Wrong?" cried Anton. He skipped down the little earth surge towards his mother. "Nothing's wrong. Everything might be just right. It has to be." He reached out and tried to dance with her.

She let him dance in front of her just a few jigs, then pulled her hands away. "What in the world are you doing? Have you been in the sun too long?"

Anton twirled and jumped with his arms in the air. When he stopped he grabbed his mother by both of her arms again. "I looked all over this farm, but I never thought to look here. I never thought about the graveyard for one minute. But there it was."

"What was?"

"I recognize the box from the cover. Pa showed it to me before. I remember it."

"What box, Anton?" Then she remembered William's box. "What do you remember?"

"Come and look!" He led her by the hand, skipping along almost faster than she could keep up, past the well and up the little knoll where the other three were kneeling on the soil and where the girls had gathered round.

"It's heavy," she heard Amos say as he helped Ned lift the metal box from the hole. "Not too heavy to lift, but too heavy to be empty. It's real heavy."

Preacher Pearsall grabbed hold of the handle on the front of the grey iron box and helped ease it down on the ground. "You're right, Anton. It's a small box to weigh so much."

Sadie looked puzzled. Anton wanted to make sure his mother understood and that the news had sunk in. "The treasure, Mama. Daddy's treasure. We found it."

She lifted the hem of her black dress and stepped closer to the pit. The strong box was covered with a layer of dirt and some clods of earth stuck to its sides and bottom, but she recognized it herself the second she laid her eyes on it. It was William's treasure box all right, in which he always hid his money before travelling. She had seen it before, the week before he had gone missing in Arkansas. "Oh, William," she spoke to the coffin beside her, touching the bier gently with her fingertips. "Thank you. Thank you for remembering us."

"If Pa hadn't been so long," said Amos. "I'm mean so tall... I wouldn't of had to make the grave wider and longer... and I never would have seen the edge of the box."

Ned wiggled the lock that held the box shut. "Don't get your hopes up yet. You either, Mrs. Williston. This may be his treasure box, but it does not mean anything of value is inside it."

Amos was exhilarated. "It's as heavy as a log."

"They could be rocks," said Ned.

"There has to be something inside," added Anton.

"What I mean," Ned explained, "is that what is in there might not be the treasure you've been looking for. You do not know for certain that he had a treasure here."

"But he always hid his money. And why would he bury a bunch of rocks."

"He's right, though, boys," decided Sadie. "Money isn't heavy. And we know the gold is down in Arkansas. Let's not count our chickens just because we can see the eggshells."

"Well, let's open it." Anton and Amos offered the suggestion enthusiastically together.

"Get something to knock this lock off," said Ned.

Amos retrieved his discarded pickaxe. Ned struck the lock steadily as though he were chiseling. Several blows. Harder each lick.

"Dear God," cried Sadie. "Please let there be some money in that box."

"Yes, Lord," joined the preacher, removing his hat and looking up into the clear sunny skies. "Thy kingdom is like a treasure buried in a field that men would give all they had to purchase. Oh, Lord, let this be a pearl of great price for their sakes, to save their little farm."

"Hurry up!" ordered Anton, falling to his knees beside the gunslinger.

Just then the latch broke loose and the lock swung uselessly on the side. Six hands reached in to raise the lid together. Ned lifted out a yellow leather bag tied at the top with a piece of frayed cord. "It is heavy," he said, smiling. "There are more little bags in there. Anton, you have looked for this for a long time. You open the bag."

Anton quickly cut off the rope and pulled the top of the bag open. He peered inside. "There's no money in here," he spoke, a subdued expression on his face.

"None?" cried Evelina.

"None." Then a wide grin overtook his face. Reaching his hand inside the bag, he drew out his clenched fist. "That's because..." He opened his hand revealing several small buttery lumps. "That's because it's gold."

Sadie had not danced many times during her hard life, but this day she swung in the arms of four men. She hugged and kissed her girls. She even hugged the scruffy dog that wandered up to see what was going on. Her eyes turned to the plains. *Where is Granger and the sheriff now?* she thought. *Let them come. I'm not worried about that man anymore. This is our land and he cannot take it.*

"Well, Preacher," she asked. "What do you think about all this?"

"I think your miracle has come."

"Cutting it mighty close," added the brown-skinned man. "But it appears that your miracle arrived at just the right time. Your God's timing in miracles is impeccable, but certainly leaves one feeling anxious for a long time."

Evelina couldn't believe their fortune. "Is this part of the stolen gold?"

Ned laughed. "No, Evelina. The stolen gold was in government bars. These are nuggets that a miner would have brought back from California."

"Thank you, God. And thank-you my dear William," Sadie lauded as the children poured the golden lumps out of the sack and into their hands, spilling them into the soil, filling the air with the sounds of laughter. They drew out the other bags and found coins and notes. "Thank you, dear William, for putting this here for your family."

The matronly plainswoman beckoned everyone's attention. "Children, your father has given us this gold, not once, but two times. The first was when he buried it and the second when he died while trying to save our home."

"What do you mean, Mama?" asked Evelina.

"If we had not dug another grave today, we might never have found the box of gold."

Even Preacher Pearsall could agree." This means that if you had not chosen to bury the old Indian man here in your family cemetery and if poor Miss Lenora had not succumbed, you would still be digging two plots over and never would have found the gold." Tears welled up in the preacher's eyes. He couldn't speak. Sadie knew that his heart had been healed.

"Let's bury your father, children. The preacher has some good words to say over him and then we can celebrate saving our farm."

Lillibet looked up into her mother's sparkling eyes and asked, "Can we plant some wildflowers on my daddy's grave when he's buried?"

"Of course we can, child," her mother replied. "You know how much your daddy loved prairie flowers. They won't last much longer this year, but every year their seedlings with come back up and cover the earth like a colorful blanket."

"And we will still live here to see them."

"Yes, honey. We don't have to leave. He called me his *Little Butterfly Weed*. I think those should grow in abundance all around these little graves."

Little Lutie tugged at her long dark dress, stepping over the soil to look closer. "What colors should we plant for him?"

Evelina scooped the child in her arms. "I'm sure he would love any colors we planted."

"I like purple."

"Then we'll plant purple ones too."

"Was that my daddy's favorite color too?" Lutie asked.

"Oh no, " Evelina said, laughing. "I'm sure his favorite color is gold."

The echoes of merriment resounded across the vast plains of Nebraska where the colorful little prairie flowers radiantly bloomed across the beautiful mounds of earth.

Printed in the United States
By Bookmasters